Voice of the Victim

Praise for Rick Ludwig

"Rick Ludwig has done it again! With *Voice of the Victim*, Ludwig expands his universe of clever detectives and intriguing mysteries with a hard-hitting examination of the past and how it shapes us into who we become. A beautiful, fast-paced novel you should pick up today!"

— RJ Johnson, *author of The Twelve Stones*

"Ludwig brings this crime-fiction reader full circle from the Hawaiian Islands to the Italian Coast and back again. He has not only created believable characters and complicated crimes, but also he's introduced me to a detective I hope resurfaces in the future."

— Elaine Gallant, author of *The 5th C*

"An auto accident destroys Detective Sergeant Keone Boyd's roadster, plunging him into and unexpected realm as he grapples with a suspect's alternate reality and unexpected plot twists. this is not your typical investigation. Eyes of the Beholder is a gripping read that leaves you wondering what comes next."

— Kenneth Andrus, author of *Arctic Menace*
(for *Eyes of the Beholder*

"If you're yearning for a page-turning tale of suspense and skulduggery, look no further. If you're hoping for some crackling dialogue and vivid descriptions, you'll find them here. And if you're yearning to go that land of myth and mystery in the middle of the Pacific, let Rick Ludwig take you. Along with the beauty, he'll show you the dark side of paradise. Don't miss it."

— William Martin, *New York Times*-bestselling
author of *The Lincoln Letter* (for *Pele's Fire*)

Voice of the Victim

Maui Mysteries
Book 2

Rick Ludwig

BABYLON BOOKS

For Jennifer

A Note on the Spelling of Hawaiian Words

After moving to Maui, I learned a great deal about the history and culture of the Hawaiian Islands. I respect this ancient and vibrant culture and have tried to reflect this in everything I've written in this beautiful place. But I am neither a native Hawaiian nor a speaker of the language. Though I have learned a few phrases that I am not too embarrassed to speak aloud, I faced a challenge in spelling Hawaiian words.

Two characters are used in proper Hawaiian spelling that may be unfamiliar to those new to the language. These are the *'okina* and *kahakō*.

The 'okina can be approximated by an apostrophe but is an actual consonant and represents a glottal stop. It may occur at the beginning or in the middle of a word and changes the pronunciation and meaning of words. An example familiar to many non-Hawaiians is the name of the island Lāna'i (Lah-nah-ee), which is very different from the word for a veranda or covered patio, lanai (Lah-nigh). Throughout the novel I have used a reversed apostrophe to represent this important consonant.

The kahakō indicates vowel length, which changes meaning and the placement of stress. In other languages it is referred to as a macron and represented by a line over a vowel. An example of how these can impact meaning in a Hawaiian word is the word kāne (kaa-nay) which means male, while the same word without the kahakō, kane (ka-nay), means skin disease.

In this trilogy, I have elected to use both the 'okina and kahakō. I apologize to Native Hawaiian readers for my other limitations.

I have also attempted to use the standard method for distinguishing non-English words, using italics for the first occurrence of such words, except for place names.

Another characteristic of the islands is the common use of pidgin in friendly banter. I have learned that there are subtle differences between the pidgin used on each of the Hawaiian Islands. What I have tried to capture, on occasion in this novel, is probably closest to the pidgin I heard on Maui. I have tried, phonetically, to capture the essence of this joyful and constantly evolving language as I heard it spoken. Born from the desire of each wave of immigrants to this lovely place to communicate with each other, despite vastly different native tongues, Hawaiian pidgin is an essential component of daily life here in paradise. One very common aspect is a tendency to end most sentences with, *yeah?* It's kind of like ending a sentence on the mainland with, *right?*

Prologue

How'd I ever get so lucky?

The shooter slogged through the ʻĪao stream to a spot where he could climb out onto rocks instead of mud. He scaled the hillside to a lone palm tree that provided an excellent vantage point, quietly climbed to the crown of fronds, and created a sniper's nest. Despite concern that the target might decide to move, he carefully prepared the site, assembled his weapon, and assumed a supported and balanced position.

The valley was so lovely and quiet at sunset. The rifle's noise suppressor would prevent anyone left in the park from hearing the shot. He could see the target with his naked eyes. The man with short grey hair in a flowered aloha shirt stood calmly on a raised area on the far side of the stream. Gazing through the scope, he lined up a kill shot. The target turned away from the stream to gaze at the stunning green expanse of the ʻĪao Needle. This change in position determined a new location for the bullet, the base of the man's skull.

Though exhausted from the frantic scramble up the stream, the hillside, and the tree, the shooter concentrated on drawing a slow, deep firing breath. The squeeze on the trigger was also slow and gentle. The only sound, a *pfutt,* thanks to the noise suppressor. Handling the recoil, he looked back through the scope to see the figure fall to the ground. Mission accomplished.

BLAM . . . Blam . . . blam.

The sound of the single shot reverberated off the valley walls.

What the hell?

The shooter hadn't made that noise. Who had?

Swinging his head in a slow arc, he saw the bushes move on his side of the stream. A small form fell out, juggling a smoking rifle a lot like his.

What's he doing here?

Part One

A Whole New World

"There are worlds beyond worlds and times beyond times, all of them true, all of them real, and all of them (as children know) penetrating each other."

P.L. Travers

Chapter One

Sunday, July 7, 2013, 6:50 p.m. HST

Detective Lieutenant Tony Alcala slumped in his chair. He was down two detectives and crime on Maui showed no sign of taking a holiday. That damn Loftus case. He never wanted to hear about it again.

A knock on the door snapped him out of his reverie. He sat up straight and wiped the worry from his face before he growled, "Come on in."

Detective Sergeant Keone Boyd, all six foot seven, two hundred seventy-five pounds of him, took a hesitant step into the office. "Hi, boss."

"You're on vacation." Tony shot back, then smiled. "But since I'm unlucky enough to be your friend, come on in. Where's Julie?"

"Unloading my cruiser."

Tony could tell something was troubling his friend. Never one to beat around the bush, he said, "What's your problem? Why does a man about to leave on a multi-week cruise of the Mediterranean look like he just swallowed bile?"

Keone hesitated.

"Spill, Big Guy. What's eatin' you?"

"I visited Sam Loftus in the Molokini ward, yesterday."

Oh shit.

"Dr. Drayton was there, observing his catatonic patient. Even that scientist, Dr. Hasselbach, stopped by."

"Sam's lost it, eh?"

"I saw a shell of the man I knew but with a faint smile on his face. I found myself hoping he made it back to his imaginary universe, if only in his mind."

"Hold onto that thought and let the rest go." Tony grew increasingly uncomfortable with this topic.

"I think Hasselbach may have acquired a touch of crazy, too. You don't think dementia could be contagious, do you?"

"Hell, no. Hasselbach's a friggin' astrophysicist. Those bastards are born on the edge. Look what happened to his assistant. He's in the same nut shop as Sam."

"Actually, no. They released Dr. Carvell three days ago. Hasselbach says Brad's given up studying the multiverse. Gonna teach at UH Maui College next term."

"Good. That multiverse crap can warp your mind" Tony paused, hoping Keone would change the subject.

Keone took the hint. "Anyway, how are you doing, boss?"

"Shitty. I'm understaffed, up to my ass in alligators, and now I've gotta waste my time taking a rogue detective and his wife to the airport."

"I appreciate what you did for me. And I'm truly sorry to leave you short-staffed." Keone paused. "But I've got a suggestion."

"Oh boy. Here it comes." Tony leaned back in his chair.

"What?" Keone looked like a giant kid caught with his hand in a cookie jar.

"I don't know yet. But I'm not gonna like it."

"Julie's adamant that I completely forget about this place while we're gone, so I have to talk fast, before she comes in."

"You used up most of my goodwill during the Loftus case."

"I know, but this isn't about me. It's about Sergeant Beyers."

"Beyers? She's the only one to come out of the Loftus case looking good. She was decorated for her work—unlike you. Why would she need my help?"

"She'd kill me if she found out I told you."

"Told me what?" For a man of few words, Keone was sure taking a long time to say something.

"She deserves a break. She's always wanted to be a detective. And I think she'd make a damn good one. But you don't need to take my word for it. Why don't you assign her to CID, while I'm gone?"

Tony was skeptical, and it must have showed.

"It could be temporary. Like you said, with me away and Kulima gone for good, you're understaffed."

"What's her background?"

"Local girl. Got her bachelor's degree in Criminal Law and Society from UC Irvine before joining the Maui PD. Currently halfway through her masters in CL&S online. And she's passed the detective exam."

"Who suggested that route to her?" Tony had a pretty good idea of the answer.

"I didn't even meet her until she was in her senior year. Gave a talk and did some recruiting at UCI for the LAPD. Since we were both from Maui, she felt comfortable talking story with me. Later we worked together when I transferred to MPD."

"Look, Keone. She has a fulltime job in Hana. I doubt her CO would let her take a temporary assignment over here without a good reason. Besides, the few weeks you're gone is hardly enough time for me to evaluate her."

"True. But I wanted to put a bug in your ear before I left. We really could use Ange here, Tony."

"I'll look at her record and if the opportunity ever arises to bring her over for an evaluation, I'll consider it." Tony stood, ending the conversation. "Let's get you and your bride to the airport." A smile creased his face as he glanced passed Keone's head to Julie, who promptly bopped her new husband on the top of that head.

"No more talking, or even thinking, about work, Mister Boyd. You're a married man, now. You must focus entirely on your loving bride."

"I know. Julie. But—"

"No buts. We're officially on our honeymoon. Lieutenant Alcala and the MPD will have to manage on their own for a few weeks." She glanced at Tony. "It'll help them realize how much they need their best detective."

Neither Keone nor Alcala risked a word.

"Look," she said. "I've been more than accommodating. I agreed to let you drop off your department car on the way to the airport. I agreed to let this overgrown cub scout take us to our flight. But I won't allow police static to interfere with the most important time of our new life together."

Tony spent the entire drive to the airport telling the lovebirds about his own romantic Greek Island tour ten years before. *Before his marriage went to hell.*

At the airport Keone unfolded his bulk from the back seat while Tony jumped out and transferred their luggage to a cart. "Aloha, you two. Enjoy yourselves."

"We plan to," Julie said, before planting a kiss on Tony's cheek. "Thanks for never doubting Keone, or me."

Keone ambled over, brushed past Tony's outstretched hand, and encircled him in a bear hug.

"Ouch. That hurts. Just get outta here. And have one great time, Big Guy."

As he watched them walk arm in arm to the Agriculture Inspection station, Tony thought, *Beyers, eh? Wouldn't hurt to glance at her file.*

His radio beeped and announced, "Shooting in 'Īao Valley State Park. One man down. See ranger in parking lot."

There's never been a shooting in the park.

"Unit one-kilo-two responding to shooting in 'Īao Valley."

Alcala hit lights and siren and sped away from the airport, grilling the dispatcher for more information.

Chapter Two

Angela Beyers looked forward to spending the next week at home. She spent most of each week in Hana and saw too little of their cozy home in the hills above Lāhainā on weekends. But this week she had training at the local division, so she could commute from home.

Her roommate and best friend, Linda Carroll, was a part-time real estate agent, part-time insurance agent, and full-time graphic artist. Neither could have dreamed of buying such a place on their own salaries. But their combined income, coupled with a foreclosure, an auction, and a terrible storm that kept other bidders away, made it happen. Technically they weren't equal partners since Linda put up the full down payment, but they shared the monthly payments and other expenses equally. Despite Linda's protests, Angela was nibbling away at her part of the down payment a little each month.

"Why are you doing this?" Linda griped as Angela handed her this month's check. "This place appreciates in value every day. We can settle up after we sell—if we ever do."

"Older places here can also **de**-preciate. I won't let you carry all the risk."

"Damn it, Ange. You look at everything so much like . . ."

"Like a crime I'm investigating? I guess I do. I always consider the possible ways something can go south on me."

"Does that include me?"

"No way, Lin. You're the one constant in my crazy world. Friends fo' evah."

"Friends fo' evah," Linda echoed.

A sharp buzz from Angela's cell brought their conversation to an abrupt halt.

"Sergeant Beyers." She always answered this way. She never knew if the call was from a friend or work.

"Aloha, Sergeant. It's Tony Alcala from CID. You worked with us on the Loftus case."

"Yes, Lieutenant. How can I help you?"

"There's been a shooting in the ʻĪao Valley. A man's been injured. I'm headed over to the scene now, but the dispatcher informed me that the injured man and his wife live near you in Lahaina. Could you possibly bring the wife to the hospital? I hate to ask, but we're really short staffed right now in CID. The wife's name is . . ." He paused. She assumed he was looking at his notes. "Lister. Nancy Lister."

Nance. Oh no. "The Lister's used to be my next-door neighbors, sir. Of course, I'll go get her. How bad, sir?"

"I don't know. I just got here. I'm not even sure if Lister's the shooter or shootee. I only know he's injured. They're gonna take him to Maui Memorial. I'm pulling into the ʻĪao parking lot right now. Thanks for your help."

In her bedroom, Angela buttoned her uniform blouse and reflected on her times with the Listers over the past five years. Good times. Nancy was the best golf partner she'd ever had.

Nancy and Rob are so close. Whatever hurts one of them hurts both.

She finished dressing, checked her gig lines, strapped on her holster, and headed for the front door.

"Got a call!" she shouted over her shoulder. Linda knew the drill.

Chapter Three

Nancy Lister loved to read sitting in Rob's study, embraced by his cushy recliner. She imagined him hugging her as she read.

When the bullet hit home, a third jogger dropped in place along the trail in D.C.'s verdant Rock Creek Park. A third blood pool spread from the jogger's ruined face to the pine needles bordering the path.

"Two young women and a jock. This silencer is fabulous. And look what's coming—a young mom with a baby stroller built for joggers, and it's a doublewide. It doesn't get better than this—"

Nancy's reading was interrupted by the Hawai'i Five-O theme erupting from her cell phone. She didn't recognize the number but decided to answer it.

"Hello?"

"Mrs. Lister?"

"Yes. Can I help you?"

"Mrs. Lister, I'm Detective Lindsay Kalani from the Maui Police Department."

"Police . . ."

"I'm afraid your husband has been injured."

Nancy squeezed the arm of her chair. "What? How?"

"I don't know the details, ma'am. The paramedics are taking him to Maui Memorial right now."

"What happened?" She willed the room to stop spinning, her heart aching at the unwelcome news.

"They'll know more at the hospital. An officer will be there in a few minutes to drive you there. Please be ready to leave when the officer arrives."

Nancy wandered into the bathroom, used the toilet, and washed her hands and face. As her shaky hands applied some minimal make-up, her restless mind travelled to a conversation she'd had with Rob before he left on last month's European book signing tour.

"Have you got everything you need together? Glasses, chargers, passport?" Nancy asked.

"Yep."

The question was unnecessary. *Dr. Anal* always had everything packed and ready a week before any major trip. Rob wasn't clinically obsessive compulsive, but close.

"Will you get a chance to write while you're there?"

"Mike promised me two free days in Florence, before the flight home from Rome. I'll try to do some character and location sketches for my new novel."

Rob changed the subject before she could follow up.

"You know, I was thinking the other day about how healthy we both are. The only time either of us was in a hospital was when we had Beth."

What you mean we, paleface? She thought, but she said, "Good stock."

"You know it. But we are getting older."

"You may be, but I decided not to, many years ago. That's why my hair remains a rich, dark brown."

"That and your hairdresser. But seriously, honey, someday

you or I may, through no fault of our own, wake up in a hospital somewhere."

"If you wake up, there's no problem," she said with a grin.

"Agreed. That's not the scenario that concerns me. Damn, you're making this hard."

"Just spit it out."

"Okay, I never want to live as a vegetable. If the doctors ever tell you there's no hope, you need to let me go."

"Will you shut up? I've told you I plan to live forever, and you'd better keep me company."

"I know you don't want to plan for negative events, but I need you to know how I feel."

"Okay. Feeling noted. Now let's discuss something important. What are you going to bring me from Italy? If only gelato wasn't so hard to transport . . ."

THE DOORBELL BROUGHT NANCY BACK TO THE present. She leaned into the living room and looked out through the screen door. They never closed the front door when they were home, allowing the trade winds to enter and keep the condo cool with just the ceiling fans.

A short, uniformed figure faced her. She recognized her friend Angela Beyers, a former neighbor in their complex, a golf partner, and a sergeant with MPD. Angela's expression did nothing to assuage Nancy's anxiety.

Chapter Four

Elizabeth Lister glanced out the window. Her plane was crossing the Maui coast for the second time, over Kihei. The first crossing was near Pāi'a. The plane would now turn one hundred eighty degrees to cross the coastline once again, fly over the sugar cane fields, and land into the wind at Kahului.

She'd made this trip so many times over the years. But this visit would be different. This trip, she would tolerate no drama from her mother.

Mom was so cool with everything before I moved to New York.

After two years working on miscellaneous theater projects throughout Southern California, Beth finally got the chance she'd been praying for. She'd grown beyond her West Coast training to develop a résumé people in the business took seriously. She was stage-managing a play on the East Coast. Not in New Haven or Albany but in New York City.

The key was receiving her Equity Card for the screwy comedy she co-wrote, directed, and starred in at the College of the Desert. When Yuri Tartov caught the play on his pilgrimage to the desert, he offered her a job in an off-off-Broadway production. It didn't hurt that the production would be her play. She negotiated her butt off to become stage manager.

Yuri received rights to produce the show. But she owned the content and had free rein to stage the show her own way. The director would have a veto but no creative input on the staging. The director was Yuri's lover, Corbin Crespi, who turned out to be a sweetheart and didn't like to be bothered with techie details.

Two years into the project and sixteen months after their first shaky previews, Beth was satisfied with her decision. Sure, she lived in a hovel in Bed-Stuy with three colorful roommates, who all worked in the theater. Sure, she'd been mugged twice, hospitalized once, and ate far less than she should. But you put up with a lot to live your dream.

She was twenty-six now. Mom and Dad would have to suck it up and let her take a few risks. The jolt of the plane's landing gear meeting the tarmac interrupted her reverie. Popping in her ear buds, she would allow Idina Menzel to ease her mind and calm her temper.

At baggage claim, she collected her rolling duffel and an odd assortment of boxes and bags, removed one ear bud, and speed-dialed Dad to tell him he could cruise on over from the cell phone lot.

After five rings, the phone rolled over to voicemail.

She waited a minute and re-dialed. A strange voice answered. "Are you trying to reach Dr. Lister?"

"Yes. Who the hell are you?" Beth was worried. Dad was never late for anything and never, ever, lent his cell phone to anyone.

"Lieutenant Alcala, Maui Police Department."

A tingle started at the base of her spine and headed upward.

"I'm Dr. Lister's daughter. He's supposed to pick me up at the airport."

"I'm afraid your father's been injured. You need to get to Maui Memorial Hospital."

His words slapped Beth. Not Dad. Not now. He had to be okay.

"Ms. Lister? Are you still there?"

"Uh, yes. How serious?" she asked and made her way to a cab.

"Gunshot wound. The EMT's took him away in an ambu-lance. They can tell you more at the hospital."

"I'm getting into a cab right now." Beth ended the call, slammed the cab door, and shouted her destination at the driver.

~

ANGELA RISKED A GLANCE AT HER FRIEND. WHAT WAS Nancy thinking? She hadn't said a word since they left Ka'anapali for Wailuku. At first, she respected the silence and concentrated on driving to the hospital. But after Nancy didn't react to the shrieking siren of a passing ambulance, Angela spoke up.

"Nance, I'm sorry it took something like this to get us together."

Nancy shook her head before replying. "You're still working in Hana full-time, yeah?"

"Sure, but I'm home in Lāhainā on weekends. I should've—"

"How bad, Ange? Tell me."

"I don't know. I know he's injured and that they took him to Maui Memorial."

"Come on, Ange, I'm not an idiot. Why are the police involved?"

Angela resisted telling her friend about the shooting, since she didn't know for sure if Rob was shot. But she needed to give her something, anything. "Whatever happened occurred in the 'Īao Valley. Do you know what he might have been doing there?"

"He liked to write there. He wanted a scene in his new novel to take place there."

"I didn't know Rob wrote novels. I thought he wrote about science and business."

"That's what he's published. But he has a vivid imagination that's wasted in non-fiction."

"Why the 'Īao at sunset? Today?"

The tears forming in Nancy's eyes made Angela regret the question.

"It's our anniversary. When he left the house, he told me he was going to get some goodies to celebrate. He always likes to surprise me." She dabbed her eyes with a handkerchief.

I need to keep her talking. "Congratulations. You and Rob met in college, yeah?"

"That's right. We knew each other, even liked each other, but never dated. We found ourselves at the same parties and often wound up sitting together. We were both fascinated by the disconnect between self-perception and reality, especially in university undergraduates in Southern California."

"Rob once told me that your first date was over ten years after you met. Was he pulling my leg?" He'd shared that nugget at the pool one evening while they were neighbors.

"No, he told you the truth. We didn't rush into anything. We both had careers to pursue and only got together occasionally after graduation. I got my med tech training and began working in LA, and he went into the Army right after graduation. It was the Vietnam era, but he became a medic and worked in hospitals, stateside. We'd get together every year or so for a Christmas party with our friends from college."

Good. Keep it up. "You lived in Europe for a while, too, didn't you?"

"In England. But that was later, after we got married and he got his Ph.D. We loved England, but until you immerse yourself in that culture it can seem a bit bizarre. I used to compete with Rob to see who could find the first bone in the minced beef."

"You sound like quite a team."

"We are. Once we got back home, we faced every challenge together, especially after Beth arrived. Beth! I need to call Beth. She needs to know what's happened." Nancy pulled out her cell.

"Wait. We're at the hospital now. Wouldn't you like to know a little more when you call her?"

"Yeah. You're right. I'm so worried I can't think straight."

When Angela pulled in front of Maui Memorial, a cab pulled up directly behind them. As Angela helped Nancy from her cruiser and gave her a hug, she saw a young woman emerge from the cab. *That looks like...*

~

"Beth," Nancy called out.

They ran to each other, and Beth wrapped her mother in her arms.

"How . . . When . . . Why?" Nancy sputtered.

"I was supposed to be a surprise for your anniversary. When I called Dad to pick me up, a policeman answered Dad's cell and told me to get over here. Did they tell you what happened, or how he is, or . . ."

"So far, they've only told me he was injured in the ʻĪao Valley. When Angela brought me over, she said we'd learn more at the hospital."

"The guy on the phone told me Dad's been shot."

At these words, Nancy collapsed into her daughter's strong arms. Although a few inches shorter than her, Beth had strong muscles from moving heavy objects on stage.

Nancy turned her head toward Angela, but saw she was back in her cruiser, speaking into a mic. Angela rolled down her window. "I'm so sorry, Nance. I got a call. Go on inside with Beth and check on Rob. I'll check in with you later."

Nancy watched her friend speed away, siren blaring and lights flashing.

Chapter Five

Keone squeezed Julie's hand as their plane taxied into position. "We're off to see the wizard, Dorothy." He found it so easy to relax around this beautiful woman, to kid with her, to open himself up to her. When he was with her, the short, clipped sentences he used around everyone else were not enough.

Her eyes met his, and her hand squeezed back.

"Keone Boyd, civilian, reporting for relaxing honeymoon, Ma'am." He leaned over and planted a passionate kiss on her lips.

"Now that's what I'm talkin' about," Julie said, then leaned her head back and closed her eyes.

Keone's eyes were drawn to the window when the plane's engines revved for takeoff. As they rose, his eyes moved to the ʻĪao Valley. The hairs stood up on the back of his neck and a shiver ran through his body. *Something bad just happened up there.*

Was he ever really off duty? His mind wandered back to yesterday, watching Sam Loftus, long, wild hair and beard tangled around his face and Hasselbach saying he'd seen Sam with short hair and clean-shaven two days before. Something didn't track.

Tony was right. So many cases on Maui had an element of weird about them, a touch of the supernatural. It was one thing for his grandmother to believe the aina had a power all its own, but he resided in the twenty-first century and his job was to follow the facts.

Didn't Julie's sister Janet see Sam the same afternoon Hasselbach did, after the wedding? *Yes, when my brothers went off to the Fourth of July rodeo, she'd headed over to Maui Memorial to give Sam the divorce papers.* She would know if he was clean-shaven or not. He'd ask to talk with her when Julie called to tell her they arrived safely in Rome. Even Julie couldn't object to him speaking with his new sister-in-law. He could wait until then to close this annoying case once and for all.

For now, he decided to follow Julie's lead, leaned back in his seat, and closed his eyes. His thoughts anticipated the sights and sounds of a different world. Of civilizations with recorded histories more ancient than the Hawaiians. Soon he was dreaming of Greeks and Romans and lives on very different shores.

~

LIEUTENANT TONY ALCALA SURVEYED THE CRIME scene near the imu pit at ʻĪao Valley State Park. Mobile spotlights shined artificial daylight on the park's lower level. The CSIs working the scene cast eerie shadows on the stage just above the imu pit.

When he'd arrived an hour ago, the EMTs were caring for the vic on that same stage, using flashlights to illuminate their patient. From their urgent efforts and how quickly they transported him from the site, Tony figured the guy was in bad shape.

On arrival, he'd given the portion of the crime site on this side of the stream a complete once-over. No sign of a perp, a weapon, or even shell casings. The only people here then, besides a frantic park ranger and some patrolmen who'd arrived on motorcycles, were some frightened locals. These native Hawaiians had found a man with his head surrounded by blood when they carried a pig to the imu pit. They'd need to find another place for their lūʻau.

The crime scene folks were currently combing every square

inch looking for evidence. Dr. Lister was on his way to Maui Memorial Hospital, a bloodstained indentation in the grass the only reminder of the victim's presence.

A survey stick marked at head height stood near the indentation with strings leading off towards the large stream that looped around the site. Tony's eyes followed the strings as he reflected on the ʻĪao Valley's violent history. After the Battle of Kepaniwai, the stream ran red with the blood of Maui's troops, decimated by the superior forces of King Kamehameha two hundred and fifty years ago. Kepaniwai translates as the damming of the waters, reflecting the glut of bodies that prevented the stream from flowing after the battle.

From the angle the technicians had projected, the shooter must have been high up the steep mountain slope on the far side of the stream. They had wisely decided to put off looking for the sniper's position until daylight, given the wild growth and sheer slope.

Nothing about this crime scene made sense. From the report he'd received from the dispatcher and his brief conversation with Beyers, Tony knew Robert Lister was a retired scientist, sixty-three years old, now writing books about his experiences in the pharmaceutical industry. He was married with a grown daughter and spent his free time playing golf. He had no record and had never made a complaint to the MPD since moving from New Jersey five years ago. No motive, no weapon, no suspect, no anything. This should be a good test for Beyers.

Before he spoke to Beyers at her home in Lahaina, he'd begun to reconsider Keone's recommendation. Keone was right that he was short staffed. The other detective on active duty today, Lindsay Kalani, was investigating a hit-and-run in Wailuku when he took this call. Had Keone had one of his hunches when he put that bug in Tony's ear?

No point in wondering. Mr. and Mrs. Boyd were winging their way across the Pacific on the first leg of their journey to

Rome. Keone had told him they'd have short layovers in L.A. and Chicago before the long flight to Rome.

A new set of flashing lights caught his eye. *That should be Beyers.*

Tony watched her exit her vehicle and approach the crime scene. She had a tight, compact athlete's body and an experienced cop's slow careful gait. She checked with a CSI before entering the site to identify both Alcala's location and a route to him that wouldn't compromise any evidence.

Tony waved her over. "Nice to see you again, Sergeant."

"Lieutenant." Beyers replied. "I was surprised to get your second call at the hospital."

"On the phone you said you knew the vic."

"I do. We used to live next-door to each other in the same condo complex. I met Dr. Lister a bunch of times. He seemed like a nice guy. But I know his wife better. She and I played golf together. Still do when I get the chance."

"Do you know any reason why someone might take a shot at him?"

"No, sir. He's a writer. I read one of his books. It described how people manage scientific research in a business environment."

"Sounds like a page-turner," Tony said.

"The book wasn't as dry as you might expect. I laughed out loud a few times reading it. He loved to point out how stupid decisions were often made for seemingly sound reasons. He could be a little sarcastic in person, too, but the neighbors all loved him. I can't imagine anything in those books or in his daily life that would make anybody angry enough to kill him."

"What about the wife?"

"She's a sweetheart. Worked in hospitals for years, in the clinical lab. She's retired now, like her husband. She likes being around people more than staying at home trying to keep quiet while he writes. Does some tutoring at the elementary school."

"Any marital conflict?"

"No. Those two are devoted to each other in that quiet, comfortable way older people are."

"What about the daughter . . . uh . . . Elizabeth?"

"Beth works in the theater in New York, off-off-Broadway. She was at the hospital when I dropped her mother off. Nancy seemed surprised she was here."

Tony paused, then decided to bring Beyers up to date. "I talked to the daughter. Said she'd arrived on a flight from the mainland and was calling her dad to pick her up. The EMTs left Lister's cell phone where it fell when they took him away. When she called, I picked it up with my gloves and answered. We'll need to confirm her alibi, but it tracks. How about the wife?"

"I picked her up at home at seven twenty p.m. When did the shooting occur?"

"Techs say a little before seven, and that jibes with what the witnesses saw and heard. Looks like she's in the clear."

"Yeah, it took me a half hour to get across in the easy direction —with my lights flashing."

Alcala deliberately said nothing for a full minute.

"Sir, how badly was Dr. Lister injured?"

"EMTs found a gunshot wound to the head, near the base of the skull. They breathed for him while they loaded him into the ambulance and started chest compressions inside."

"A load and go," Beyers said. "Can I ask why I'm here, sir? This seems like it's in your ballpark."

"It is, Beyers, but I'm thinking of getting you temporarily assigned to help us. With Keone on his honeymoon and another detective . . . uh . . . terminated, I'm understaffed and swamped with cases. I thought your familiarity with Lister and his family might give you a leg up on the investigation. Are you game for a little detective work, Sergeant?"

Tony saw her suppress a smile. "I'm always happy to collaborate with my colleagues on the force, sir. But I'm stuck in a training class in Lāhainā right now."

Now it was Tony's turn to hide a smile. It would be much

easier to get her reassigned from training than from her duty station. Besides her CO was an old friend. "Consider yourself unstuck. I'll clear it with Lieutenant Keola. Come and see me tomorrow morning and we'll discuss the case. I'm outta here. Sunday's my day off."

"Mind if I hang around a little bit and check out the scene, sir?"

"Not at all. It's your case. Better have those two patrolmen over there seal the site before you leave. But don't stay too long. I get to work early and expect to find you at Wailuku headquarters when I get there." Tony turned and walked to the parking lot, leaving Sergeant Beyers at the crime scene.

He had no doubt that Keone knew about the training assignment when he made his pitch. But it would take more than wanting to be a detective to earn his acceptance. He hoped he'd made that clear to both of them.

Chapter Six

The shooter walked home, a duffel bag slung over his shoulder. He often got home this late and always carried a duffle or backpack with him when he went out.

He went directly to his bedroom, shut and locked the door, and gently placed the duffel on the bed. Donning latex gloves, he removed the rifle and carefully wiped every inch. There would be no prints.

Another duffle bag rested at the foot of the bed. Inside was a second rifle. He removed it and replaced it with the one he'd used. And yes, it had been fired recently, too. *That damn kid.*

He left the room carrying his duffel bag with the other rifle inside. It may have been fired, but the ballistics wouldn't match. Walking out to the carport, he unlocked a footlocker and placed the other rifle inside, along with the sniper scope and cartridges. He threw the empty duffle in, too.

Back inside, he stripped down and entered the shower, the cool water enlivening his senses. He'd always hated warm showers. They were for pussies.

He still couldn't believe his luck. *I not only find the bastard, but he's alone in a secluded place.*

The shooter scrubbed his body with cheap, hard soap.

When he spotted that idiot kid at the scene, the shooter was sure he'd ruin everything. But the fool never saw or heard the actual kill shot, just managed to make a lot of noise and turn himself into the perfect stooge.

Drying off, he pulled clean boxers from his dresser and climbed into bed. He was tired. Tonight, he would sleep like a baby knowing he'd nailed that son of a bitch.

~

BETH COULDN'T REMEMBER BEING THIS EXHAUSTED. They'd spent hours at the hospital. And when they finally got to see her dad, he wasn't really there. They'd told Mom she could come by in the morning and see him, while they run another test. But what was the point? The doctor had left no doubt what he thought.

She'd left that awful room to order a cab. And when she finally got her mom to leave the hospital, it was well after ten p.m. The guy that picked them up was friendly but must have realized from their icy silence that something was very wrong. He drove them home without a comment.

This whole nightmare was too horrible. Beth needed time to sort it out.

Beth didn't speak until she unlocked the front door. "Go inside and sit down, Mom. I'll get us some water." The fact that Mom did as she suggested confirmed how hard this was hitting her.

Her mother sat on the sofa, while Beth stowed her luggage in the study. The bright floral pattern surrounding her mother reminded Beth of other times in her parents' dream home filled with laughter and fun. Seeing her mother just staring into space, Beth grabbed two bottles of water from the fridge and plopped down hard on the sofa, getting her mother's attention.

"Here's that water, Mom," she said.

"Sorry, honey. I'm just . . ."

"I know. I know. Do you mind if I sleep in tomorrow? I'm still on New York time, where it is now six a.m."

"Don't you want to see him?"

"Not like that."

"I need to. It's horrible with him lying there like that, but he's still my love. And maybe the second EEG will surprise them. He's tougher than they think."

"He's not really there." *Did I say that out loud?*

Her mother's face twisted in a way she'd never seen before. "Don't say that. Ever." As she said the words, Nancy's fist clenched.

Beth resisted the reflex to turn her face away. She knew her mother would never strike her. But she hadn't expected Mom to be consumed by denial, either.

The anger left her mother's face as quickly as it came. A look of shame replaced it.

"I'll make up the pull-out," Beth said, grabbing sheets, pillows, and a light blanket from the linen closet.

Mom wrapped her arms around Beth as she walked past. Beth didn't pull away, needing the embrace as much as her mother.

"I'll see you tomorrow morning when you get back. But do try to get some sleep tonight. Remember, you can't see him until after nine. I love you, Mom."

With the efficiency she normally applied to dressing a set, Beth prepared the bed. With each step, she challenged herself to answer the questions that were troubling her.

Her mother was the realist in the family, not a dreamer like Beth. *Why is she having such a hard time with this?*

She loves him, you dolt.

Tired of the tumult, she went into the attached bathroom, washed her face, and donned her drama-queen pajama bottoms and a roomy Disney T-shirt.

When she climbed under the sheet and flipped off the light,

tears came. Despite her mother's fervent hope for a miracle, Dad was gone and with him a piece of her heart.

~

ANGELA PULLED INTO THE DRIVEWAY OF THEIR COZY little home. She was used to arriving home late, with her long drive back from Hana every Friday. She hadn't left the crime scene until the two patrolmen were in place and replacements arranged for the next eight-hour shift. Then she stopped by the Lahaina station to read online transcripts of all the communications regarding the case. It was well after eleven p.m. when she unlocked the door of the quiet house.

Linda had wrapped up the leftovers from the dinner they'd planned to make together. Without a sound, Angela took a helping of chicken and dumplings from the fridge, re-warmed it, and ate alone. She rinsed her dishes and thought of her friend Keone and his new wife off on their honeymoon. How far would they be by now? Had they made it to the mainland? She decided to send her old friend a text.

"Enjoy that honeymoon, Big Guy. I caught a case with your boss. Will tell you all about it when you get home. Aloha."

Her bedroom shared a bathroom with Linda's. She gently closed the door into her friend's room to avoid disturbing the inert form gently snoring there.

Linda wasn't just her housemate, she was her best friend. The one person she could let down all her barriers with. She had an urge to wake her and tell her about the new assignment but decided to wait until she had more to tell. Besides, Alcala expected her in bright and early the next morning. She set her alarm for five a.m.

She'd leave a note. Linda would understand. She always understood. That's why they did so well together.

With this thought on her mind, she dozed off. In her dream, she was back at the crime scene, her subconscious re-constructing a version of what happened. She saw a small figure holding a rifle across the stream. The rifle was pointed straight up in the air when it fired. The imagined sound of the shot jarred her awake.

Could the shooting have been an accident? No way. It's just a dream.

Chapter Seven

Monday, July 8, 5:30 a.m. PDT (2:30 a.m. HST)

Julie watched her husband duck his head as they left the plane that brought them from Maui to LAX. With an hour and a half before their flight to Chicago O'Hare and the gate nearby, they felt comfortable grabbing some coffee and a snack for breakfast. She was glad they'd both been able to sleep on the flight from Maui. But she had to wake Keone once when he cried out in his sleep. After a few hugs and kisses, he slept the rest of the flight. She wondered at the words he'd cried out, *No Beard!*

Finding no shortage of empty tables outside the snack bar, Julie settled in with their carry-ons and Keone walked over to order. She watched as he took a surreptitious glance at his cell. *I'll need to do something about that.*

~

"I'd like two coffees, one black and one with cream and one sugar," Keone said to the young woman at the counter. "Oh, and one jelly doughnut and a chocolate croissant, please."

"It'll be a minute. You can pick it up over there on the right." The cashier took his money, and he put the change in the tip jar by the register.

While waiting at the pick-up counter, he read the message on his cell, keeping his back to Julie at the table. After all, the message was from Ange and could have something to do with work. He wished he'd never made that silly promise to Julie.

Enjoy that honeymoon, Big Guy. I caught a case with your boss...

Keone smiled. *Tony did take my advice. Good. Angela won't let him down, and I won't have to worry about either of them.*

When the young woman brought his order, he carefully transported the coffees and pastries to Julie. The look on her face told him she'd noticed him check his phone. *Better come clean.* "Julie, you'll never guess who sent us a text while we were on the plane."

"Tony?" she asked with a smirk on her face.

"No. I told you that you'd be surprised."

"Someone else from MPD?"

Busted. "Well, yes, but it's not what you think. Just my friend Ange wishing us a happy honeymoon. Remember, she was on duty and couldn't make the wedding." Keone feigned a hurt expression.

"Uh huh. And she didn't mention anything about work, right?"

This telling her the truth all the time was gonna be hard. "She told me that she was working with Tony on a case, but that's it."

Julie held out her hand. "That's enough. Phone, please."

"Aw, c'mon. I need to be reachable. I'm still a detective."

"An off-duty detective on his honeymoon. Give it!"

Keone complied but said, "You will check it in case there's a real emergency, right?"

"I will, but only if it's a real emergency." Julie stuffed the phone in her purse. "Thanks for the coffee and the croissant. Chocolate's my favorite."

Keone swallowed the last of his jelly doughnut and shoved his chair back, "Better make tracks."

He'd noticed Julie was already finished and fidgeting. "We're scheduled to arrive in Chicago at 11:30 a.m. What time is that back home?"

Keone smiled. "That would be 6:30 a.m., Hawaiian Standard Time." *Ange had better be at headquarters by then if she doesn't want to disappoint her new boss.*

~

Angela Beyers walked into the Wailuku headquarters at six thirty a.m. Monday morning to find Tony Alcala waiting for her. *That proves it. This guy never sleeps.*

"Sergeant Beyers, you've been officially assigned to CID for three weeks. Since Detective Sergeant Boyd is away, you can use his desk. If you're lucky, his instincts will rub off on you." Alcala walked her to a battered old desk in a typically small cubicle.

"Thank you, sir."

"I want you to spend the day at this desk, using this computer and the resources here in CID to develop scenarios consistent with the evidence as to what might have happened in the 'Iao Valley last night."

"May I visit the scene again before the crime scene folks open it back up?"

"Yes. But I don't want you interrogating any suspects until you run your ideas past me. I'd rather you take it slow, to make sure you don't . . ."

Angela kept her cool, "Embarrass the department. I understand completely, sir."

"Detective Kalani can tell you how to obtain any resources you need." Alcala nodded toward a tall, Hawaiian woman at a nearby desk, who smiled at Angela. Angela smiled back and turned to find Alcala gone.

"Hi. I'm Lindsay," the young woman said as she strolled over to Angela. "It'll be great to have another female around here for the next few weeks."

"I'm Angela. Nice to meet you."

"I know your name. You're Keone's friend, right?"

Angela nodded.

"He told me how you helped him on the Loftus case. If there's anything I can help you with while you're here, let me know. Keone's one of the good guys. So is Lieutenant Alcala, though you probably can't tell from the gruff front he puts on. Don't let him get you down." Her smile told Angela that Lindsay was one of the good guys, too.

She found the crime scene reports on Keone's desk along with a report from the hospital on Rob's injuries. She'd already read the former last night and focused on the hospital report. An autopsy would have been more helpful but wasn't possible yet. Rob was still alive, legally.

She had potential scenarios running in her head, including the one from her dream. To rule out that least probable and most annoying scenario, she'd have to return to the crime scene.

❧

MONDAY, JULY 8, 1:00 P.M. CDT (8:00 A.M. HST)

JULIE DISCOVERED KEONE HAD A SURPRISE WAITING for her in Chicago when they boarded their flight to Rome.

"Hey, Big Guy, you never told me we're in first class. I could get used to this." Julie sighed with pleasure as she slid into her cushy seat.

"Don't. We're flying back business class from Venice to New York, and then coach pretty much forever after that."

Julie thought of punching his arm, but the flight attendant interrupted with two glasses of Dom Perignon, adding, "Congratulations. Happy honeymoon."

They clinked glasses and kissed. "Nothing you say can bother me or detract in any way from my first ride in first class. I love you, you big, tough Kahana."

"*Aloha au iā ʻoe e kuʻu ipo wahine,*" he replied.

"I know what aloha and wahine mean, but . . ."

"It means, I love you, my sweetheart."

Chapter Eight

Monday, July 8, 11:00 a.m. HST

Angela loved the ʻĪao Valley. It represented something very Hawaiian. Breathtakingly beautiful, but treacherous if you wandered off the beaten path. Some parts had never been fully explored. She'd read legends of Tahitian navigators still buried in remote areas in the West Maui Mountains, including the ʻĪao Valley.

Calming, but strong, the ʻĪao Stream had a substantial flow. After a downpour it could be wild. Flash floods were a danger elsewhere on the island, but especially in this narrow valley.

The sky was completely clear, a rarity in the West Maui Mountains. And the ʻĪao Needle stood out verdant against the pale blue sky. She knew its Hawaiian name, Kūkaemoku.

Their island home was a blanket of green highlighted with the beautiful colors of the rainbow. A garden of multicolored flowers, fruits, and vegetables atop a bubbling red cauldron of magma, ever ready to spew forth, then cool to jet-black lava and create more land for the garden.

Crime scene tape doesn't belong in our garden.

This thought brought her back to her reason for being here. This morning, with Detective Lindsay Kalani's help, she'd followed up on her scenarios as much as she could from her desk. Scenario one assumed Rob had seen something he shouldn't and been silenced. With an area as wild as the 'Iao Valley, the first thing that came to mind was illegal growers. One constant with drug growers and dealers, they could always be reached on their cell phones—business was business. She'd contacted two-dozen known to have operations in or near the 'Iao Valley. Each had an alibi, but she had a network of informants who could confirm or deny them. The informants had cell phones, too. By the end of the morning, she'd confirmed all but one.

Efren (Hopper) Alavezos had sworn he was miles from the 'Iao Valley and Wailuku. But an informant saw Hopper bringing down harvest around the same time as the shooting. Her informant, known as Blue, also knew where to catch up with the guy. He'd keep an eye open for Hopper and shoot her a call or message if he showed.

She wanted to follow up on scenario two as well. The idea that someone from Rob's past had a grievance that triggered the shooting was always a possibility. Before leaving the office, Alcala had told her visiting Nancy would not violate his rule against interviewing suspects, since they'd confirmed neither she nor her daughter could have shot Lister. Nancy was at the hospital but would be home for lunch, so she planned to head to Lāhainā next.

But first, she had time to come here and pursue her shaky third scenario, which had no evidence to support it except the vivid dream she'd had last night. After she woke up this morning, she'd realized the dream was just her subconscious mind putting together disparate facts from her memory. She knew kids shot at birds and rodents in the valley, although it was strictly prohibited. She'd done it herself and always worried about where the bullet might travel if she missed. She also knew that a kid shooting at birds and nailing a retired scientist by mistake was a long shot, in more ways than one.

After reviewing the areas taped off by the crime scene folks, she told them they could start packing up this side of the stream. She walked back to the parking area and looked over the edge to find a spot in the ʻĪao Stream narrow enough to cross to the far side on protruding boulders. That crossing was directly below a chain link fence that she'd seen in her dream. She climbed over the fence and followed a path to the boulder crossing.

Reaching the stream, she knew she'd never find footprints on the boulders. But once she crossed to the other side, a set of footprints decorated the mud. They were from bare feet, the bare feet of a child. A dozen yards above her, Angela saw a crime scene tech start to remove yellow tape from an area of hillside. She shouted and waved to catch his attention. The CSI carefully worked his way down the hillside with his pack on his back.

"Find something, Sarge?" he asked.

"Do you have what you need to take an impression?"

"Hell, yes. I was hoping to take some up there but found nada." He looked at the prints Angela had discovered. "A barefoot kid made this and the angle's way too low to allow a shot at the stage."

"I know, but I'm gonna follow it and see where it ends up. I doubt he's the shooter, but the kid could've seen something." She didn't wait for a response.

The tracks ascended the hillside to below treetop level, well below the area the crime scene team suggested for the shooter. The tracks ended by a large root surrounded by mud. She knelt, and her eyes followed the only other tracks as they descended from this point towards the earlier trail and paralleled it back to the stream. He'd stopped here.

She spotted a large scrape on the root, as though someone might have slipped on it. Surveying the surrounding area, she caught a glint of sunlight off a metallic object. She photographed both sets of tracks and carefully moved over to where she saw the glint. She took another picture of the cartridge case she found there and used a pen to pick it up and place it in a plastic evidence bag.

What if the kid tripped over that root while he or she was carrying a loaded rifle? The shot would have gone over the trees in an arc.

Climbing up a few more feet so she could see over the trees, she saw the stage. Could a fluke shot have caused this tragedy? Unlikely, but she'd need to follow up. She waved up the crime scene guy, air-dropped her pictures onto his cell phone, and handed him the cartridge. "See what you can do with this before you open up the site, will you?"

"Sure, Sarge. Thanks for the help."

"What's your name?"

"Jenkins. Officer Ed Jenkins, Sarge."

"Didn't you work on the Walden case with Keone Boyd?"

A small smile lit Jenkin's face "Yes, I really enjoyed working with him. Great guy."

"Did you also enjoy saving him from an explosion that put you in the hospital?" Now it was Angela's turn to smile.

"Oh, you heard about that. Just doing my job." Did Jenkins blush?

"Keone told me you're very good at your job," Angela said. "As far as I'm concerned you found this. But be sure to have them send the report directly to me, okay?"

After Jenkins nodded, Angela re-crossed the stream, returned to her cruiser, and headed back to the station.

Okay. Make it three theories consistent with the evidence. No way I'm telling Alcala about this until I have more.

~

ONE HUNDRED FEET ABOVE THE ʻĪAO STREAM, THE shooter was concerned.

When he saw a woman in plain-clothes cross the stream, he

figured the crime scene folks had opened the site. Using mini binoculars, he saw she was the same lady cop that met the other cop at the scene Sunday night.

He'd been relieved last night when everyone left without checking out his side of the river. When he was sure they'd left, he returned the nest to its native state. He'd only come back today to double check and make sure CSI hadn't found it. They hadn't. They'd been looking on the hillside at about the same altitude he'd attained in the tree.

So, what the hell's that lady cop doing back here?

CSI staked off a spot fifty yards farther up the narrow valley from his tree. It had a good line of sight to the stage, but insufficient cover for him. A tech was still searching it when the lady cop hollered at him to join her.

The shooter clasped his Glock semi-automatic the whole time the two cops were together. When the lady cop climbed up the hillside towards him, he screwed on the silencer. She stopped well below his tree, looked around, picked something up, and headed back down the slope to where the tech waited.

She must have found that damn kid's trail. I wouldn't be surprised if that little shit was so scared, he forgot to pick up his brass.

He watched as the CSI made casts of the kid's footprints.

This could work in my favor. He unscrewed the silencer and returned the Glock to his backpack.

They think some kid fired a wild-ass shot and took out a dumbass in the process.

He liked their thinking.

Chapter Nine

Nancy Lister was off-balance. She drove back from Wailuku on autopilot. She'd done everything she could at the hospital. The sound of that machine breathing for Rob got on her nerves. She'd listened but refused to believe Dr. Carver's gloomy update after they ran the EEG. They would take the next EEG readings at 10 a.m. Tuesday and Wednesday. She'd watched them put all those leads on Rob's head, tape his eyes closed, and tape the breathing tube to the side of his mouth. He looked so . . . *No. I can't think about that now.* She had to concentrate on other things.

Someone had shot her husband. The police would want to know who might want to hurt Rob. He had no enemies here that she knew of, and she couldn't think of any off island either. There were competitors when he was developing new drugs but mostly colleagues. He loved to collaborate and share ideas. He was more of a teacher than a competitor.

But someone had shot him. Near the base of his skull. In the tranquility of the ʻĪao Valley. *Why?* It made no sense.

None of this makes sense.

When she got home, she took her time relinquishing the known of the car for the unknown of the condo. How would

Beth react to her harsh words from last night? *Everything's just happening too fast.*

Beth had left the door open. Through the screen she could see her daughter perched cross-legged on the couch, typing away on her laptop. Nancy took a deep breath and swung open the screen with a loud creak. *Rob never got around to oiling that.*

"Hi, Mom. Welcome back."

Nancy let out a breath she hadn't realized she'd been holding, relieved at her daughter's pleasant greeting. "What're you working on?"

"I've got an awkward entrance in the second act that I'm moving around. I had to change the lighting cues. And . . ."—with a final tapping of keys, Beth announced—"I'm done."

"Were there any calls?"

"A couple neighbors who heard us come in late last night. I thanked them for their concern but didn't tell them about Dad. They just assumed I came in on a late flight. The only other call was from Mike Butler. Said he needed to speak with you."

Mike was more than an agent for Rob's books. He was *'ohana,* family.

The fact that he divided his time between his house in Wailea and an apartment in New York City made him the perfect go-between for Rob and his publisher.

Nancy set down her purse and called Mike's cell.

Mike answered on the second ring. "Hello, Nancy. I'm so sorry about Rob. Is there anything I can do?"

"Nothing right now. But I'm sure there will be."

"I'm at your disposal. Look, I know you need time right now and I don't want to intrude. But when you're ready, I'm here to help with financial and legal matters. Just pick up the phone."

"I will, soon. I promise."

"My thoughts and prayers are—"

"I know." She heard a tapping on the screen door. "Mike, I've got to go. Somebody's here."

"Understood. Aloha."

Angela Beyers was standing on the other side of the screen door waiting patiently to be asked in. She wasn't wearing her uniform this time.

~

Angela, Nancy, and Beth sat around the dining room table sipping iced tea and trying to ignore the elephant in the room. The hug Angela gave Nancy when she entered the condo was heartfelt and meant to show them that she was here as a family friend, not just a cop. The fact that she was authorized to wear plain clothes helped.

Alcala wanted her to interview the Listers and search the home. He'd obtained a warrant and passed it on to Ange. But she cared about these people and decided to ease into things.

Angela took a sip of the tea and turned first to Beth. "I hear you're working on a play in New York. I bet that's exciting."

"It can get crazy sometimes, but I love it. I'm surprised big city people get my play."

"It's about your experiences in college, right?"

"Yeah. We put a lot of humor into it about real people, so I guess it rings true."

"Your dad told me he liked it. Quite a compliment from a guy who's not much for fiction."

Nancy jumped in. "Why does everybody think he hates fiction? He enjoys a good thriller now and then. He prefers movies, especially if there's a lot of action." With a slight smirk on her face, she added, "Don't ever tell him I told you, but he loved the first Star Wars movie."

Angela looked at Beth, who gave her head a quick shake. Her meaning was clear. *Nancy hadn't accepted Rob's prognosis.*

Surely the doctor had been clear. Denial must be lasting longer for Nancy than Beth. She'd have to tread carefully.

"About Rob. I've been assigned to the case. My lieutenant thought it might be easier for you to answer questions from me, here in a friendly environment, than from a stranger down at the station."

"They wouldn't be that thoughtful in New York City," Beth interjected before Nancy could react. "I'd forgotten how nice people are on Maui."

"We want to help you find whoever did this to Rob," Nancy said.

Beth was more direct. "Do you know who shot my dad?"

Angela stiffened. Here it was. The unspoken question on everyone's mind. She wished she had an answer. "So far, we believe Rob was shot with a rifle from the other side of the ʻIao Stream. Because he was struck near the base of his skull, it's unlikely to be an accident or a suicide attempt."

"We knew Dad didn't try to kill himself. Wait, could they have been shooting at someone nearby and hit him by mistake?"

"Unlikely. Your father was alone. The nearest people to him were in the parking lot. The crime scene team is still analyzing every inch of the site. I'm sure they'll find something. But while they do their job, I need to do mine."

"Of course." Nancy and Beth said at the same time.

"I'll need to ask each of you some questions. I know neither of you saw the crime, but you may remember some little thing that Rob said or did beforehand that could put us on the track of the shooter or reinforce what CSI finds."

When neither Beth nor Nancy said anything, she continued. "I also need to look around the condo. Rob may have written something or gotten an email or letter that could give us a clue." Her fingers brushed the warrant in her pocket.

"Which would you like to do first?" Nancy said.

"I guess I should look around for clues first. I'll start in the study. You can stay here in the dining room and finish your drinks. I'll have a look on the bookshelves and in the drawers and cabinets, but don't worry. Unless something's relevant to the investigation, I never saw it. Oh, and just so everything's legal, here's a warrant."

"I haven't had a chance to straighten anything up since I got the call yesterday. Please, be kind."

"I will. But as a cop investigating a crime, I'm glad you haven't had time to straighten anything up." Angela entered the study.

She proceeded quietly and efficiently. She was mainly interested in correspondence, and most would be on Rob's computer or tablet. But she needed to look everywhere for notes or scraps of paper, including the trash, as well as filing cabinets and bookcases. Rob was organized, so she found everything physical she needed quickly.

She returned to the dining room after twenty minutes, carrying Rob's open briefcase, filled with files. She had Rob's published books under her other arm. "Nancy, I'd like to take these back to the station to look over more carefully. They include Rob's personal correspondence and your financial documents, including his writing income."

"That's fine. Mike Butler has everything essential. As Rob's agent he handles our finances."

"I'll need to take Rob's computer and tablet with me. But I'd like to talk separately with each of you first."

For the first time, Nancy looked uncomfortable.

Beth walked her to the door and opened the screen. "Can I help you carry anything?"

"No, I've got it." When she popped the trunk, she could hear raised voices coming from the condo.

Nancy spoke up as soon as Angela returned. "There are personal items on that computer. I don't want strangers looking through our dirty laundry."

Angela set her jaw. It was time to educate her friend about some facts. "Nance, I know how hard this is, but you need to understand something. A person shot Rob, and he might die. That makes this a potential homicide investigation. An evidence team would normally do this search, but I came personally. My lieutenant let me do this for two reasons. First, he knows the timeline excludes you both as suspects. Second, both the nature of

Rob's wound and the absence of any weapon at the scene make it clear this wasn't a suicide attempt. I agreed to do it because you're my friend, and I don't want an evidence team going through your dirty laundry, either."

"And they would literally go through our laundry, right?" Beth asked.

"Right."

Nancy crossed her arms, prompting Beth to intervene. "Don't you get it, Mom? She's bending over backwards to help us get through this. She has a shooter to catch and there could be clues here as to who might have wanted Dad dead."

"He's not dead," Nancy shouted.

Angela held up her hand and spoke in her calmest voice, "I know he isn't, Nance. But trust me, whoever did this wasn't trying to wound him. They were trying to kill him and probably think they succeeded. We haven't given the press any specifics to keep it that way."

"Mike Butler knows," Nancy said, calmer.

"I know. He was listed as an emergency contact in Rob's wallet, so my lieutenant had me call on him this morning. He had a solid alibi and was devastated by the news of Rob's shooting. I told him what I'm going to tell you. Don't discuss this with anyone else. He specifically asked permission to call you. I agreed because I know you have financial issues he'll have to help with."

"I'm sorry I shouted," Nancy said, eyes glistening. "There's so much to deal with. I know you and Beth are trying to help me get through this. It's just so hard."

Nodding her understanding, Angela said, "I'll talk to Beth first, in the study, and let you know when I need you."

Chapter Ten

Angela's interview with Beth provided no new clues. With Beth living so far away and seeing her father once a year, she hadn't expected very much. But Beth did help her regarding Rob's computer. Beth explained about the auto back-up feature and showed her how she could disconnect the square back-up drive. The small drive would be much easier to carry and backed up every one of her parents' electronic devices in one place. Beth told Angela that being able to keep Rob's computer would make this easier for her mother.

Why? Nancy had her own computer and tablet.

Angela decided to wait and ask Nancy that question.

Nancy seemed recovered when Angela brought her into the study for their session. Beth withdrew to the living room with her tablet as Angela closed the door.

Nancy was helpful and even listed Rob's old rivals from when he worked as a scientist. But she couldn't come up with any enemies he might have made since they moved to Maui, only friends.

When the interview was over, Angela turned to Nancy. "You need to know my thoughts and prayers are with you, Beth, and Rob. We will catch the person who did this."

"I believe you, Ange. I do."

"Okay. Let's look at Rob's computer."

Angela saw Nancy tense. "Beth showed me how to get everything I need without taking the computer or the tablet with me. Would you like that?"

Nancy relaxed. "Oh, yes. It would mean a lot."

"Beth thought it would but didn't say why." Angela waited.

"Beth knows that, whenever Rob was away and I'd get lonely, I'd come in here and read something he wrote. Sometimes I'd read a published piece. But usually, I'd look for a work in progress. Rob didn't mind, as long as I never talked about what I read to anyone else. I'd read his electronic journal, too. If he was away for a long time, he'd leave little notes in there for me. I felt connected to him, you know. I couldn't bear both Rob and his writing being out of reach at the same time. Do you think I'm crazy?"

"No. I think you love your husband."

"Thank you, Ange. Now, what do you need to do on the computer?"

"I need to check the backup and confirm it has everything that's on the drive. Beth didn't know her dad's password. Do you?"

"Yes. Only he and I know it," Nancy said and logged in.

After spending ten minutes going through files, Angela could tell the backup was complete. One file, however, caught her by surprise. "Nancy, I picked you up at seven twenty-five last night. When did you and Beth get home?"

"A few minutes before eleven. I checked my watch when we parked the car."

"That's about what I figured. Is there anyone who might have come into the house while you were gone? A neighbor with a key?"

"No. Rob, Beth, and I are the only ones with keys, except the site manager. And he'd have no reason to do so unless there was an emergency."

"Do you have his contact information?"

"Yes, he lives off-site. I just sent everything to your cell."

Angela looked at her cell phone. "Got it." She turned back to Nancy. "Looks like I have everything I need. I'll return the back-up drive as soon as I've downloaded everything to Keone's computer at the station. In the meantime, you have everything on Rob's computer and Beth can hook you back up to the Internet."

"Thank you for understanding, Ange," Nancy said as they walked to the screen door. Beth had gone into the study to reconnect things.

Angela opened the door, turned back to Nancy, and said in a soft voice, "You might want to glance at the last file loaded and when it was saved. I think you might find it interesting."

She gave Nancy the filename and location before she left. She could tell she'd piqued Nancy's curiosity. Hell, that file had piqued Angela's curiosity.

NANCY WAS INTRIGUED BY WHAT ANGE TOLD HER about the file and by the title—*Something More*.

Beth had everything up and running in the study when Nancy returned. "Honey, thank you for doing that and for showing Angela how I could keep the computer. You were right about how important it is to me."

"No prob. Everything's all set to go."

"I'd like to commune with your dad's computer for a while. But I know we missed lunch."

"I'm fine. I was thinking we might have a nice *linner,* anyway."

Nancy loved Rob's term for a late lunch/early dinner. "Perfect. I owe you. I shouldn't be too long."

"I can keep myself occupied for a little while. I'll come and get you if hunger pangs overtake me."

"Fine."

They each settled into different rooms and busied themselves in different ways. Beth slid into the living room, plopped onto the couch, and withdrew into an eBook on her tablet. Nancy remained in the study and sat in Rob's chair at the computer.

After a minute, she opened the folder that Angela said contained the newest file. This same folder held Rob's journal. A borderline obsessive-compulsive, Rob saved each month's journal entries in a subfolder.

That can't be right.

The file Angela mentioned was in the subfolder for July. He saved it on . . .

No. That's wrong.

The date was unlikely, but the time . . . That had to be a computer glitch. And why hadn't he renamed the July folder? It still sat right between June and August, daring her to open the document it contained.

She opened the file and blinked. It contained a completed manuscript.

He would have taken months to write this.

She searched the computer and found no earlier drafts.

No way. His first book went through over fifty revisions before he considered it good enough to submit. Those fifty revisions still resided on the computer along with the five that followed after submission and every galley proof. He never deleted anything. Yet, she found no earlier drafts. No outline. No raw notes. Nothing.

The document's location disturbed her as much as the time stamp. Rob's electronic computer journal had gaps, as did everything he wrote.

She recalled a conversation they'd had two days ago in this very room:

"Why you lazy bum. Nothing in the journal for the whole month of July?"

"I have a rule never to write in the computer journal after the fact. I kept a paper journal during the Europe trip that ran through

July second. When I got back, I filed it there on the bookcase with my older paper journals."

"But how will you ever find it again?"

"Do you know me? I know the location of every scrap of paper in this room. Now, how about we watch the sunset with a couple gin and tonics?"

Nancy found that paper notebook, right where he said it would be. In it, Rob described in detail the landscape around Florence, the last city he'd visited on the tour. That wasn't unusual.

But an entire manuscript, sitting patiently on the computer in a folder that had contained a different file with thirty-one blank dated pages the day before was unusual—damned unusual.

Confused, Nancy found the first few sentences, written in that odd typewriter font he always used for drafts:

Silence. Absolute. Unrelenting. Silence.

Usually, when confronted by extreme quiet, I first notice an insistent ringing in my ears. Next, I hear the gentle rush of my breathing. Finally, I feel blood pulsing through my body.

Not this time.

Sound doesn't exist for me.

The world isn't quiet. It's silent.

This silence is wrong.

Everything has changed...

~

NANCY GLANCED AGAIN AT THE TIME AND DATE AFTER reading the first few pages.

It's a mistake. A computer glitch.

Only she and Rob knew the password. Neither of them could have saved a file—then.

Afraid Beth might walk in on her and ask questions she wasn't prepared to answer, she sent the file to the printer in their bedroom.

The moment Nancy closed the document, Beth walked into the study. "You need to eat something and so do I. Let's hit the deli, okay?"

"Sure," Nancy replied, "but don't expect me to eat much."

Beth's look told her she'd be watching. Nancy could wait to read the manuscript. She'd have to. But she couldn't erase what she'd read from her mind.

Chapter Eleven

Something More

By

Rob Lister

Day: Unknown; Time: Unknown

Silence. Absolute. Unrelenting. Silence.

Usually, when confronted by extreme quiet, I first notice an insistent ringing in my ears. Next, I hear the gentle rush of my breathing. Finally, I feel my heart beating and blood pulsing through my body.

Not this time.

Sound doesn't exist for me.

The world isn't quiet. It's silent.

This silence is wrong.

Everything has changed...

The total darkness disturbs me less, as logic explains it. My eyes are probably closed. The pain in my head happened about sunset and I've probably been unconscious for some time.

The pain?

That's right. My last memory was pain. A sharp pain at the base of my skull.

Closed eyes and night can combine to create inky darkness. But why can't I open my eyes? Why can't I feel them rolling around behind my eyelids?

Why can't I feel—anything?

No pain, thank God. But I can't tell if I'm sitting up, standing, or lying down. I'm not dizzy. My mind seems clear. Yet something is definitely wrong.

"How do you know your mind is clear?"

I can test my cognitive skills. Ten times seventeen equals one hundred seventy. The square root of forty-nine is seven. Math's okay. How about general knowledge? Shakespeare wrote *Hamlet* and *Coriolanus*. I add the latter to make sure I'm making this a challenge. DNA self-replicates through the auspices of DNA-polymerase and is transcribed into RNA, which is translated on ribosomes into protein. The nascent protein molecule then folds and is either innately active or activated by phosphorylation or some other modification to carry out its functions. My biochemistry and molecular biology expertise remains intact. Gallia est omnis divisa in partes tres. Three branches constitute the United States government – executive, legislative, and judicial. Today is Sunday. My name is Robert Thomas Lister, and I'm sixty-two years, eight months, and thirteen days old.

The old synapses seem to be firing. But I can't feel anything or move anything. Fingers—gone. Hands—gone. Arms—gone. Toes—gone. Feet—gone. Legs—gone. Chest—gone. Abdomen—gone. Shoulders—gone. Neck—gone. Face—gone. That's the most unsettling. I can't feel my face. I can't even frown.

What spinal injury makes your face numb? Those senses come

from cranial nerves that don't travel down the spine. "On Old Olympus' Towering Tops, a Finn and German Viewed Some Hops."—Olfactory, Optic, Oculomotor, Trigeminal, Trochlear, Abducens, Facial, Auditory Vestibular, Glossopharyngeal, Vagus, Spinal Accessory, Hypoglossal. I can't believe I still remember this from physiology lectures. Those were over forty years ago.

"Paralysis?" I ask the question in my mind, thinking it's rhetorical.

"No, pan aesthesia."

The response seems to materialize in my mind.

"Okay, let's go through the possibilities here: Possibility One: I'm completely paralyzed, on a respirator in a hospital somewhere. Then why can't I hear or see or feel my face or my eyes? Am I in a coma? If so, how can my thoughts be so lucid? Possibility Two: I'm unconscious and dreaming the above. But I don't feel unconscious. Possibility Three: I don't want to acknowledge this one, but as a scientist I must. I'm dead. If so, the afterlife's pretty damn disappointing."

"Not really."

There's another one of those unusual thoughts in my mind.

"This isn't my thought. It doesn't sound like me. I don't even agree with it."

"Good. You're starting to get it, Robert. May I call you Robert?"

Somehow, I'm now certain the other voice in my head is male and equally certain it isn't mine.

"Sure. Does this mean I have pan aesthesia and schizophrenia?"

"What do you think?"

"A head trauma shouldn't cause that."

"What are your hypotheses then?"

"Hypothesis One: I'm carrying out a thought conversation with myself. Hypothesis Two: I'm unconscious and dreaming the above. Hypothesis Three: I don't like this—same as Possibility Three?"

"I was called Calla when I lived on Earth."

~

AM I DEAD?

In my mind I hear John Cleese from the old *Monty Python* sketch, *This parrot has ceased to be. It is a former parrot.*

I need to remember more about what happened immediately before . . . this.

That voice—Calla—interrupts. "You are about to try to remember something, are you not?"

This is becoming annoying. "I thought I might recall what happened to me right before I . . . uh . . . met you. Do you have a problem with that?"

"No, but you might. Memories are vivid here. They can overtake you. You can become lost. The consequences could be . . . quite serious."

"You're saying I shouldn't try to remember?"

"No, I am explaining the danger. If you allow me to accompany you, I can protect you from that danger."

"Uh, sure, come on along. I was on my way to the airport to pick up my daughter Beth—a surprise for my wife Nancy for our anniversary."

I find myself in our grey VW with the top down, driving on the Pali from Lāhainā, preparing to plunge toward Māʻalaea Harbor. It's a half-hour before sunset, the view soft and kind. No whales in July, so I don't need to look out for quick-braking tourists, anxious to take the three-billionth picture of a humpback—after it disappears.

The sun slowly descends through clear skies to the water's surface . . .

I hear Calla's thoughts again in my mind. "Robert."

"Whoa. That was scary. My memory seemed to be sucking me in. I only wanted to remember how I got injured, but I got sidetracked."

"I know. Getting lost in memories is easy here unless you discipline your mind."

"Okay, I'll focus. I'm driving to Kahului via Wailuku. I came early to allow for a little side trip. I love the ʻĪao Valley's natural calming influence and want to spend a few minutes there and maybe do a little writing before heading to the airport's bustle. Look, we're heading up the road now." I notice we seem to jump ahead in the memory as if I've discovered the fast forward button.

"This road is narrow and winding. It is also poorly lit." Calla seems concerned.

"That's why it's fun."

I'm driving a little faster than normal. I've got to keep moving to beat the sunset. I envision the verdant valley and the ʻĪao Needle proclaiming its wildness. A different shape from different vantage points, the Needle's smooth, inverted cone pushes up the lush vegetation to pronounce this place truly Hawaiian.

These memories are in my head. We don't float above the car observing, we're inside the mind of an earlier version of me behind the wheel. Brilliant light in our eyes shatters our reverie. We're only immobilized for a moment. I'm thinking, "Why's a truck coming down this way? Probably hauling some private agricultural contraband."

These thoughts take less than a second. I struggle to make my arms turn the damn wheel, but I can't. I'm in this body. I can feel and experience everything it does. But it won't obey me. The mind in control sees the problem and tries to give the barreling truck a wide berth.

As the truck slows, the driver, his passenger, and I exchange surprised stares as the vehicles swerve to avoid each other. Something about one man's expression—fear, recognition, I don't know, something—commands my attention before I shake it off and continue to the ʻĪao Valley.

When we reach the nearly empty parking lot, we see a local family struggling to remove a huge leaf-wrapped pig from the back of a well-used pick-up. Looks like somebody's having a lūʻau tomorrow.

I approach the path to the viewing site and notice movement in the bushes across the lot from where I parked. A small form climbs over a chain-link fence and down to the ʻĪao stream. From the height I assume it's a child, but I can't be sure. Maybe it's a *menehune*. These fictional little people supposedly inhabited the islands before the Tahitians arrived. Shy, they only come out at dusk and work until dawn on their many projects to protect the *aina*, the Hawaiian word for land.

I don't walk onto the bridge over the stream for the perfect view of the ʻĪao needle. Instead, I climb down a stairway past a reconstructed taro garden. Water pours from level to level through pipes to keep the base of each plant submerged. In truth the pipes should be bamboo, but the park employees use PVC to maintain the essence, if not the detail.

At the stairway's end, a level area spreads out that includes a large planter shaped like the Island of Maui, complete with a pointed stone to represent the ʻĪao Needle. A variety of native plants flourish here and are changed with the seasons to reflect different aspects of the island's ecosystem.

Directly beyond the planter is an imu pit, the probable destination for the pig I saw in the parking lot. Beyond the pit, a raised, grass-covered area provides a stage for dining or entertainment. As sunset approaches, the birds in the surrounding trees erupt in song. They'll continue for about fifteen minutes until the sun is truly gone.

I climb onto the stage and watch the ʻĪao Stream churn past. I'm immersed in this symphony of sights and sounds, grateful to live in this wonderful place. I slowly turn to face the bridge and the needle.

Wham!

Something slams into the base of my skull.

Pain.

I don't even have time for a last thought before I'm ejected from my body.

Once I'm outside my body, I'm back in silence and darkness.

The pain is gone. "What would have happened if we hadn't left when we did? Would I have died?"

"Once your living-self lost consciousness, you had nowhere to go in the memory. Thus, you returned here."

But where is here?

Chapter Twelve

B ack from linner, Nancy excused herself for some personal time in her bedroom. Before she slid the pocket door closed, she saw Beth slouch on the couch, open her tablet and become one with Brent Week's latest fantasy epic.

A large portion of the manuscript had printed before the paper ran out. Nancy pulled a stack off the printer and set it on the bed, then added fresh paper and resumed printing.

I should call Angela.

She didn't know if Rob's description could help her friend with the investigation but felt obliged to disclose it. Of course, the fact that the eyewitness was in a hospital bed in a coma might make Ange question its relevance. Still, she reached for her phone.

"Good afternoon. Maui Police Department, Sergeant Beyers speaking. How may I help you?"

"Hi, Ange. You even answer your cell phone like that?"

"I do during work hours. You never know who might be calling."

"I'm sorry to bother you."

"You're never a bother, Nance. What's up?"

"I took your advice and started reading the file you pointed out. Have you?"

"I've been chasing down other leads, but I'll take a look before I go home."

"I think that would be a good idea. I think the first part might help you with your investigation."

"Thanks. How are you doing? I'm sorry if I upset you today."

"You didn't upset me. Everything upset me. But I'm starting to find some focus. Your visit forced me to do that. Mahalo."

"I'm so glad. You're lucky you've got Beth there with you. She's a bright young woman, you know."

"Yes, I know. We'll talk again soon. I'm interested in what you make of the story. Aloha."

"Aloha."

Nancy sat down on the bed, turned over the pages she'd already read and dove back into Rob's story.

Beth looked up from her tablet to realize two hours had passed since she last saw her mother. She'd heard no sounds coming from the bedroom. Two hours on her own, and her mother hadn't cried once. Had she fallen asleep? Beth decided to check on her. After only one meal today, Mom needed something to eat, if only a snack.

She paused outside the door, hoping to hear sobbing, or at least snoring. Instead, she heard papers being turned and tossed. She knocked. The paper shuffling increased, and Mom blurted, "Just a minute, Beth. I'll be right there."

Beth didn't wait.

Her mother tensed, then relaxed. "Come on in, kid. I've decided to ask for your help with something. I wasn't going to involve you. But the more I get into this, the more I realize I need another perspective."

"What is this?" Beth pointed at the papers scattered across the bed and onto the floor.

"It's a story. I've been reading it since we got back. Well, I started before we left, but . . ."

"You're reading a story?"

"Somehow, it's helping me. I think it could help you, too. Please humor me and don't ask why."

Beth watched her mother carefully collect the scattered pages and place them in a pile next to a much larger stack she assumed were unread.

Between both piles Beth estimated over three hundred pages of double-spaced text rested on the bed. "Where'd you get this tome?"

"I found it on your dad's computer. Well, Angela found it and pointed me to it. I'd like you to read up to where I am while I fix us a snack."

"Did Dad write this?"

"Read first." Mom pointed to the smaller stack. "We can talk about it while we eat."

Beth's surprise that her mother was going to leave her alone allowed her mother to glide out to the kitchen before she could ask any more questions. She was left with a stack of pages and a mountain of unanswered questions.

Beth began to read.

Dad did write this. He'd put his name on the first page. Even if he hadn't, she would have recognized his style. But the content was nothing like his usual writing. Critics chastised her dad for the lack of imagery in his books. This was so vivid—so focused on internal thoughts and external perceptions.

She flew through the pages. Rapid reading was a pre-requisite in her line of work. She soon caught up to her mother and understood why Mom was so rattled when she'd walked in. This would disorient anyone. On its surface, her father's story was a fantasy. His other books were non-fiction, focused on science and the business of science.

She wanted to learn more about this mysterious Calla. But the part that gave her goose bumps was when Dad described his own shooting, where it would occur, and when. Sure, he hadn't provided a date in the manuscript, but his age and the general time of day were the same as those on the night he was shot.

Given her mother's denial about everything else, she'd be careful when they discussed this new impossibility. But they needed to discuss it.

If this story was what she believed it to be, it represented the most astounding discovery imaginable. Could her father be speaking to them from beyond their physical world?

She read on.

Chapter Thirteen

Day: Still unknown; Time: Still unknown

That other voice in my mind is very persistent. "Your recollection is quite comprehensive."

"Okay . . . Calla, is it? You can read my thoughts and I can read yours."

"Yes, when they are directed."

"Why can't I see or hear you?"

"To see, you need eyes. To hear, you need ears."

"What are you saying? My ears were cut off and my eyes gouged out when I hit the ground?"

"Nothing so gruesome. You left your body."

"Elvis has left the building."

"Yes. In a manner of speaking."

"Am I dead?"

"Do you feel dead?"

"No, I don't feel anything. That's the problem."

"Ask a different question, one that I can try to answer."

"Okay, am I unconscious?"

"Do you feel unconscious?"

As I receive this thought, I realize something I'd missed before. How can a thought in my mind have an accent. "Are you going to answer all my questions with other questions?"

"What do you think?" Calla asks.

"I think I'm losing ground."

"What is your religion, Robert?"

"I was raised in the Christian faith, but I don't belong to a church."

"What does your faith tell you?"

"I see where you're going. It tells me there's life after death."

"So?"

"So, this is . . . what? My afterlife?"

"I am impressed by you, Robert."

"Am I in heaven?"

"Does it feel like heaven?"

If I'm honest with myself—no way. As a scientist, having no ability to perceive my environment would be much more like . . . I've got to change the subject. "Do you have a body?"

"Not what you would call a body. I have what you have—existence, sentience."

"Why can I still think, if I have no brain?"

"You still exist. Cogito ergo sum. You understand this. You were a scientist."

"I am a scientist."

"Yes. I apologize. I misspoke."

"Apology accepted. So, I exist, but as what?"

For the first time, Calla pauses. "I cannot describe it precisely, but I can approximate. Consider a point of light. Now consider that this point has a huge amount of energy but occupies no space. Finally, imagine this point has consciousness—your consciousness, or my consciousness."

"Am I visible?"

"No. But you can be perceived."

"Light is visible."

"Visible light occupies only a small portion of the full spectrum of electromagnetic radiation. When I said light, I paraphrased. You will find that you have quite formidable abilities."

"Abilities? I can't even see."

"Yes, but you can perceive that which is visible, and more. What do you perceive directly in front of you?"

"Nothing."

"Am I there?"

"No. You're off to my right."

"How do you know?"

"Your thoughts are coming from there."

"You are correct. You have perception."

"So what, if I can only perceive other people who have no bodies? No offense."

"None taken. But is my position the only thing you can perceive?"

His question takes me by surprise. I can't see anything, but he says I can perceive visible objects. I open my mind, which is basically all I am now, to discover whether I can perceive anything directly in front of me.

"I do sense something. It's like when your eyes adjust to a dark place, and you start to see . . . stars. There's a field of stars. I can't exactly see them. I can sense them. They have energy and light, but they're far, far away. There's no consciousness, though. Only matter and energy."

"Good," Calla replies. "Now, what is directly beneath you?"

I perceive enormous energy, heat, and light. Much closer than the objects in front but somehow similar. "The sun." I shout out in my mind. "It's the sun, our sun."

Then somewhere around here . . . Aaah, yes, there it is, directly opposite where I sense Calla. Home. Earth. How could I have missed it before? It's breathtaking. I feel the oceans and the deserts and the mountains and the towns and the cities and the fields. Oh, it feels so good. If I had eyes, I'd be crying.

"I've found my home, Calla. Can I go closer?"

"You can, but you must not—you could be lost forever."

"I knew it. I'm in hell."

"I am telling you that you cannot go, yet. You are not ready."

"Then I'm in purgatory."

"Why must you put a name on everything?"

"I'm a scientist. We do that."

"Must this existence fit neatly into a box you define?"

This stops me. Am I being tested, or have I already failed? I need to find out what Calla's keeping from me.

"Calla, who are you? Are you an angel?"

"I am a guide."

"Do you believe in God?"

"That depends on how you define God. I commune with *an astounding entity*." This last thought doesn't precisely translate into English.

"Are you a Christian?"

"When I lived on Earth, Jesus Christ had not been born."

"That's not an answer."

"Oh, but it is. I am a guide, not a teacher. You must learn on your own the answers to the important questions. And you will. Nothing will be hidden from you, but I cannot deny you the opportunity to discover the answers yourself."

"Why not?"

"It would cripple you. You studied biology. Think. The butterfly in the cocoon."

He knows my mind better than I do. He's referring to a classic biological experiment. If you open the end of a cocoon, to help a butterfly get out, it will never be able to fly. The struggle to break free from the cocoon pumps fluid into the wings and causes them to open fully. Otherwise, it crawls around a bit, then dies, never fulfilling its mission to reproduce.

"What good is perception if I can't feel, hear, taste, smell, touch, or see anything?"

"You are a scientist. You can perceive a molecule, measure its effects, even determine if it has been changed. You spent your career in research doing this."

"Right, because a molecule was too small to be seen with my eyes, even with advanced optics. Some larger forms can be visualized using electron microscopy or crystallography, but you don't see the molecule, only a graphic representation."

"A moment ago, you told me you perceived the sun. We are precisely equidistant from your Earth and your Sun. Describe to me what you perceive."

"Intense heat and enormous energy."

"When you were mortal could you perceive directly the sun's surface from this distance with your senses?"

"Of course not. I'd have been vaporized before I had a chance to die from the vacuum of space."

"Then you will admit that perception has some advantages, despite its disadvantages?" Calla asks.

"Obviously. But when I was remembering my, uh, event, I was able to experience my usual senses, even extreme pain."

"Yes. What have you learned?"

"I can experience the sensations of life when I'm in my memories, but I can only perceive that which can be sensed when I am here."

"Not quite."

"Okay. I can also perceive energies that are beyond the range of my mortal senses."

"Perception is less intimate, but more comprehensive. As a scientist this must hold some appeal for you, yes?"

"I understand that you"—*or my subconscious mind*—"want to help me accept my new situation, but I'm too overcome by what I've lost to concede any gain."

"I appreciate your honesty. You have taken an important first step in discovering your situation. I am proud of you."

"Can I be alone for a while? I have a lot to think about."

"Call my name when you want to commune again."

This will take some getting used to. I spend the next few

seconds (minutes? days? months? millennia?) alone with my thoughts. I've got to discover where I am—and when.

I'm still unclear about my status. The possibilities have been reduced to two in my mind. Either I'm close to death and imagining this. Or I'm dead and in some afterlife. As a scientist, I must critically evaluate these options. I've read about people having experiences when they were near death. They exhibited highly active EEG tracings inconsistent with their comatose state. Could I be lying in a hospital bed, apparently comatose, while still experiencing this alternate existence? Yes. It's possible.

On the other hand, I do believe in the basic tenets of my faith —or want to. I hope that there's life after death. Although Calla did suggest *he's* not alive—I was called Calla when I lived on earth —he never actually said *I'm* dead.

If Calla's real, I'm probably dead. But if he exists only in my mind, I could be in a coma. I reflect on the vivid moments I've experienced so far. If this is from my subconscious, I need to take it out for a walk more often. I guess I'll play along for a while and see what I can discover. Where else do I have to be?

~

"Calla."

"Yes, Robert. I am glad that you are back."

"What day is it?"

"What day do you believe it is?"

"Sunday, assuming I arrived here before midnight."

"It is indeed Sunday—for you."

"For me?" I consider the implications. "What is it for you?"

"Sunday—right now."

"You give strange answers, Calla. They always seem to suggest more questions."

"I am a guide. I will not lie to you."

"Could you be at a different day if you wanted?"

"That . . . is an excellent question, Robert. It demonstrates your investigative abilities—important for a scientist. The answer is yes. Does a related question occur to you? I know that, as a biochemist, you had to study physics."

"I sucked at physics. But I know what you're getting at. Okay, I'll play. Could you be in a different place if you wanted?"

"Yes. Now finish the question."

"Could I?"

"Yes." A pause. "You have taken your first step into a larger universe."

"Didn't Obi-wan Kenobi say that to Luke Skywalker?" I project this with great sarcasm. This elicits a chuckle from Calla. Although how I know this, I can't imagine.

"All right," I ask, "how can I change my position in space and time?"

"Before you learn this skill, I must make sure that you realize the need for extreme caution. I mentioned before that you could lose yourself if you do this rashly. I am allowed one demonstration. We will move twice as close to earth as we are currently, for precisely one second, then return to where we are now in space."

My consciousness explodes. The input is too intense. I seem to be experiencing every voice, every thought, every sight, every motion, and every pain from every inhabitant of the earth at once. Then we're back, and I'm able to bear my perceptions again. But something else has changed, something much more frightening. "Calla, I'm perceiving in multiple directions at once. What happened?"

"A reflex. You diluted the overload by including the full spectrum of perception. You could not direct it, so you perceived everything simultaneously. That is one of your new abilities."

Simultaneous perception in every direction is astounding, but hard to get my head around. My perceptions extend outward in a sphere, from the point of my consciousness. But there's a problem.

"Calla, now that we're back where we started, I perceive much more than before."

"Yes. The overload also forced you to open your perception to every wavelength in the electromagnetic spectrum. As we discussed before, what is visible to the human eye is only a tiny fraction. You now perceive X-rays, radio waves, ultraviolet, and infrared, which are detectable by contemporary human technology. In addition, you now perceive wavelengths undetectable even with your most sensitive scientific instruments"

"And I perceive these in every direction at once."

"Yes."

"When we were closer to the Earth, I also perceived the life forms teeming over its surface. I could understand their thoughts, even primitive, animal thoughts."

"Did any specific thoughts catch your attention?"

"No. No. Too many voices competed for my attention. The cacophony was unintelligible. But I could tell they were there, distinct and available to me. How am I doing this?"

"You will understand more as we move forward. You have only scratched the surface of your new capabilities."

"I notice no magnification capability in these perceptions. Is that because I haven't learned how to do something or is this an innate feature?"

"If it were not so, can you imagine the overload you would be experiencing even now? Proximity has meaning even here and allows us to buffer our perceptions."

"Amazing. But I'm finding it hard to concentrate. Can I block part of it out somehow?"

"Yes, but you must leave a small portal for me to call to you. You must promise."

"I will. I don't have any desire to be completely alone."

"You know how you used to be able to blur your vision when you wanted to think about something intensely?"

"Yes. I remember doing that as a child, when I needed to concentrate on a math problem in class."

"First, find the exact point where you perceive me. Keep this open as you blur out the rest. If you don't return, I will contact you. But I think that you will come out on your own. You might want to spend some time with your memories."

Finally, he's providing some direction. The key to figuring this out might be in my memories.

"Where should I begin?"

"To quote the lovely Julie Andrews, as Maria von Trapp, *Begin at the very beginning, a very good place to start.*"

"Two movie references in one encounter—it's time for me to leave. Here goes."

I concentrate on defocusing my perceptions everywhere except precisely where Calla's presence seems to be. The sphere becomes slightly blurred, then the blurring deepens until I perceive only blurring, except for one small crack that I leave open to Calla.

I concentrate on memory and feel completely at ease. I remember my first landing in Hawai`i over thirty years ago.

But that wasn't the very beginning.

Chapter Fourteen

Monday, July 8, 7:00 p.m. HST

Angela Beyers dropped the papers she'd been reading as if they were on fire. *What the hell was that?*

She was up to where Rob Lister decided to go back and remember his early life. She wanted to stop several times when it got too cerebral but kept scanning for information helpful for her investigation.

The overall story couldn't be true, but some descriptions were so vivid, she felt a need to check them out. Someone was on that trail across the stream. And what about that truck that sideswiped him on the way up to the ʻĪao Valley? What if that wasn't an accident?

Angela couldn't share any of these *clues* with Alcala. He'd laugh her all the way back to Hana. She'd thought about printing the manuscript so she could read at home, even share it with Linda, but didn't want the lieutenant to happen by and catch her. Instead, she mailed it to her department email.

Keone once told her everything associated with a case should be investigated, even facts that seemed unlikely on the surface. They'd discussed the unique connection people born on Maui, like them, felt to the island. Some, like Keone's grandmother, felt the aina had a life force. Many of Angela's cases were touched by it in some way. Ideas mainlanders would call weird seemed more reasonable to people close to the aina. Hell, that last case she helped Keone on had plenty of weird in it. That guy, Sam, believed he'd crossed over from another dimension.

On her way to her car, she slid out her cell phone and called home.

"You are alive then," Linda cracked as she answered the call.

"I'm sorry about the craziness, Lin, but you got the note I left, right?"

"Yes."

Angela picked up on the terse response and tried another tack. "How 'bout I treat us to dinner tonight at your favorite restaurant?"

"No."

"No?" *This isn't going well.*

"That's right, no. I'm currently preparing a perfectly good meal right here at home. You do remember where that is, don't you?"

"Ouch."

"Anyway, I thought you'd call it a day about now, which should put you home by about eight p.m., if you're actually calling to tell me you've left."

"I left the parking lot in Wailuku a minute ago."

"What have they got you working on?"

"It's complicated. With some pieces I can't quite get my head around."

"Get yourself home. I'll straighten you out, girl."

"You always do."

～

Tuesday, July 9, 8:00 a.m. CEST (Monday, July 8, 8:00 p.m.)

Eight thousand miles away from Maui, Julie and Keone's flight from Chicago approached Italy. A flight attendant's gentle touch awakened Julie for breakfast allowing her to arouse her husband. The flight attendants all seemed a little nervous around Keone. Probably just his size.

Julie followed Keone's eyes, as he stared out the window sipping the sweet bubbly wine served with delicate pastries. She hoped it was the stunning view of the Italian alps and not thoughts of work that held his attention. As they ate, snowy peaks gave way to the dark green hills and valleys of Northern Italy. What a lovely way to greet a new day.

An announcement interrupted her reverie. "We are now flying over Italy. If you wish to set your watches to local time it is 8:00 a.m., Central European Summer Time. We will be landing at 8:30 a.m. CEST at Rome's Fiumicino Airport."

Julie watched Keone adjust his watch. She kept hers on Maui time, just for fun. It was still yesterday at home. Time was such an interesting concept.

Chapter Fifteen

Monday, July 8, 8:00 p.m. CEST

Throughout dinner, Angela thought about what she'd read. Last night she'd been anxious to share everything with Linda, but now?

"Okay, girl. You've been quiet long enough. Tell me what's going on."

"Sorry, Lin. I have so much news I didn't know where to start. First off, I'm temporarily assigned to CID."

"Really?"

"I think Keone may be responsible for that."

"Uh-huh. For a moment I'd like you to pretend I'm not a cop and don't know all your cute little abbreviations? What the hell's CID?"

"Sometimes I forget you're the creative one and I'm the cop. CID is Criminal Investigation Division." When Linda still registered no recognition, she added, "Where the detectives work. Where Keone works."

"Do you think it's because you passed that detective exam?"

"No. Many people pass that exam and still wait months or years before being contacted by CID. The lieutenant suggested it's because he's short-handed and because I know the victim. But I think there's more to it."

"You know the victim. What's the case? And, before you spew some bullshit about how you can't discuss an ongoing investigation, you know I never share anything you tell me."

"A shooting."

"That sounds juicy. Where?"

"'Īao Valley, in the state park."

"Who got shot?"

"A friend." Angela's eyes glistened. "Actually, a friend's husband, but I liked him, too."

Linda stood, walked over, and gave her a hug. Looking into her eyes she said, "Is he alive?"

"Barely."

"Do you have any good leads?"

"Leads—yes. Good—no. But there's something else. Something a little weird."

"You know I love weird."

"The victim's a writer, and he left something on his computer."

"Somehow a writer leaving something on his computer doesn't seem all that weird."

"The file was created over two hours after he was shot and describes the shooting in detail from his point of view."

"Ooh-la-la. Très creepy." Linda's faux French accent prompted a chuckle. "This I must read, Mademoiselle l'inspectrice."

"I'm not some female Poirot, but I would like you to read it. You couldn't discuss it with anyone, ever. You'd be working as an informal consultant to Maui police department. I'm up to my eyeballs in work, the damn thing's three hundred pages long, and most of it has nothing to do with my investigation."

"That means some of it does?"

"Some parts *might,* but others are pure fantasy. I'll need you to focus on hints about possible motive or suspects. In the part I finished, the guy plans to re-experience his entire life."

"You want me to read it front to back and highlight sections of interest, right?"

"Right. Oh, Lin, there's one more thing."

"Uh-oh. I hate it when you sound like Columbo."

"Well, you can't print it out and can only read it on my department laptop. Oh, and you won't be able to open any other files. They're all encrypted."

"I'd prefer my tablet, but I understand. Just set me up in the study, and I'll get started tonight."

Angela did as she was told while Lin cleared the table and put the dishes in the dishwasher. When Linda came into the study, she already had the manuscript up on the screen. "Okay. You are now officially an unpaid consultant to the Maui police department, with access to one secure file. Linda, I need you to take this seriously. It could mean my badge."

"I will. I'll share anything I discover with you in person or over your cellphone while you're at work. Okay? Now take a nice warm bath and get to sleep."

Angela was too tired to protest. "I've got a copy on Keone's computer at work, if I need to look at anything you discover. I can't thank you enough, Lin."

"What are friends for? Now, shut up and take your bath. I've got some reading to do."

Chapter Sixteen

Day: Sunday; Time: Still unknown

Although I arrived a bit too late to be a Thanksgiving baby, I did give my mother the pleasure of a short labor. She prepared a turkey dinner with all the trimmings for Dad, his parents, and my sisters, never mentioning her contractions to anyone, especially not my grandparents. She refused to ask Dad to take her to the hospital until she'd done the dishes and put away the leftovers. Dad dropped my sisters at his parents' house on the way to the hospital. He left before they could bog him down with questions. Of course, I learned this much later. Now my memory takes over.

President Harry S. Truman leads the United States as I emerge into the light, according to the news on the radio in the delivery room . . .

. . . The U.S. 17th Infantry has reached the Yalu River in North Korea. The river, which forms the border between Korea and Manchuria, has been the goal of these forces since the beginning of the conflict. Reports are circulating that the military is proposing a

final offensive which is being called the "Home by Christmas Offensive." This news is sure to brighten the day for family and friends here at home as well as our boys overseas.

In other news, a new musical comedy is set to open on Broadway tonight called Guys and Dolls. *Based on the works of Damon Runyon, the musical has music and lyrics by Frank Loesser and a book by Jo Swerling and Abe Burrows. Mr. Robert Alda will play the lead role, that of a gambler named Nathan Detroit.*

The U.S. House of Representatives is poised today to approve citations against the Hollywood Ten for contempt of Congress for refusing . . .

I'm amazed at how real the sounds and other sensations are for me as I reside within the tiny body that just emerged.

Baby Rob isn't aware of much beyond being cold, scared, and famished, but through my access to his senses, I am aware of much more. This isn't just a memory . . .

～

"Welcome back," Calla said. "You are making good progress, my friend. What do you wish from me?"

"Advice," I reply. "I've begun to relive my earliest memories . . ."

"Robert, one cannot relive. You are re-experiencing what you already lived."

"Whatever. But these experiences pop at every level. I love having senses again, but I experience everything on two levels. I have the sensations and thoughts I had at the time. But I also perceive things I couldn't then, as the person I am now. These aren't recovered memories, are they? I was an infant. Yet they're as sharp and clear as those from the ʻĪao Valley. How is that possible? I'm tempted to re-experience more of my life. But is it good use of my time? Will I miss a great deal if I do this? Help me, Calla."

"I will, but in my own way. I will guide you as a great countryman of mine would have. A man who died while I still lived.

His approach was to answer questions with questions. Some considered him the wisest of men."

"I may be a practical and worldly biochemist, but I recognize the Socratic method. So, you were born Greek and were alive at the turn of the fourth century B.C."

"I continue to be impressed by you, Robert."

"You still haven't answered my question. I need some of that guidance you keep talking about."

"How much time do you think has passed since you first encountered me?"

"I don't know. A little while ago I couldn't tell if my thoughts took minutes or years. But when I re-liv . . . uh . . . experienced that little piece of my old life, it seemed to pass in real time."

"Do you have any idea when you were struck?"

"Yes, shortly after sunset. I'd planned to leave to pick up Beth when it got too dark to stay in the park. I never made it."

"That is correct. What do you think struck you?"

"I don't know."

"Think."

"Well, I know it penetrated my skin. It burned as it went in. It felt like I was punched in the head by an iron fist. Oh hell, I was shot, wasn't I?"

"Yes."

"But who'd want to shoot me?"

"Let's keep that for a later discussion. Right now, we are concentrating on time."

"Okay. But given where the bullet hit me, I'd probably be paralyzed and wouldn't be able to breathe unless someone gave me CPR."

"After an injury of that magnitude, how long do you think your brain remained aware?"

"Not long. I probably lost enough blood to trigger unconsciousness in a few seconds."

"And brain death would follow in . . ."

"About ten minutes, if no oxygenated blood reached the brain."

"Then what time do you think you moved on?"

"Seven p.m.?"

"Close enough that I can help. 7:02:06 p.m."

"So what time is it now?" I ask. "It must be after midnight, or a year from then, or a thousand years. I don't know."

"Yes, you do. Tell me the time you believe we occupy right now."

"How should I know?" But before, when Calla let us move closer to the earth, he'd said, "We will move twice as close to earth for one second, then come back to where we are now in space."

"Calla, I don't know why I'm saying this, but—7:02:07 p.m., today, Sunday?"

"Precisely."

"I can move in time and space, but it takes a conscious effort to do so. Unless I start the clock, or you do, it stays at the exact moment when I lost awareness."

"Your body lost awareness. You moved on, remember?"

"Okay, but what about the rest?"

"You will move in time when you wish to do so."

"I thought time was frozen, not me."

"Can you describe your perception of time when you lived on Earth?"

"Time went forward at a constant speed, and I went with it."

"And now?"

"Now time can stop?"

"Try again."

"I can stop my progression through time?"

"Yes."

"Can I start it up again?"

"What do you think?"

I need to play his game. "I can start my progression through time again, if I want."

"Yes. Go on."

"Well, you already confirmed I could move in both space and time."

"Yes."

"I'm no longer limited to moving forward in time."

"Yes."

"How will I know when time . . . No, I mean, how will I know when I start progressing through time again?"

"How do you know when you start progressing through space?"

"I move."

"Yes."

"I won't progress forward, or backward for that matter, in time or space until I decide to move and learn how to do it, right?"

"That is correct and enough guidance for the present. You need to answer your initial question. You said, 'I'm tempted to re-experience more of my life. But is it good use of my time? Will I miss a great deal if I do this?'"

"I won't miss anything, because I'm not progressing through time."

"Correct. You can re-experience your entire life and when you return it will still be 7:02:07 p.m., Sunday."

"But what about my first question?"

"I believe you already suspect the answer, based on your phrasing of the question, 'These aren't recovered memories, are they?'"

"Are you saying I actually travelled through time?"

"No. I'm saying you travelled to a time tied to a memory and then moved forward through that time, but that doesn't cause you to move forward in this point in time."

"But why wasn't I overwhelmed by all the perceptions, like I was when we moved closer to Earth?"

"Why do you think?"

"Because I was focused on a specific space and time, by my memory, right?"

"That would be my opinion."

"Okay, I'll give re-living my life a try."

"Not re-living!"

"Okay, okay, re-experiencing my life."

"Better. You might want to check with me occasionally to discuss what you have learned. Many have found this helpful when doing what you are doing."

"So, you've guided others. What if I check in every few years?"

"I'd suggest five, at first."

I allow the blurring to refill the gap where Calla waits. This time I leave a tiny hole. I must be getting better at this. I return to my memories and don't plan to stop until my fifth birthday party. In my perception this will take five years. But I know when I reach out to Calla it'll still be the exact same time I left. I realize I'm not wasting his time either.

Chapter Seventeen

Nancy warmed up some leftover meatloaf for sandwiches and listened to Neil Diamond. She found the routine activity calmed her. The disorientation she'd felt reading Rob's story gradually faded as reasonable explanations surfaced in her mind.

Sure, Rob wrote it. It's him trying to write a fantasy.

But the details?

Coincidence. He never provides a specific date or year. Our anniversary's the same day every year. It's logical he'd use an occasion he remembers for his story.

But he described the shooting exactly the way it happened and precisely where it happened?

He's driven up that way so many times it's an obvious location for him to use. I've heard him talk about how eerie it can be around sunset.

Life imitating art?

Sure. The fact that he was writing this gave him a reason to be up there at that time of day. He probably planned to write some description to use in the novel, like he did in Florence.

What about where we found the manuscript?

He probably stuck this in the blank space in his journal long after he wrote it, to pay me back for kidding him about leaving those pages empty. He could have written it anytime, even months ago. He probably wrote the drafts by hand so I wouldn't see it prematurely. This last thought calmed her.

AN HOUR LATER, AS NANCY POURED THE WINE, BETH emerged from the bedroom. Lines on her forehead and a faraway look in her eyes told Nancy her daughter was still pondering what she'd just read.

"Dad really did write this, didn't he?" This sounded more like an accusation than a question.

"It appears so. Angela found it on his computer this morning."

"It's good. I didn't know he could write like this. It's nothing like his other work. Isn't it weird how close his description is to the real shooting? It's even on your anniversary and about the right time. When did he write it?"

Nancy hesitated. Even though she was sure a logical explanation existed for the date and time on the file, she wasn't ready to discuss this part with Beth. "It must have been some time ago. But I agree it's eerily close to what happened. Do you think your dad's a closet psychic?"

The question brought a smile to Beth's face. "And the Pope's a closet Hindu. Uh, no."

BETH LINGERED AT THE TABLE AFTER THEIR SNACK.

"So, why do you think it's good?" Nancy asked.

"It's the story every writer would love to write but can't—a firsthand account of what happens after your soul leaves your body. I'd buy it."

"But it's a fantasy."

"So was *The Divine Comedy*, but it did okay."

"I think it's good, too, but we have a lot more to read." Mom stood up to clear the table.

Beth glanced back to the bedroom, thinking what to share. "Dad's story blew my mind a little. That part about perceiving in every direction at the same time intrigued me. That's like three hundred and sixty degrees squared, or circled, or whatever. I can't even imagine it."

"Your dad didn't mess around when he decided to write a fantasy, did he?"

"When are you going to tell Mike?"

Her mother stopped midway to the kitchen. "Oh, you thought about that, too, did you?"

"Not everyone's as oblivious as Dad. In the theater, it's important to keep your eyes, ears, and mind open. You never know when you might discover something useful."

"We need to read a little bit more before dealing with Mike. Let's do the dishes and save the leftover potato salad."

Beth was happy to hear her mother use we in that sentence. She appreciated how hard this was for Mom. But this stage manager would apply the same skills she used with a temperamental actor or director to make sure she didn't lose her mother's trust after just regaining it.

Deciding she had work to do, Beth didn't follow her mother back into the kitchen. "I want to convert the file to a pdf so we can read it on our tablets. I can check Dad's computer to see when this file was last saved when I do. Is the password written down somewhere?"

She heard a plate hit the tile floor and shatter. Walking back from the study she saw her mother staring at what remained of the plate.

So much for my people management skills. "You know when the file was saved, don't you?"

Her mother walked into the study and sat in Dad's desk chair.

Beth followed and stood by her shoulder while Mom typed

the password into the computer. "I'm going to show you this, but I want you to know that this is just a computer glitch. The story is a fantasy."

Beth saw the date and time the file was saved, surprised that she wasn't surprised. The file was saved at 9:11:15 p.m., Sunday, July seventh—yesterday. This was around the time they'd finally seen what remained of her father, over two hours after he was shot, and almost two hours before they returned home. Someone saved this to the computer when none of them were at home. But who?

Without another word, they returned to the kitchen and finished washing up. Beth cleaned up the broken plate.

Soon they stood in the bedroom looking at the three stacks of manuscript pages. What they'd both read, what Beth had read when she got ahead of her mother, and what they both had left to read.

"Mom," she said, "let's read the rest of Dad's story together. I caught up and read the next few pages to see where he's going." She'd changed her mind about moving it to her tablet. It was important to do this with her mom. "I'll pass the pages to you after I finish."

"That makes the most sense, I guess. You do read faster than I do."

"Let's solve this mystery together."

Mom nodded and they each picked up pages to read. She suspected her mom needed to hold the pages in her hands to feel closer to Dad. Maybe it would be the same for her. She'd stay alert to her mother's moods as they continued reading to avoid another incident like the shattered plate.

Part Two

The World of Yesterday

"*Here you leave today and enter the world of yesterday, tomorrow and fantasy.*"

Walt Disney
Words at the entrance to Disneyland
Anaheim, California

Chapter Eighteen

Sunday, 7:02:07 p.m.

When I return from my re-experiences, I feel Calla's presence before I hear his greeting. "Welcome back, my friend. What have you to share with me?"

"I re-experienced almost five years and feel we've been apart that long."

"You realize that no time has passed for me. You left and returned."

"I understand but still find it challenging. I was embedded in a three-dimensional, spherical movie, starring me, viewed from within a tiny body I once occupied. I could feel, smell, and taste, in addition to see and hear, everything I had the first time through. I loved the return to sensation. But as before, I could only experience, not act."

"Yes, and?"

"And when I was not quite three, I ran face-first into a clothesline pole. I knew it was going to happen, but I couldn't stop it.

And, like when I was shot, I felt the pain. But this time I wasn't knocked out, so I got to experience the whole thing. It hurt like hell. Knocked my two front teeth out. I thought of leaving but knew there were better times ahead, so I just kept going."

"It is good that you remained."

"I found another event so vivid, I felt I was there. I wish you could have perceived it with me."

"I can. Go to that memory while we are in contact, and I will perceive it precisely as you do."

Boy, this sure saves time. There's that word again. "This experience was when I was four and a half. During it I discovered a new ability. Will you experience it with me now?"

"I will."

CALLA AND I TAKE IN THE VIEW AT THE MAIN ENTRANCE to Disneyland within my much younger body. My father is talking.

"After we watched the grand opening on television a couple weeks ago, I decided we were all going to experience this wonder in person. And here we are."

"You certainly did, Bob. I just had to scrape up the money," Mom adds with a roll of her eyes.

"Remember when we saw Art Linkletter and Bob Cummings on TV, Robby?" my sister Terry asks me.

"Sure. And that tall guy from Death Valley Days was there in a white suit," I reply, always wanting to be included.

"Ronald Reagan," Tammy says. "He used to be in movies, too."

"I remember some old guy, too. I think he was the gardener of California," I add.

"That was the governor of California, Robby. He's like the president, but for the state," Mom explained.

"Oh."

"The park has the same four lands as the TV show," Dad says, reclaiming control of the conversation. "Tomorrowland, Adventureland, Fantasyland, and Frontierland. There's also something called Main Street, USA. It's supposed to be like Walt Disney's hometown, when he grew up at the turn of the century."

"That last place sounds boring to me, Daddy. Maybe they should call it *Boring-land*."

Mom hands some cash to a smiling woman in a brightly painted ticket booth at the entrance then turns and hands us each a pass to get in. We show our admission tickets and walk through a turnstile.

Dad's company did some work on some of Disneyland's attractions, so he knows a lot about the magical place we're about to enter. "Right now, they only sell general admission. We'll have to pay extra to go on some rides. Later this year, they'll sell ticket books at these booths. The tickets will be different colors and labeled with a letter from A through C."

I tolerate Dad's ticket dissertation but cut right to the chase. "How many rides are there?"

"When they opened, they had eighteen. I think they're up to more than twenty now."

My current mind sees twenty-three open rides listed on a board near the entrance.

"Let's go see what they've got," Dad says. The curly red hairs on his arms glow in the sunshine as he hurries off with me in tow. Mom and my sisters struggle to keep up. Luckily, our first stop is mere steps away. Multiple flowerbeds adorn the slope below a train station. Together they create the smiling face of Mickey Mouse.

"Come on, Robbo, let's get our picture with the man." Dad lifts me up and holds me in the air next to Mickey's face. I enter Dad's thoughts and realize that he's as excited by this fantastic place as I am. It triggers warm memories of special times with his own dad, back in Missouri.

After Mom clicks the camera, I turn around to look at Mickey's face, up close. I enjoy the sweet smell of the flowers. *Even the pictures smell good here.*

We walk through a little tunnel and see a vision right out of a movie. Bright colors and motion fill my eyes. I see three vehicles drawn by horses: a fire truck, a streetcar, and a surrey. The surrey even has fringe on top, like that song my sisters sing.

My sixty-two-year-old self marvels at how open the park seems. The trees are still young, making the streets look broader and the buildings taller than they do today. Everything's so new and, from a five-year-old's eye level, enormous.

"Daddy, I want to see the horsey," I say. Dad picks me up and carries me over to pet the horse in front of the surrey. I feel dizzy as he lifts me high into the air. The driver welcomes us with a huge smile as we climb on board the surrey to take our first ride down Main Street.

We swivel our heads right and left to take in buildings that look like pastel gingerbread houses. I even look behind us and see a steam train parked at the station. White clouds billow from the black smokestack to dissipate in the bright blue sky. A loud-speaker growls something about the Santa Fe and Disneyland Railroad.

"The train next, Daddy! Please, the train."

"Sure, if you want. But look what's up ahead."

"A castle!" Terry shouts. "It's just like the one on TV."

I can't form words. A castle? In America? How can it be? And it's pink. Well, pink and baby blue.

When the surrey pulls to a stop right in front, Dad points over the drawbridge and into the castle. There's a merry-go-round inside, spinning and sparkling in the sun. I run over the wooden planks of the drawbridge and forget about that train.

We go on the merry-go-round first, which they call the King Arthur Carrousel. I ride with Dad on a hand-carved horse—the most beautiful creature I've ever seen. We go round and round to the clear notes of a huge music box. Every horse goes up and down, too, but only one is white. The one we're riding.

I give our horse a little pat as we get off. Straight ahead I see Dumbo, the flying elephant. But not one Dumbo, an entire herd of flying elephants flies up and down and around in a circle. I drag Dad over to watch. We end up standing by a man who seems to be testing the ride.

"John, how much weight do you have in there now?" he calls to the man at the controls.

"We're up to eighty pounds and it's staying in synch. I think we can try one twenty."

"Okay. But take it slow. I don't want sandbags flying off those things." He turns and smiles at me and I notice he has a moustache—the first one I've seen on a real person. But he doesn't look like a villain.

I pull on the guy's pant leg when he turns back to the ride. "When can I go on it?"

He leans down to me and says in my ear, "Next time you come, for sure. But a lot more fun rides and things are open. Do you like Peter Pan?"

"Uh-huh, sure."

"Then you and your family come with me." Terry, Tammy, and Mom have caught up by now, so he waves them over. He leads us to a small building with Peter Pan painted on it and little boats going around in front and into the building. The boats aren't in water, though. They seem to be flying. There's a line, but he takes us to the front. Bending down to look into my eyes, he asks, "What does Peter teach Wendy to do?"

"He teaches her to crow, and he teaches her to fly." I know this stuff.

"Let's see if he can teach you," he says, and we climb into our ship.

Mom sits on one side of me and Dad on the other. "Hang on, Robbo."

The observing me notices an expression pass between my sisters as they sit in their own miniature flying pirate ship behind ours.

"Terr, do you know who that man was?" Tamara asks

"Sure, Tamm. Walt Disney."

And so he was. I enter Walt's thoughts to find these few moments shared with a family enjoying his park together take his mind off the risk of ruin he faces if his beautiful park fails.

"Calla," I say as the memory fades. "I want to meet that man again. Can I?"

"No, that man died."

He feels my spirits fall.

"But you can do something better. The entity you are now can commune with the entity he is. And you will, as you are communing with me now."

"But can't I travel back in time?"

"Yes, you did in this re-experience, but he could not perceive you as you are now, only as you were then. You cannot change anything. You cannot make your five-year-old self go over and talk to him more or ask what he thinks about Disneyland now. Trust me, nothing can compare with communing with what he has become."

"I'll have to take your word for the present, or the past, or whenever the hell we are."

"You have learned how to do a bit more through your re-experiences, and I am pleased. But take it one step at a time. Remember that ride they were testing?"

"I get the point. If I try my new abilities without sufficient planning and guidance, the damage could be much greater than a few sandbags flying off."

"Moving too quickly has made many lose their way, never to find their way back. So, what have you discovered about yourself so far?"

I pause again before replying, "You know, I think it's the immense hope and faith I had during these first five years. That faith was in my parents and sisters. They would always keep me safe and fix anything that went wrong. I felt free to try anything new. I was brave."

I feel Calla disengage and re-close my perception sphere as he withdraws, leaving an even smaller contact point as I turn to years six to ten.

Chapter Nineteen

Tuesday, July 9, 12:00 p.m. CEST (12:00 a.m. HST)

"We're really here." Finished unpacking and staring out the window of their beautiful hotel suite, Julie finally allowed herself to admit it out loud.

The airport and the train trip into the city had been a blur, but the walk through the streets of Rome from the station to the hotel, rolling their bags along the bumpy sidewalks made it all real. She couldn't help feeling like she was looking into the past. This truly was the *old world*, parts of it older than anything she'd seen before in her life.

Julie had packed their itinerary for the second day with places she'd read about all her life, but not knowing how tired they would be when they arrived, she hadn't planned anything for today. They had slept well on the flight from Chicago, and it was only noon here in Rome. She glanced over at Keone. "How about a little walk around the town, Big Guy?"

"Weren't you going to call Janet to tell her we made it safely to our hotel?" Keone asked.

"I sure was. Let me see, what time is it back home." She glanced at her watch, which she'd kept on Maui time. "Is this right, Keone? My watch says it's midnight yesterday."

"It's noon here and twelve hours earlier there. So, yeah." Keone replied.

"I don't want to wake her, but I don't want her to worry either."

"Just send her a text saying we got in safely and that you'll call her in the morning—her morning. And say, when you call her, I'd like to say a few words to my new sister-in-law, okay?"

"I think that could be arranged." After she'd sent the message she said, "Now, about that walk?"

"You think we might be able to find the Colosseum?" Keone asked with a grin.

Julie spoke to her cell, "Hey Siri, give us walking directions to the Colosseum?"

"How about this," Siri replied. The phone displayed a walking route of about twenty minutes from the hotel to the Colosseum.

"Think you can follow this, Mr. Detective?"

"You bet," Keone said and held the door open for his new bride, who kissed him on the cheek as she passed.

Along the way they discovered Trajan's Forum, one of many *fora* built over the centuries. Surprisingly well-preserved ruins captured the vibrancy of a place that was more than just a center of government but a gathering place for the people of the city, complete with offices, shops, and even apartment blocks. Exploring this forerunner of the modern town center, Julie thought of their own Banyan Tree Park in Lāhainā and felt a link to these ancient people.

Keone found a restaurant nearby called Castellino. The modest seating area was surrounded by glass display cases filled with delectable cold and hot entrees and glistening fresh pastries. The late lunch warmed their stomachs and assuaged appetites developed over almost twenty-four hours of air travel. Their waiter snapped a picture of them enjoying their lunch.

~

"Are you *pau*?" Keone asked, using the Hawaiian word for finished.

"I couldn't hold another bite," Julie replied. "I know you can't wait to see the Colosseum. Lead the way. You're in charge today, but tomorrow we follow my plan. We have so much to see tomorrow and still get back to the hotel in time to pick up our bags and make it to the station for our train to Civitavecchia."

"No problem. When I checked in, I arranged to leave our bags at the front desk. We can pick them and up take a taxi to the station, tomorrow." Keone rose first and took Julie's hand in his as they walked from the restaurant to the entrance to the giant amphitheater.

He knew Julie wouldn't be surprised at his desire to see this spot first. *Gladiator* was one of his favorite movies. Julie stood beside him as he stared across the reconstructed portion of the sand-covered floor and on to the uncovered sections that once housed gladiators and wild animals awaiting their contests. Although basically a man of peace and justice, Keone also understood the conflict and violence prevalent in this ancient society, and their own.

He led Julie from the Colosseum through the Arch of Titus into the oldest and largest of the Roman Fora, the Forum Romanum, ignoring her quizzical expression.

"See that brick building over there?" Keone pointed and watched his bride's eyes follow. "That's where the Senate met, the Curia. Julius Caesar had it rebuilt on this spot and Augustus had it covered with marble, but that was all stripped away after the fall of the empire."

"How come you know so much about this place?" Julie held her hands open and shook her head, clearly amazed.

"My interest in law enforcement drew me to the origins of law. Many of those foundations were laid during the Roman republic and empire. I didn't just study forensics at UC Irvine, you know."

"You surprise me, Mr. Boyd. What other secrets are you hiding about yourself?"

Keone smiled. "I'm not hiding anything. You just need to ask. Come on, let's go inside."

When they were in the old building, Keone surprised Julie again.

"*Quo longe, Catalina, abusarunt patientia noster?*" he announced in a booming voice that echoed from the walls. Some tourists turned toward them, probably thinking he was a guide.

After they were outside, she pulled on his sleeve. "What was all that?"

"You didn't think Hawaiian and English were the only languages I've studied, did you? That was Cicero, from one of his Catalinaria."

"Huh?"

Keone smiled again. "You've heard of the great senator and orator Cicero, yeah?"

Julie nodded.

"The Catalinaria were a series of speeches he gave denouncing the revolutionary actions of another senator, Cataline. The quote I recited means, *How long Cataline will you abuse our patience?*"

"Do you know any less lofty Latin expressions?" Julie asked.

"Sure. *Non se tibi illegitimi carborundorum.*"

"What does that one mean?"

"Don't let the bastards get you down." They both laughed and Keone guided her to what looked like a pile of rocks in an enclosure a few feet away.

"This is where the Dictator for Life's body was burned after his assassination."

Chapter Twenty

Julie Boyd watched in silence as her husband stood totally still and bowed his head at the site of Julius Caesar's cremation.

She was surprised at the respect Keone displayed. As they walked away, Keone discussed Caesar's life. She quickly realized that Keone didn't respect the dictator he became, but the brilliant leader of men and rule breaker that he was before overthrowing the Roman Republic.

"His leadership skills remind me of Tony Alcala, and his tendency to break the rules . . ."

"Remind you of *you*."

Keone laughed but didn't deny it.

"Let's keep walking outside," she suggested. "It's such a beautiful day."

Arm in arm, they continued their outdoor walk down a street of two- and three-story houses with brilliant flowers on every balcony.

While she was enjoying the friendly atmosphere of the street, Keone tapped her shoulder and pointed. "Do you see that rock outcropping up there?"

"Yes. What is it?"

"That's the Tarpeian Rock. In ancient Rome, wrong doers were thrown to their deaths from there."

Always a policeman at heart, her Keone.

~

THEY WANDERED BACK TOWARD THEIR HOTEL ARM IN arm, stopping frequently to enjoy a view and share a kiss. But Julie didn't stop at the hotel. She'd decided to buy their train tickets first for tomorrow's trip to Civitavecchia, where they would board their cruise ship in the evening.

Determined to show Keone she was capable of handling things on her own, she sent him off to find a newspaper in English. She quickly discovered buying a train ticket was not quite as simple as buying a metro ticket. While she was staring at a machine trying to figure out which buttons to push, an Italian woman came up to her and asked, "You have trouble with machine-a, cara?" Her English wasn't great, but she had no trouble making herself understood.

"Actually, yes . . . Si . . . Signora," Julie answered.

"I can show how to buy ticket. My name-a Angelina."

Trying to be a good tourist and not an ugly American, Julie agreed to the woman's offer of assistance.

"Where you go?"

"Civitavecchia."

"What class?"

"First."

After a few minutes, clutching their tickets in her hand, Julie was grateful to the woman for helping her prove her competence to Keone and said so. "Grazie mille signora. You are very kind."

"Yes, I am. One euro, please," the woman said.

Julie was embarrassed to have been taken in so easily, but she handed the woman a one-euro coin quickly, before Keone returned.

"How much did she get?" Keone asked.

"One euro," Julie replied reluctantly.

"That's pretty good. While I was buying my paper, I asked a cop at the news stand about the lady talking to you. He said they usually ask for five. Let's go get dinner at the hotel and order some room service, yeah."

Back at their hotel room, after a light snack, they were both spent. They fell asleep in each other's arms watching Italian TV before it was late enough to make that call to Janet.

Chapter Twenty-One

Tuesday, July 9, 9:15 a.m. HST

The digital clock above the stove told Nancy she'd slept more than eight hours. She planned to let Beth sleep in, but thought she heard noises from the study and decided to get dressed.

"Did dad really knock his teeth out on a clothesline pole? And what is a clothesline, anyway?"

"Rob told me the story about how a little boy's silly escapade lost him his two front teeth. And we didn't always have clothes dryers, baby child."

"Just playin' with you. I've heard of clotheslines, even used them on stage in some classic musicals like *Oklahoma* and *Newsies.*"

"Anyway, isn't it nice learning things about your dad that we didn't know?"

"So, you believe it's true."

"I believe he is filling his fantasy story with true stories about his childhood. Don't make more of this than it is, Beth. How about a walk to breakfast?"

"I'm in."

~

THE WALK TO KING KAHEKILI BEACH PARK FROM THE condo was four-tenths of a mile, and the first leg was downhill. Nancy watched Beth emerge from the lush foliage of the condo complex onto the adjacent golf course. Its manicured fairways and greens contrasted with the surrounding wildness.

Farther down Puʻukoliʻi Road a tiny train station waited hopefully for the return of something called the Sugar Cane Train. A little steam locomotive had once pulled brightly painted cars from Lāhainā to Kāʻanapali, but the ride was too expensive for locals and attracted too few tourists, so the enterprise went in and out of business at intervals.

They crossed to the station and Nancy gave the local produce displayed in the little farmer's market a once over. Beth continued over to the adjacent shave ice stand. A "Gone Fo' Surf" sign hung askew on the shutters. Nancy waited for Beth to return before crossing the tracks, to Honoapi'ilani Highway.

When they got the stick-figure signal to walk, Nancy recalled Rob calling it the little haole man, due to its bright white color. She also remembered Angela explaining that, although the word haole refers to non-natives, the word doesn't literally mean Caucasians.

Beth pointed to the artificial waterfall at the entrance to the Westin Kāʻanapali Villas. "Welcome to tourist land."

True, but Nancy didn't mind. The landscaping was dominated by lush vegetation and hinted at wildness despite being well maintained.

Beth's comment broke the silence, though, and opened the way to continued discussion. "Your dad loved to take this walk. Sometimes he'd keep going and walk all the way to Lāhainā or the other direction up to Napili. It helped him clear his mind when he was writing."

Beth found a break in the walkers and joggers whizzing by and they stepped onto the Beachwalk. Broad strips of plastic composite formed the path, which resembled a boardwalk. The Beachwalk ran the length of North Beach with a brief detour through the grounds of the Maui Kāʻanapali Villas and the Royal Lāhainā before continuing down the length of South Beach.

"I love these houses," Nancy said as they passed the mini mansions running from the beach park to the Villas.

"Your dad imagined building on that empty lot over there when he wrote his first best seller."

"I think it would have taken more than one," Beth said.

Nancy led the way along the path as it veered away from the beach through a parking lot and onto the Villas' grounds. Beyond the pool, the quaint Castaway restaurant enticed both locals and strolling tourists to leave the Beachwalk.

"Sit anywhere," the tall, blonde waitress directed with a smile. And they did, right by the partial wall that separated indoor from outdoor seating. A row of palm trees surrounded by luscious ground cover opened to a broad beach and the vibrant hues of the ocean. The cool tradewinds off the ocean calmed Nancy's body and mind.

When the waitress returned for their order, Nancy found she was hungrier than she'd expected. "I'll have The Paniolo over-easy, with Portuguese sausage, hash browns, and an English muffin."

She saw Beth nod with respect, then immediately put her mom's order to shame. "I'll have a Loco Moco. And could I have Tabasco for that?"

"Do you know what you're getting yourself into?" the waitress asked.

"Oh, sure. I used to eat these all the time with my dad . . ."

Nancy remembered the first time Rob introduced Beth to the concoction combining two scoops of steamed rice with a large hamburger patty topped with two fried eggs and smothered in brown Maui-onion gravy Even Rob was amazed to see their petite daughter put this mountain of comfort food away and still have room for a shave ice on the way home.

Their orders in progress, Nancy and Beth gazed back at the ocean. They both seemed to appreciate its calming influence.

"I can't believe Dad was such a little cut up."

"I've heard many tales about the irrepressible Little Robby. I think growing up with two older sisters who liked games, especially word games, gave him a head start."

"He had such a rich imagination back then. I wonder what happened to change that." Beth's eyes peered at her over the rim of her cup.

When Beth remained silent, Nancy picked up the discussion. "Rob never wrote anything like this before, even in his journals. His stories were always realistic, but they never involved childhood—his or anyone else's. He told me they went to Disneyland right after it opened, but he certainly never mentioned meeting Walt Disney."

"I'm not sure he remembered it until the re-experience," Beth said.

"Or added it for the fantasy, like that psychic link between his twin sisters. Rob must have found it disorienting to write about something so far from reality."

"I never dreamed Dad could write a story about being in Fantasyland. You could tell he enjoyed himself. I wonder why he would never go with us. Something doesn't add up."

Nancy was relieved when the waitress slid their plates on the table, focusing both of them on the delicious task at hand.

Chapter Twenty-Two

Tuesday, July 9, 10:30 p.m. CEST (Tuesday, July 9, 10:30 a.m. HST)

Keone was wrenched from sleep by another vivid dream. At first, he thought this too was about Sam Loftus. He was in a rainforest like the one near Hana where Sam kept Julie captive in his cabin. But it wasn't that cabin. It was a shack, and this time Angela wasn't the one viewing from a sniper's nest, he was. Angela and Tony were about to enter the structure, and he knew they shouldn't. He tried to yell out to warn them but couldn't make a sound. Shortly after they went inside, he heard gunfire.

What he thought were shots was the sound of his arm hitting the glass-topped coffee table by the sofa where he'd fallen asleep. Nothing broke, but their coffee cups from last night were scattered across the carpet.

Julie was nowhere in sight. He quickly remembered they were in the hotel in Rome, got up quietly, and tiptoed to the bedroom, where Julie was sound asleep. *She probably woke up and decided to find a more comfortable place to sleep,* Keone thought to himself. It reminded him of another night when he'd slept on the couch before they admitted to each other they were in love.

Although his cellphone was still hidden, he saw hers lying on the bed. He silently collected it before closing the door with a soft click. He had an idea, but first needed to check to see if she'd called Janet when she woke up. She hadn't.

He saw no reason to wait until morning here in Rome to give her a call, given it was now mid-morning on Maui. Besides, he had an important question to ask his new sister-in-law and preferred Julie not hear it.

"Hello?" Janet's voice said on the other end of the line.

"Aloha, Janet. I'm calling from Roma. Did you get Julie's message?"

~

Tuesday, July 9, 11:30 a.m. HST

Angela Beyers was about to tuck into a sandwich she'd brought from home when a special ringtone indicated her housemate, Linda, was calling.

"Hi, Ange. I now know what you meant about this story being a little weird. But I just finished a section that relates to your investigation. I think he put some valuable clues in there for you."

"I already read the part where he remembered going back to the crime scene, Lin."

"So did I. This section comes later, after he's gone back and re-experienced a couple of five-year periods of his childhood. He's learned he can filter out the noise and decides to return to— Oh hell start on page eighty-two, and you'll see what I mean. Trust me. It's worth it."

"Could you summarize what you've got from the manuscript in a few words?"

"I'll try. There's more about the form he saw on the other side of the stream and a gun firing into the air. And there's a license plate number for the truck that sideswiped him."

"Okay, give me the page numbers for the plate and the form in the bushes."

"They're both in the same part. Just start on page eighty-two but don't let the weird parts side-track you."

Angela cringed at the words 'weird parts' but said, "I'll read what I can while I eat lunch."

NANCY AND BETH FINISHED EATING, THE PLATES WERE cleared, and coffee refills were provided. As they sipped their coffee, Beth spoke up. "Mom, we need to talk about tomorrow."

Nancy saw an image in her mind—the two of them sitting on either side of the bed holding Rob's limp hands as a stranger flipped a switch.

Beth waited.

Nancy tipped her head back and closed her eyes, preparing herself. "We'll go to the hospital tomorrow, and I'll do what Rob would have wanted."

Beth nodded.

"I've known it's what we'd need to do since that first night, but I wanted a miracle. Tomorrow, I'll have to let that go. I hope you can forgive me for hanging on to hope until then."

"Mom, there's nothing to forgive. But I have a different take on that miracle. I think Dad's story is a miracle."

Now Nancy paused. "I agree. No matter what the story is, it gave me the strength to make this decision. I feel him beside me when I read his words."

Beth looked serious but seemed satisfied with Nancy's answer.

As she paid the bill, Nancy said, "Want to check out that shave ice stand again on the way home."

"You bet. And I'll accept nothing less than a rainbow of mango, *lilikoʻi*, and guava."

"Fair enough."

"And, Mom, when we get home, let's set up a comfort zone on the living room couch, like we used to in Newark. We can read 'til we fall asleep."

The suggestion brought back wonderful memories of the two of them snuggling when Beth was little and Rob away on business. "I'm in, but such a cozy environment might cause an early bedtime."

"I know. I also know you barely slept last night."

Smart young woman, my daughter.

Chapter Twenty-Three

Sunday, 7:02:07 p.m.

"Robert?"

For the first time, Calla needs to call me back. These years absorb me completely. I re-experience the most interesting parts more than once. I know I should return to the present but hesitate. My experiences provide so much more information now that I've discovered how to . . .

"Robert!"

Calla's voice in my mind commands me to break free. I'm slow in opening my perception sphere, but Calla is waiting.

"Calla, was I lost?"

"No, my friend. But I sensed a risk."

"I'm glad you're looking out for me. Something unusual and new happened during this re-experience."

"You can share anything with me."

"I do have an experience to share with you. But before we start, I need to discuss something with you."

"Continue."

"While re-experiencing years six to ten, I realized I was able to perceive everything that was happening not only from my perspective but also from the perspective of every person present, like I had for Mr. Disney and my dad in the Disneyland re-experience. I could hear what was said, what was intended, and what each person heard. These perceptions were often quite different from what I perceived at the time. Though confused at first, I eventually learned to deal with it. My re-experiences became so much . . . I don't know . . . more complete than before."

"That is why you didn't want to leave," Calla says. "You had a good reason. There are other reasons, which could have caused you to get lost. I need not have interfered."

"I'm glad you did. Before, during my first five-year experience, the time felt shorter. I'd skip through the times when little Rob was asleep. This time I was able to remain and move into someone else's mind for a while when my younger self slept, so long as they remained conscious."

I sense a nod.

"When I'm here with you, I only see my perspective. Yet, when I came closer to the Earth with you, I was inside everyone's mind at once—even the animals. Is that why it overwhelmed me?"

Another nod.

"Why can't I see inside your mind?"

"You could, if I let you. But you are not ready for that. As you are able to limit my access during your re-experiences, I can control your access to my thoughts. You will be able to do this someday as well."

"But why don't the people in my re-experience feel my presence? Is it because they're in the past?"

"You are moving through it with them, but as you have already lived it, you can only observe, not interact. Your reasoning is sound."

"When I move forward in time, am I in danger of being perceived? Is this why you wanted me to start with the past?"

"I wanted you to start with your memories, which you did. At an early point in the process, you truly moved into the past, anchored by your memories."

"When I could sense other people's perceptions."

"Correct. This skill will be helpful for you, essential when you explore times and places for which you have no memory. But that will come later."

I let this soak in for a minute.

"You are also correct about entering minds in your present. You could be perceived. This could be extremely damaging to the people whose minds you enter. It can even trigger insanity. How did it feel when you were one with the perceptions of others in the past?"

"It was a lot like experiencing from within my own body. But I didn't feel at home. You know, like I was wearing someone else's clothes and they didn't quite fit. If you come with me this time, will you go everywhere I go, both into myself and into others?"

"Yes. I will go wherever you go. Are you asking me to accompany you?"

"Yes, definitely."

When we return, I wonder why I chose the experiences I did to share with Calla. The last one, when the Dodgers were still playing at the Coliseum was a lot of fun, but I had other fun times. Maybe it was the huge crowd. That exhibition game between the Dodgers and the Yankees in honor of Roy Campanella had the largest crowd in baseball history.

"Re-experiencing these events have changed you, Robert. Enhanced your abilities. You need to realize something before you continue with your re-experiences. You mastered a new and crucial ability in your Disneyland memory and the memory we just shared about your trip to the baseball game."

I sense pride from Calla and try to think what those two re-experiences had in common. "I focused my perceptions. In the other re-experiences, only one or two other people were present. At Disneyland hundreds of people surrounded us and at the L.A. Coliseum, tens of thousands. But I focused only on Mr. Disney's and Dad's thoughts in the first and only those of my family members in the second. That's good, isn't it?"

"Yes. Let's repeat our experiment and see how you handle it this time."

Instantly, we've moved half the distance closer to earth again, but this time I'm not overwhelmed. I perceive the earth and its gradual rotation. I perceive the billions on the surface, but I focus my thoughts on Nancy and Beth and find them. Beth's on her plane off the Maui coastline, thinking about her life in New York. Nancy's in our study at the condo reading a thriller.

I decide to find my own consciousness in the ʻĪao Valley but discover Calla has pulled us back to our previous location.

"You are progressing briskly. We stayed a full ten seconds this time and you exhibited no signs of discomfort."

"But, Calla, didn't you say you were only allowed one demonstration?"

"Yes. But I did not say the demonstration had one part."

"You're a sly one. But you're right. I had no difficulty filtering input this time. I even found my wife and daughter. Don't worry. I didn't enter their minds."

"I know. I monitored your actions. You are learning skills that you will require in the future."

"What future? I thought you said I was dead."

"Did I?"

"Not in those words, but I assumed."

"Never assume. You can experience everything in the universe accurately and completely, but you must never assume."

These words require some consideration, but before I have a chance to reflect further on what he's said, Calla redirects me.

"You must close the sphere and return to your re-experience, Robert."

"I may take a while this time. I'd like to make it through high school."

"An excellent plan."

I realize as I close the sphere that going through high school might not be such a great idea.

Chapter Twenty-Four

Tuesday, July 9, 4:05 p.m. HST

Tony Alcala peered inside Keone's cubicle. Angela Beyers seemed at home there. The desk was covered with contact reports and files. She was so immersed in what she was reading on her computer that she didn't notice him until he tapped on the cubicle entrance.

"Would you join me in my office in five minutes, Sergeant?"

He watched her clear the computer screen before turning to answer.

"Yes, sir. I'd be happy to," she said, and began combining some files.

"What's that you were reading? It didn't look like a police file?"

"I'm reviewing more of the vic's writings. I found some scattered sections that mention the ʻĪao Valley. I'm trying to see if they offer any clues as to why he was up there when he got shot."

"I see," Tony said, but sensed there was more she wasn't telling him. "I expect a full and complete update. See you in five."

116

When Tony returned to his office from the restroom, Angela sat across the desk from his large swivel chair with various folders set out between them and her flip notebook open in her hands. She seemed ready.

Time to throw her off balance and see how she handles it.

"Sergeant Beyers." He paused. "How does it feel sitting at a detective's desk, trying to do a detective's job?"

"I've collected some new information and developed a few theories, as you requested, sir."

"You're doing us a favor by being here, and I'm grateful. I want you to relax and talk to me as if we're colleagues, since we are. How do you feel?"

He saw her hesitate and studied her face. Was this young woman ready to trust a stranger who happened to outrank her?

"I feel fine, sir. Detective Kalani has helped me get up to speed. I find the work challenging and stimulating."

"No. You find it boring and can't wait to get out of this office and get some real work done."

"Sir, I—"

"Don't worry, that's a compliment." He leaned forward. "I'm going to level with you. Keone thinks you might make a good detective—someday. I make it a habit to listen to what he has to say. For the next few weeks, you have a unique opportunity to show me what you're capable of. I'm difficult to please, but fair. This is your shot. Impress me."

"I plan to, sir."

"Good. I have two questions before we move any further. Number one: Do you want to be a detective?"

"Yes, sir." For the first time, her broad, friendly face revealed informality and even vulnerability. She was letting him in, and Tony appreciated it.

"Number two: Do you honestly believe you're ready?"

Angela paused but maintained eye contact. "I believe I am."

Alcala noticed that, for the first time, she neglected to say sir.

"Tell me what you have so far."

"I have two main theories. The first is that that Dr. Lister may have seen something he shouldn't have and was killed for it. The second is Dr. Lister was shot by someone from his past, someone who held a grudge."

"What do you have to support each of these theories and what are your next steps?"

As she detailed her efforts and plans, Tony was impressed by what she'd accomplished in two days and by her ability to share her thoughts and supporting facts in a concise, lucid manner.

Keone may be right about her. *But she isn't telling me something.*

"Two reasonable theories consistent with the facts. You should pursue them. What about your trip to the crime scene yesterday? Did you manage to get over there before the team opened it back up?"

"Yes, sir, I did. I had another scenario I wanted to run. I felt being at the site would be helpful."

"Has that effort provided any additional thoughts or evidence?"

"Yes, sir, but it could be nothing."

"Let me decide that."

"As I told you, I've been reading over the victim's writings, looking for relevant information to advance the investigation. While doing so, I became concerned that I was neglecting one possible scenario, so I decided to follow up on it."

"Go on." Tony had a bad feeling about this.

"The nature of the wound bothered me. The surgeons found a slug in Lister's head."

"I read the report."

"Ballistics has confirmed that it's from a twenty-two-caliber rifle cartridge. But the limited damage suggests the bullet was travelling slower than one would expect if the shooter were in line-of-sight on the far side of the river. The shot should have shattered the skull and passed on through, but it didn't."

"Do you have any theories as to how this could occur?"

"Yes, sir, two. First, the shot could have been made through an external noise suppression device, like military snipers use to make it hard to pinpoint their location. Second . . ."

"Yes?"

"The shot could have followed an elliptical path."

"You're suggesting Lister was shot by accident? A random shot that happened to nail him near the base of his skull?"

"I agree it's unlikely, but it is consistent with the evidence."

"What evidence? The fact the bullet didn't get through his thick skull? It could have taken a weird bounce inside the guy's skull or nicked a tree branch before impact. We can't tell without an autopsy report. And we can't get that while he's still on life support. You're guessing."

"No, sir, I'm deducing. The family in the parking lot and the ranger all heard a loud report from the weapon." He noticed Beyers hesitate again.

"Which they shouldn't have heard if the shooter used a suppressor."

"Yes, sir. And CSI discovered some additional evidence when I re-visited the site." She looked at her notebook. "Officer Jenkins found new evidence consistent with the accidental scenario."

"What did he find, Sergeant?" Tony shifted in his seat.

"A spent twenty-two caliber shell casing and footprints on the far side of ʻĪao Stream but well below the trees."

When Angela finished describing everything they found, Alcala was the one who hesitated. "Sergeant, did Jenkins look down there on his own or did you help a little?"

Beyers remained silent.

"I know, you want him to get the credit, but it's clear to me you did some good detective work there. I still think the accident theory's extremely improbable, but you can keep pursuing it—if only to rule it out. Don't allow your investigation of the first two theories to be delayed while you invalidate the third. A good detective needs to follow up on everything consistent with the evidence. You've had a productive start to your investigation, Sergeant. Now, go home and get some rest."

~

Angela left for home at five thirty after finishing her reports, Tidying Keone's cubicle, and calling Linda.

She was grateful Alcala hadn't grilled her further about the victim's writings. What Linda found for her to read was beyond bizarre, but totally backed up everything she'd found at the scene.

In the manuscript, after his guide had shown Rob that he could filter out excess perceptions, Rob took a little trip on his own and risked getting lost. But by doing so, gave her a more complete view of the crime scene, the crime itself, and the nature of his injury.

Damn, she wanted to ask Keone about this. She would never forget what she read in that lengthy section Linda pointed out to her. Never.

Chapter Twenty-Five

Sunday, 7:02:17 p.m.

I'm alone with my memories again, but far from the memories I told Calla I was going to re-experience.

In my sphere out here in space, I decide I'm torturing myself for no reason. I miss Nancy too much to keep playing Calla's games. To hell with the next ten years, I want to re-experience my honeymoon.

Instantly, I'm standing in the Honolulu airport with my sweetheart.

"Nancy, I love this place. It smells like flowers."

"We're surrounded by lei stands, Sherlock," my new bride replies.

"Oh, yeah."

Having this impossibly wonderful woman tell the world she loves me and wants to be my wife has rekindled my belief in dreams.

A fresh breeze permeates the airport. No walls or windows

separate us from the environment. An invisible weight falls from my shoulders, and I relax.

Nancy's in her element, too. She introduces me to everything she fell in love with during her earlier visits. She's happier than I've ever seen her. So am I.

Our honeymoon trip will begin with a few days here on O'ahu, then we head to Maui and finally Kaua'i. We leave the Honolulu airport by shuttle bus for our Waikīkī hotel. After check-in, we go to our room, freshen up, and still have time for a refreshing, tropical beverage before dinner. We sit in a bar over-looking the beach and sip our Mai Tai's. Waikīkī's familiar to me from TV. A thin beach bordered by luxury hotels extends to the exclamation point of Diamond Head. It's swarming with pink-skinned tourists, some scantily clad wahine with significant chestage and small nimble posteriors.

Nancy, equally nimble, places her hand on my cheek and turns my head so I am looking into her eyes. "I'm over here. Remember, you're married now ..."

~

SORROW YANKS ME BACK TO MY POINT IN SPACE. WHAT the hell have I been doing? I need to get back to Nancy—now.

If I'm in a coma, the doctors may be advising Nancy to let me go. My living will directs: *if the doctors determine there is no hope of recovery, my life shall not be artificially maintained by machines.* I even talked to Nancy about it before my European trip.

I've got to get back and climb into my body before somebody makes a terrible mistake. But how?

A wedge forms in my blurred perception sphere opposite the tiny crack I left open to Calla. I open a portal to where the bright, blue earth sparkles in the distance and slowly close the one to Calla.

I'm going home. And Calla can't stop me. That celestial figment of my imagination has distracted me enough.

The sense of movement I perceived with Calla remains with me. I attempt the same now, prepared to filter the cacophony of perceptions as I did on our second visit. But the stimuli are absent. I perceive the beautiful blue orb, but no activity. My filter must be switching on automatically.

Maybe I'm less sensitive now, able to ignore unimportant stimuli. I move closer. Still nothing. I take a chance and go the rest of the way to our condo. No problem. I'm here and yet no movement or sound or anything.

I arrive in the living room, but Nancy isn't there. That's right, she's probably still in the study reading that book. As I move to the study, I notice that I haven't entered a body. I seem to be floating a few feet off the floor. I'm still able to move from place to place but not conventionally. I'm one place, I think of being another place, and I'm there. I've finally achieved what my three-year-old self took for granted when he ran into that clothesline pole.

Nancy's presence is here, in my recliner with a book in her hands. I'm not surprised that she doesn't perceive my presence, but I am surprised that her eyes aren't moving back and forth as they normally do when she reads. She doesn't blink, although I concentrate on her for what seems like minutes. I know she's alive, but she seems frozen. The second counter on the clock on my desk is frozen, too. It displays 7:02:17 p.m.

That's the exact same time Calla and I returned from our second trip towards earth. I've moved in space, not time. I don't know how. I decide to ask Calla for help and open the crack in my consciousness sphere where I last perceived him.

He's not there.

~

WHAT WAS I THINKING? I DON'T FEEL CALLA'S presence anywhere. Maybe if I concentrate on broadcasting my thoughts . . .

"Calla"

No response.

"Calla," I shout the word in my mind.

No response.

What have I done?

I'm lost. He warned me not to go too close to earth too soon or this could happen.

I struggle to control my thoughts.

Hold on. Don't freak out.

I can't be lost. I know when and where I am, don't I? But I don't know how to restart the clock. I'm frozen along with everyone else.

This didn't happen when I was with Calla because he knows how to move in space and time in the present. I haven't learned that yet. I came too soon. Before I was ready.

When I was by myself in my re-experiences, I moved forward in time. No, wait. I didn't move forward. The person whose mind I shared did. I tagged along.

I wonder if I can do that in the present, too.

There's an easy way to find out. Nancy's right beside me. I can join with her thoughts and see if we move forward. But I've got to be careful. Calla said that in the present I could be perceived.

I hate the idea that I could hurt Nancy but can't ask Calla for instructions. It should be safe to enter her mind for a second, then leave and see if time moves forward. I stare at the digital clock on my desk frozen at 7:02:17 p.m. and take a chance.

Entering Nancy's mind feels like coming home. I perceive everything in an instant. She's focused on her book, so I don't have to deal with confusion or strong emotions. I jump out and see that the clock has advanced five seconds. My guess was right. I can move forward if I'm sharing thoughts with someone.

I know I should leave now and go to the ʻĪao Valley but hesitate. I can't resist the chance to spend a few more moments in my love's thoughts.

She's reading a book by William Bernhardt about a serial killer sniper that I found a bit too violent for my taste when I read it. How ironic, given my current predicament. I probe beyond her conscious mind to focus on her subconscious. Myriad thoughts percolate there at once. Some are about me. When will I get back? What present did I get her for our anniversary? Will I ever start writing again?

This last thought carries real concern. She realizes how much trouble I've had writing anything in the last six months. I also perceive a few special memories from our years together that form a canvas for the rest of her thoughts. Her mind is so bright and active, even when she's quietly reading. Damn, I miss her.

Her cell phone interrupts my thoughts and hers. The Hawai'i Five-O ringtone—someone she doesn't know. I leap from her thoughts and see that the clock has moved forward to 7:17:00 p.m. What seemed like a few seconds had been thirteen minutes.

I need to get moving if I'm going to get back into my body before they take me to the hospital. I try to jump in space, like I did in my re-experiences. Instantly, I'm in the 'Iao Valley. I perceive a man standing near where I was shot and enter his thoughts.

Chapter Twenty-Six

Sunday, 7:17:00 p.m.

From his thoughts, I can tell the man's a policeman. Not an ordinary policeman—a detective. He scans the site with experienced eyes. At his feet, a blood-stained depression in the grass near the imu shows where I fell. He's looking over at the family I saw in the parking lot, but frozen like everyone else. They must have found me. But who shot me?

The detective wonders the same thing. His name is Alcala, and I've entered his mind.

A cell phone rings. Alcala looks around and locates the source next to the depression. He carefully lifts the phone from the grass by its edges. By then it's stopped ringing.

Just as he's about to replace it where he found it, the phone rings again. This time Alcala answers.

I hear Beth's voice on the other end of the phone. She must be calling from the airport.

Alcala says, "I'm afraid your father's been shot. You need to get to Maui Memorial Hospital."

Much as I'd like to stay and listen to Beth, I realize time is passing, and I now know where my body is. I leave the detective. I must get to the hospital and re-enter my body.

Wait a minute. I don't need to rush. I'm not moving forward in time anymore.

I look at the detective's watch, just to make sure. It's frozen at 7:29 p.m.

I decide to find out who shot me and why. I know I can return to my own memories from the time right before I was shot without moving forward in the present. I've already done it with Calla. I decide it's time for me to revisit that experience again.

I BEGIN BEFORE THE TRUCK ALMOST HIT ME. THIS TIME I notice there's actual contact with the back of my car. I focus on the license plate. It's a Hawai'i plate, JAC 276. Mud obscures the plate. But because I can perceive, I get the full license.

I park my car in the parking lot. There's the same local family struggling to remove their leaf-wrapped pig from the pick-up. I again notice movement in the bushes across the parking lot. I see a small form beyond a chain-link fence.

I jump into the form and find myself in the mind of a ten-year-old boy. He's nervous about something. The rifle. It isn't his. It belongs to his grandfather. He snuck out with it to prove he was old enough to hunt like his older brother. He knows the birds like to congregate in the trees around the stream near sunset. He'll shoot one and bring it home. That'll show his gramps he's ready.

The trail on this side barely exists. The boy finds a row of boulders spanning the rushing stream and hops from one to the next until he reaches the far side and sinks into the mud. With careful steps, he slogs far enough up the hillside to have a shot into the trees. A beautiful white bird rests in the branches of a Cook's pine. The boy takes aim, adjusts his stance, and slips on a soggy root. As he falls back, his finger pulls the trigger, and a bullet sails in a high arc toward the far side of the stream. The sound of the shot reverberates loudly through the valley.

Thank God there's nobody left in the park, the boy thinks.

Blocked by foliage, the boy can't see the bullet hit my head, but the timing's right. I didn't hear any shots before I was hit, but the bullet would have reached me before the sound. The shot he fired could've hit me.

The boy wastes no time leaving the area. He falls through the bushes, juggles his rifle, regains his balance, and retraces his steps back to the parking lot. Then he runs.

I return to the present and decide to head for the hospital. In my re-experiences, I entered my mind at a specific point in time and was carried forward with it. If I enter my living mind here in the present, I should be able to move forward. It worked with Nancy and the detective. This could be precisely what I'm meant to do. Everything that went before might have been the training I needed to climb back into the cockpit and start piloting my body again.

Once I merge with my living mind, I can wake up from this craziness. That's what I've needed to do from the beginning. What a dope I've been. It's so obvious. Calla, my subconscious mind, was trying to prod me to do this. It must have predicted I'd eventually get bored with re-experiencing and try something like this. It even provided warnings to keep me from doing it wrong.

SUNDAY, 7:29:00 P.M.

AT THE HOSPITAL, I GO FLOOR-BY-FLOOR AND ROOM-BY-room but can't find my body. I even check the morgue. I spot an EMT filling out some paperwork at a desk in the ER and enter his mind.

Through his eyes, I watch him write. It's a shooting report

with my name listed as victim. I stay with him until he writes *transferred to OR-3 for immediate surgical intervention.*

I move to the operating suite and perceive my inert form. Unconscious, my body lies face down while they open the skin at the base of my skull. Exactly where I felt the pain.

Well, this won't work. I don't want to enter my mind under anesthesia. I'll have to wait 'til I come around. That means moving forward in time with someone. But whom?

I think about this for a minute and decide the surgeon's the best person. Entering the surgeon's mind, I move forward with time again. Focused on his work, he's especially concerned about how much blood has accumulated inside the skull at the base of his patient's brain—my brain. He asks another doctor in the room, "How long has it been since the shooting?"

"About a half hour."

The surgeon working on me shakes his head. "We're probably wasting our time here, given the amount of trauma, but the police will want the bullet. If by some miracle this guy didn't lose fresh circulation to the brain for more than ten minutes and the bullet managed to skirt the brain stem, he could end up alive. Either way, the bullet needs to come out."

He locates the bullet, extracts it, and drops it into a metal tray with a clink.

"I can repair some of the damage the bullet did before it entered the brain and what we did getting to it, but there was massive pooling here. I've debrided what I could and put in an intraventricular catheter for drainage, but it's doubtful oxygenated blood made it any higher than the brain stem before we did. This guy's only hope is if the bleeding didn't begin in earnest until after we got him on the table."

My surgeon works diligently, closing every bleeder and restoring structure to the tissue for another half-hour.

This guy's good.

"You did some fine work in there, Steve," the other surgeon says. "Why don't you get out of here? I can finish up."

"Thanks. I'll order a post-op EEG. We'll need a baseline. If it's as bad as I think it'll be, we'll need two more, after the anesthetic clears the blood stream, twenty-four hours apart. I need to clean up so I can go out and talk to the family."

He turns to the nurse at the patient's head. "Nora, notify recovery, will you?"

"Yes, Doctor. I'll record the time as 7:55 p.m."

I have a choice to make, stay with my body or stay with the doctor. I decide on the former and jump into Nora's mind. I find she's also been providing my anesthesia. She's a CRNA, Certified Registered Nurse Anesthetist.

I'm prepared to jump again if I need to, but Nora stays with my body for the next half hour, through my time in recovery and the EEG.

When Dr. Steve comes into the recovery room it's eight thirty p.m. Nancy and Beth follow him in and come to opposite sides of my bed so they can each hold one of my hands. But I can't feel them. Nora remains in the room, so I stay in her mind. Another nurse hands the doctor a file. I assume it contains the raw EEG tracing. The doctor gives nothing away with his expression.

"As I told you downstairs, Mrs. Lister, I was able to remove the bullet from the base of your husband's brain and repair some of the damage. Our biggest worry once we took out the bullet was the condition of his brain. There's a significant amount of damage and swelling that can cut off circulation, depriving the brain of oxygen. Do you both understand what I've explained to you?"

"Yes, Doctor Carver," Beth says.

Nancy only nods.

"Here in the recovery room, I had them run an electro-encephalogram on your husband, to give us an early indication of whether the impediments to circulation were catastrophic. I've reviewed the EEG results. I'm afraid my fears were justified. We detect little to no brain activity."

"You mean he's in a coma, right?" Nancy says.

Beth is silent.

"No. It's worse than that. Your husband's brain was without oxygen too long. We'll proceed carefully, as the law requires. But I'm certain what the results will be." Doctor Carver says this as gently as possible, but his face conveys the absence of hope.

"What's next?" Beth asks.

"We'll do two more EEGs, twenty-four hours apart, beginning tomorrow morning at ten a.m. By then, the anesthesia will be out of his system and the swelling will be reduced. I must caution you, if they're both like the one we did in the recovery room, and I believe they will be, he will be declared legally dead. Life support would be ended sometime on Wednesday, as he's arranged to be an organ donor."

"But he's breathing," Nancy interrupts. "His heart's beating. He's warm. He's not . . . That EEG is wrong. Tomorrow. Tomorrow will be different."

The doctor looks at Beth and shakes his head. She nods to let him know she understands the truth of his statement. "Thank you, Doctor. What time can she see him tomorrow?"

"After nine a.m. A couple people will be in to talk with you before you leave the hospital this evening. You can stay with him for a while now. Keep it under an hour, though, okay?"

"We will," Beth says. "I know you did everything you could for my dad."

I'm shocked at the doctor's words. Doesn't he know I can climb back in, and my brain will start ticking over?

The time has come. Here I go. Back into my living mind.

As I form this thought, I find my consciousness falling through the bed. I pass through my body but can't become one with it.

I hop to the brain of an old woman in the next bed. I can tell she's dozing, but I'm in her mind. I can hear through her ears. I can feel her arm against the bedrail.

I leave her mind and try again to return to my own. But, with nothing to hold on to, I slip right through again.

This didn't happen when I entered little Rob's sleeping body. I entered, experienced his sense of calm, and exited. I didn't just fall through. It happens now because my brain no longer functions, and its thoughts have fled. That's what I am now, those fleeting thoughts.

The other people in this time and space are alive, thinking, reasoning, sensing. But my brain . . . is not.

Calla's been telling me the truth. What an arrogant, ignorant fool I've been. I can't return to life in my body. I'm stuck. He wasn't preparing me for this. He was trying to prevent it. Hopelessness closes in. I'm lost.

Chapter Twenty-Seven

Tuesday, July 9, 6:05 p.m.

Beth finished the chapter about her dad's failure to return to Calla or enter his body with tears in her eyes. She always knew he'd try to get back to them. How horrible for him to discover that he couldn't.

Beth had gotten several chapters ahead of her mother, who'd dozed off. She left the pages she'd read for her and took the rest into the study.

The fact there was a large pile remaining provided her cause for optimism. If he was really lost, what was the rest of the story? She understood why he couldn't get back in his body but refused to believe he was lost. She read on.

~

IS THIS REALLY THE END FOR ME? DO I JUST FLOAT around here like a ghost, with no body of my own to connect with? Isn't there someplace I can go?

Wait one stinking minute. I got here, didn't I? Shouldn't I be able to return the way I came?

I retrace my steps back to that point half the distance closer to earth than my starting point. This time I don't call or shout. I scream, "Calla? Calla? Calla?"

Silence.

His words haunt me. "*Memories are vivid here. They can overtake you. You can become lost.*"

I fell into the trap. I was warned and went ahead anyway. Another conversation plays in my mind.

"*I've found my home, Calla. Can I go closer?*"

"*You can, but you must not, or you will be lost forever.*"

But I did. Fear and anger threaten to relieve me of my sanity.

"*You realize that no time has passed for me. You left and returned.*"

But that's no longer true. I spent two hours in the present and moved forward with Nancy, the detective, the surgeon, the nurse, and the old lady in the next bed. What if Calla sensed this and quit waiting?

What if he believes I'm lost? Wouldn't he come for me? Or would that violate one of those strange rules he follows?

I realize that I have only one shot left. I must return to the precise place where I left Calla and hope he's still there. I'm terrified to take that final step. What if my aim's off or Calla isn't there? What if . . . ?

There lay madness.

Think clearly.

He came to me in the first place. He could still be waiting where I left him, hoping that I figured this out.

I have one more move in space to return to where he is— where I hope he is. I hesitate, afraid to make the last jump. What if I'm wrong?

I hate this.

I jump.

~

I say a silent prayer and call out, "Calla?"

"Yes, my friend. What is wrong? Why did you move forward?"

I could hug him if I had arms. If I had eyes they'd be overflowing with tears.

"Now that you are back, your thoughts reveal what happened. I am disappointed but not surprised."

"I missed her so much." I'm sobbing in my mind.

"I know, my friend. But you discovered the problem."

"I'm not ready. I have more to learn."

"Not that problem."

"I died."

"Your brain died. Had you asked me that question, I would have answered it honestly. Now I have a question for you. Am I a figment of your imagination?"

"No. You're my guide. And I need you."

"Then you must follow my guidance—without question—from this point forward. And this point is 8:50:18 p.m., on the same Sunday you left your body. It will be more difficult as we move forward. But you must do as I say, or I must leave you." For the first time, Calla's voice in my mind contains no hint of compassion.

I've reached a critical point. This isn't a dream or hallucination. This is my existence now. I must commit. My future hangs in the balance. I've discovered an essential truth.

"I will. I want you as my guide and need you as my friend."

"Return to your memories then. But limit yourself to the direction you have been traveling and leave nothing out. You may not skip around. Is that clear?"

"Yes."

"Proceed."

~

Beth returned the rest of the pages to where her mother was sleeping, relieved that her dad had made it back to Calla. She put a clip around the entire section to assure her mother would read up to where she had. Returning to the study, she plopped onto the sofa bed and let her exhaustion do the rest.

Chapter Twenty-Eight

Wednesday, July 10, 10:30 a.m. CEST (Tuesday, July 9, 10:30 p.m. HST)

As they left the Vatican Museum, Julie was absolutely flabbergasted by her husband. He'd gotten them there right on time. His questions to their guides displayed familiarity with ancient Roman and early Christian history. And he really seemed to be enjoying himself.

"Where to next?" Keone asked.

"St. Peters Basilica, the Capitoline Museum, the Circus Maximus, San Pietro in Vincoli, and as many more fabulous and historic sites as we can manage before we catch our train. I plan to keep you moving today."

"Great."

"Wait. I forgot to call Janet. How could you let me do that?" Julie said, glancing at her cell. A frown crossed her face

"Before you say anything, let me explain. Okay?"

"This better be good."

"I woke up last night on the couch, noticed you'd moved to

the bedroom, went in there, and picked up your phone to see what time it was. When I saw it was 10:30 p.m. here, I realized it was mid-morning at home, so gave Janet a call. I thought you'd want me to tell her how much fun we're having." Keone's face was the image of innocence.

"I want to be mad at you, but I never specifically banned you from using my phone or calling my sister. Since you didn't call anyone else, and it's unlikely you'd talk to her about work, I'm going to cut you some slack this one time. But no more using my cell on the trip. Got it, Big Guy?"

"Yes, ma'am."

"Okay, let's go."

"Andiamo!"

~

Keone held his breath as they walked to the metro station and Julie blissfully chatted with her sister on her cell. His new sister-in-law had promised not to tell Julie what he'd asked her about, and from Julie's half of the conversation he could tell Janet kept her word.

Janet's answer to that one simple question could have calmed all his concerns but did the opposite. When he asked her how Sam looked when she visited him on July Fourth, she confirmed everything Hasselbach had said. Sam was freshly shaved, his hair was trimmed, he was dressed in his best suit, and he was completely alert and talkative.

Yet, only two days later, Sam was catatonic with wild, long hair and a beard. It wasn't possible. But he had two, independent witnesses that confirmed the fact. Knocked off balance by Janet's revelation, he felt much like Sam must have when left became right for him in an instant. But as a detective, he knew he had work to do. He also knew it could wait. Sam wasn't going anywhere, and he had to concentrate on making sure every moment of Julie's honeymoon was as fantastic as this morning.

He'd spent so many years hiding his emotions. But with Julie, he wouldn't hide anything.

~

IT WAS JULIE AND NOT KEONE WHO WAS EXHAUSTED when they arrived at the Hotel later that afternoon to collect their luggage. She was glad Keone had arranged for a cab to take them the short distance to the train station to catch their express train to Civitavecchia. Once installed in their first-class compartment, she leaned back and watched people walk past by the window into their compartment from the passageway. She felt the train pull away from the station and was soothed by the sound of the wheels on the rails.

Just before she dozed off, she noticed a tanned, expensively dressed man with a bushy mustache walk past. *Had he just peered in at Keone?*

Now who's imagining things, she thought and let her eyelids close the rest of the way.

Chapter Twenty-Nine

Wednesday, July 10, 5:30 p.m., CEST (Wednesday, July 10, 5:30 a.m. HST)

Keone Boyd carried three bottles of champagne out onto the veranda of their luxury suite onboard the liner *Argonaut*. "You know, Julie, people must think we're *lolo*."

"Why?" Julie asked, setting two glasses and a basket of fruit on the little table. "Because we married so soon after meeting?"

"No." Keone popped open the first bottle, and they both watched the cork fly over the railing.

"Because we met while you were investigating my crazy brother-in-law, who suddenly decided I was his wife in a parallel universe?" Julie asked, as Keone poured.

"No."

"Okay, Mr. Boyd, why must people think we're crazy?" She clinked her glass against his.

"Because, Mrs. Boyd, we both live on a small island and are spending our honeymoon visiting a series of other small islands, halfway around the world—on a boat, no less."

Julie grinned and flashed her eyes. "It's called a ship. And I think they're the crazy ones. We just know how to live. Think about it. What are your favorite things—next to me, of course?"

"Large expanses of saltwater punctuated with beautiful little islands filled with interesting, local people."

"Me, too. Plus, I love to experience cultures completely different from my own. I think getting married on a ranch in Makawao one day, flying into to Rome three days later, and boarding this beautiful ship today to cruise the Mediterranean is the most intelligent thing either of us has ever done. Except for deciding to get married in the first place."

He raised his glass to clink against hers. "When you're right, you're right. Nice of Tony, Lani, and Angela to provide these three bottles, wasn't it?"

"Janet's gift is nice, too."

"Sure. I love fruit baskets." Keone flashed a guilty grin. He'd barely touched the fruit so far.

Their eyes wandered beyond their glasses, beyond the rail of the veranda, and caught the last evidence of Civitavecchia disappearing over the horizon.

"Keone, I just realized that for the rest of the trip we will be hopping around through time. We'll dock at modern Naples and travel to ancient Pompeii, frozen in time by an erupting volcano. Then we'll go to Athens and see ruins from the even more ancient Greek society, like the Acropolis. Then it's on to the Greek Islands which mix ancient with modern as tourist meccas. Finally, we'll end up in Venice with a vast array of Renaissance architecture. I hope I can keep it all straight."

"I've been surrounded by ancient artifacts and tourists all my life. Ain' no big ting. Look at those fish popping out of the water from the ship's wake."

Julie looked where her husband was pointing. Words were no longer necessary.

Three bottles of champagne later, Julie's eyes wandered back to the strong square features of her new husband's face. He looked completely relaxed on the deck of their private veranda. Of course, the lion's share of three bottles of champagne could relax anyone.

When she leaned forward and brushed her lips against his, he came back from his own mental meanderings and tried to enclose her in his arms. She deftly twirled away through the sliding door into their suite, gave him a teasing look, and let the simple, flowered shift she'd worn onto the ship drop to the carpet. His surprised look revealed that her detective husband had failed to realize she'd worn nothing underneath it all day.

He followed her through the sliding glass door and lifted her sun-warmed body in his arms.

Somewhat later, the Cruise Director's perky voice announced, "The first dinner seating will begin at seven p.m. Central European Summer Time in the beautiful Poseidon Room. Although we traverse more than one time zone during this cruise, ship time is based on the time zone of our port of departure, Civitavecchia, Italy—CEST." She might as well have been speaking Greek and not English for all the newlyweds cared. They ignored the auditory intrusion, absorbed in more strenuous and far more rewarding activities than simply eating.

Four decks below, an individual, alone in his cabin, prepared for the second of nine special events that would make this cruise his crowning achievement:

Europol?

Fools.

FBI?

Morons.

My adversaries would be amazed by my love of cruises. Couldn't the oh-so-intelligent members of their respective Behavioral Analysis Units realize that their profiling target could enjoy simple pleasures?

I like to go to exotic ports of call and kindle relationships in the process. Of course, mine are a bit complicated. I have fourteen days and nine ports of call, and I plan to make good use of my time.

Preparations for this adventure took a full year of research and meticulous planning. One can't leave anything to chance.

Nine worthy children came for this cruise. And I have already cradled one in my arms and sent her home to Elysium.

My fellow gods will delight in my kindness.

Tomorrow I will help another. No feeble Roman imitations of the true gods can impede my mission.

Thanatos will have his day.

Chapter Thirty

Wednesday, July 10, 7:30 a.m. HST

Angela was well into her second day as a detective, if only a temporary one. She didn't mind that Alcala closely monitored her actions. It proved he was seriously evaluating her as a potential member of his division.

Whittling down the number of suspects was an important part of her assignment. But she might have whittled a bit too far. Her list of pot growers in the ʻĪao Valley was down to one without a confirmed alibi. Her list of potential enemies from the vic's past was also down to one. The accidental shooting theory was still wide open but had little hard evidence. The footprints suggested a young person, but it could be male or female. Rob's story alone said it was a boy. She hoped the shell casing she found would help point her toward the shooter.

She opened a drawer and pulled out one of Keone's yellow legal pads and created a to-do list:

1.Extend pot grower/transporter list to include those who live farther outside the 'Īao Valley but have transported loads through there recently.

2. Touch base with Blue to obtain any new information on Efren (Hopper) Alavezos – the man with the faulty alibi.

3. Contact Lister scientific rival on-island and set up interview.

4. Follow up on new information from the shell casing, when available.

5. Touch base with consultant to see if manuscript divulged any additional potential enemies or other relevant information.

She was on her last bullet point when Lindsay Kalani appeared holding a manila folder. "There's supposed to be reports in there from ballistics and fingerprints. Where did you find fingerprints?"

"CSI found a cartridge casing on the opposite side of the 'Īao stream from where Dr. Lister was shot."

Angela looked over the reports as Lindsay waited. She couldn't help but smile.

"Catch a break?" Lindsay asked.

"The shell casing is compatible with the round recovered from the vic and with the postulated weapon. They did a calculation for me based on an elliptical trajectory for the bullet. They confirmed such a trajectory could account for the wound and the lack of deformation on the bullet the doctor recovered."

"Sounds interesting. Any prints?"

"They recovered two prints from the cartridge casing. They're running them now. They confirmed that casing was from a cartridge that had been fired within the past forty-eight hours."

"Sounds like you're on top of things," Lindsay said and turned to leave. Over her shoulder, she added, "Go get 'em girl"

Angela was still focused on the contents of the folder when Ed Jenkins, the CSI from the 'Īao Valley, leaned into her cubicle. "I see you got the initial reports on the ballistics and fingerprint evidence. I brought the rest personally to thank you for what you did."

"Happy to do it. What more did you discover?" She took a red folder from his outstretched hand.

"I was right. The footprints were from a kid. The experts say aged eight to ten. Probably a local kid by the way the feet are calloused. We also found powder residue on some leaves above the root where he slipped. He definitely fired a shot upward."

"Thanks. Good work."

"Oh, there's one more thing," Ed added. "It may not be important, but we've finished processing Lister's car and . . ."

"Yes?"

"It looks like he had a new scratch on his driver's side rear fender. It's green and probably from a minor collision. We missed it at first with all the other scratches and dings on the car. The guys in the lab think it happened the same night as the shooting. Hope it helps."

"Thanks. And don't release the car yet, okay? I want to have a look."

"Sure thing," Jenkins said, then left her on her own.

Angela thought about the near-miss Rob described. In that newer section Linda shared, the green truck tagged the back fender, probably just enough to leave a mark.

She couldn't decide if the tingling at the base of her skull was due to the ballistics report or what she'd just heard from Ed Jenkins. Maybe both.

Chapter Thirty-One

Wednesday, July 10, 8:00 a.m. HST

As always, the discordant serenade of island birds outside her window told Nancy morning had come to Ka'anapali, Maui. She reached over to touch Rob only to find Beth in his place. The reality of the past few days broke over her like a tsunami.

Her head dropped back on the pillow, and her entire body shook with sobs, waking Beth. Eyes still closed, her daughter surrounded Nancy with her arms.

After fifteen minutes, she was cried out. Beth held her the whole time and didn't say a word. Nancy placed a gentle kiss on her daughter's cheek. She was ready to face this day.

"You so needed that, Mom. I've been waiting for that dam to break for three days."

"I know, sweetheart. But it had to come in its own time. I'm sure it'll happen again over the coming days and months. Probably when we least expect it."

Nancy watched as Beth eased herself from the bed and shuffled into the kitchen, returning with her mug and the Pyrex pot from the automatic coffeemaker. Her thoughtful daughter poured a substantial dose of caffeine into Nancy's oversized Tinker Bell mug.

Nancy stared at the mug, a gift from Rob. On one side, a disheveled Tink held a coffee cup, her hair in disarray with a strikingly non-Disney expression on her face. On the other side, the cup read, "Mornings are NOT Magical," a sentiment with which Nancy totally concurred.

"So, did the two of us cozied up like that on a couch last night bring back a few memories, honey?"

"Scads. All those snowy nights in Newark, when Dad was away at a meeting or off investigating some new technology. I want to have times like that with my kids someday."

Nancy smiled.

"Did you read all the way up to where I stopped last night?"

"I did. It's a gift. Your dad let us know that we're doing the right thing today. I want to be at the hospital by nine a.m."

"They won't do the test until ten."

"I know but I have a very large stack of papers to sign so they can do what they need to do . . . after. His organs are going to help a lot of people. He'd be glad about that part."

Beth and Nancy sat on either side of Rob's hospital bed, each grasping one of his hands. It reminded Nancy of that first night they saw him after the shooting. They'd already hugged and kissed his inert form one last time.

Nancy leaned over Rob's ear and whispered, "I love you so much. You know I don't want to let you go, but it's time. Aloha, my sweet love."

She sat back up and nodded to Beth, then Dr. Carver.

The nurse turned off the alarms and other sounds from the monitors. Then she switched off the respirator.

Nancy had grown so used to the recurring beeps from the monitors and whooshes of the respirator that she found the silence deafening.

Without disturbing Nancy or Beth, the nurse gently disconnected the respirator from the tube in Rob's mouth and removed the tape that held it in place.

Nancy saw Beth focus on the remaining monitor read out, tracing with simple up and down waves Rob's final heartbeats. But she looked at her husband's face one last time, a face that seemed more familiar and relaxed.

In this eternal moment, she tried to recall all the expressions he'd shared with her over the years. The gentle flow of images calmed her. The last image, before Carver's hand softly settled on her shoulder, was Rob's impish smile.

"He's ready to help others now, Nancy," Carver said.

Beth moved to her side and helped her to her feet.

There was nothing more to say.

Chapter Thirty-Two

Angela rewarded herself with a doughnut from the box next to the coffee pot. She had managed to schedule an interview with the elusive Dr. Thomas Francis O'Rourke, M.D. later that afternoon at his home in the hills above Wailuku. Over the phone, he'd confirmed that he remembered Lister but didn't know he lived on the island. He also claimed he'd never encountered Lister on Maui or anywhere else since O'Rourke was forced to retire from Rosen Pharmaceutical Company. They moved in different circles.

Was it just a coincidence that an old adversary, who'd single-handedly halted Rob Lister's rapid rise at Rosen Pharmaceuticals lived on the same island where he lived—and died? Like her friend Keone, she never trusted coincidence. And why was O'Rourke forced to retire? She hoped for a motive in there somewhere.

With hours until the interview, she decided to follow up on the *evidence* from Rob's story. She'd consider it a coffee break. The part about the boy was reassuring but hard to prove. But the license plate was something she could rule out in a couple hours.

She picked up the phone and punched in a number from memory. "Hey, Cille, it's Ange. How's life at the DMV this morning?"

"Hi, Ange. Boring as usual. What can I do for you? I heard you're kicking around CID."

"Yeah, temporarily. It's a long story. Anyway, I've got a plate that could help us out on a shooting in the ʻIao Valley. Could you run it for me?"

"Sure. I should be able to get it for you in a couple hours. I assume you want address, phone, any outstanding violations, registration problems—the whole enchilada."

"That'd be great. I owe you, Cille."

When she ended the call, she realized she'd just sent a license plate number from a fantasy novel in for an ID. She decided not to think too much about it.

Beth spent the drive back from the hospital on the phone with Mike Butler. She arranged to use his boat to scatter her father's ashes at a spot Dad had selected midway between Lanaʻi and Molokaʻi—a spot you could see from her parents' lanai.

Before ending the call, Beth looked over at her mother. "Would you like to talk to Mike?"

"Yes, put him on speaker. You should hear this, too."

She was surprised by the determination in her mother's voice.

"Hi, Mike. I need to tell you about something," her mother began, not giving Mike a chance to share the condolences he'd just shared with Beth. "I found something Rob wrote on his computer. Beth and I are reading it."

"How long?"

"I think it's a complete manuscript. The thing is, it's so . . . different from anything he's written before. I haven't decided if it should be published. But I wanted you to know."

"You've got me intrigued. But I won't push you right now. Like I told Beth, you both deserve time to work through your loss. I'm here for you."

"I do have a favor to ask you. I need to know more about the shooting and the insurance. Could you talk to the police and the insurance company and find out where we stand? I'd do it, but I . . ."

"No problem. You've got enough on your plate. I know some people. I'll call you tomorrow. We can talk over dinner. All my thoughts and prayers—"

Her mom ended the call before he could finish the sentence.

"I can see why you wanted to tell Mike about the story, but what was that about the insurance?"

"We need to make certain the story won't make the insurance company think your dad arranged his own death before we share it with anyone. I know Angela told us the police are confident it wasn't suicide, but the insurance company might have other ideas. It was a big policy, and they might just be dragging their heels. We just need to be careful."

"Dad didn't kill himself or pay someone else to do it." Beth crossed her arms across her chest.

"I know that, but I want to move carefully. I'd like to see your dad's book published. It shows what a great writer he is. Was. But I won't risk our security."

"I understand. But I think you're worrying about nothing. He couldn't have shot himself in the head with a rifle from the far side of the ʻĪao Stream. And Angela will find out who fired the shot. From the story, it sounds like it might even be an accident."

"I know. But we'll let Mike make extra certain for us, okay?"

"Sure. On another topic, you need to tell me who you want invited on the boat Friday, and I'll contact them."

"I'm sure most won't be able to come on such short notice, but I'd feel bad if we didn't invite them."

"You might be surprised."

"Well, there's your uncle Jon. Rob's old boss Tom Byron lives in San Diego so he might be able to come . . ."

Beth typed the list on her tablet and checked to see how many she had contact info for as her mom continued to list names.

~

ANGELA ROCKED IN HER SEAT, STILL WAITING FOR fingerprint IDs. To clear her mind, she walked over to Lindsay's cubicle. The detective was writing up a contact report and looked as though she could use a break.

"May I interrupt?"

"I wish you would. This report is . . ."

"Dry as a popcorn fart? That's what Linda says mine are." Angela snorted and Lindsay laughed out loud. "What's the case?"

"Hit and run on South Main Street. Right across from Brandy's bar and grill. That's where I was headed Sunday when the call came in about your shooting. I was glad the LT was around to take it. He had me call Mrs. Lister from my car. Hey, want some spicy ahi poke, it's lunch time and I brought enough for an army."

"That is the nicest offer I've had since I got here."

Over lunch outside, Angela felt comfortable enough around Lindsay to ask her a few questions.

"What can you tell me about the boss? I don't even know if he's from Maui."

"He's not. He was born on O'ahu and grew up in Kapolei. He's got Hawaiian blood, so he was able to attend the King Kamehameha schools, but he has Portuguese and Puerto Rican roots, too. I'm guessing the grey eyes came from the Portuguese part."

"Has he always been a cop?"

"No. He was a top student. Transferred to Punahou after his first few years at Kam'. Finished high in his class."

"College?"

"U of H in Mānoa, history major. Even taught high school for a while after he graduated. I think that's what got him interested in law enforcement. Lost too many students to drugs and gangs."

"How'd he end up here?"

"Tony went through the academy on O'ahu. Top of his class.

Then worked his way up to detective on the streets, mostly Chinatown. He saw a better chance for advancement over here on Maui and thought he could make a difference. Moved the whole family over."

"Family?"

"Yeah, he was married then. He and Moani had been married for four years, had a little boy and one on the way. But you know how tough it can be for a cop to give a hundred percent at both work and home. He thought Maui's less urban environment and slower pace might help revive their marriage. It didn't. They divorced right after he made sergeant. And she moved back to O'ahu with the kids. Everything was amicable, though. He spends one weekend a month with his kids on O'ahu, and they spend time each summer with him here. They usually come in August."

"How long have he and Keone been friends? I got the sense they go back quite a long way."

"He was Keone's first partner, when Keone made detective. They worked together until Keone made sergeant and he made lieutenant, about a year ago. He treats Keone tough in front of people, but they're close. I think his friendship with Keone got him through the divorce."

"Thanks for the background. It should keep me from stubbing my toes."

"Happy to help. I better get back to my case. Thanks for the break."

Angela returned to Keone's cubicle to find the fingerprint report in the in box. She flipped open the file and was pleased to see a positive ID from one of the fingerprints. The print matched a seventy-year-old Vietnam Vet, Koa Maleko Kaleho, who lived in the ʻĪao Valley. The other produced no hits. *Probably wouldn't if it was from a kid,* she thought. Reading further, she discovered the old man lived with his daughter, Esther Anuhea Kaleho Hernandez and two grandsons, one fourteen and the other . . .

Ten years old.

With Rob's account in her mind, Angela decided the grandfather, younger grandson, and especially the house deserved investigation.

She'd already scheduled her visit with the scientist suspect at his home in the hills above Wailuku. The boy's neighborhood was not far away.

Before she could collect her gear and head for her car, the desk phone rang.

She was pleased to hear her friend Cille's voice. "I've got your truck."

"I'm in your debt. Who owns it?"

"A deadbeat named Alavezos. The only legal thing he's done over the past six years is to register his truck. I'm surprised it passed inspection. You'll find he has an impressive rap sheet, too. Multiple arrests for—"

"Growing, transporting, and selling illegal crops," Angela finished for her. "His first name wouldn't be Efren, by any chance?"

"It would, but I hear he goes by Hopper."

Bingo. She'd heard that name before. And it had no alibi for the night of the shooting.

"Oh, he had the heap painted recently, too."

"What color?"

"Kelly green."

Angela thanked Cille again, ended the call, and headed for her car, with viable suspects for each scenario.

The tingle was back, stronger than ever.

Chapter Thirty-Three

Wednesday, July 10, 2:30 p.m. HST

Finished with all the tasks needed for Friday's memorial service, Beth plopped on the couch next to her mother and picked up unread manuscript pages. But Mom was still working on what Beth had already read. After a few minutes, she saw her mom fighting to keep her eyes open before giving in to the exhaustion that Beth knew was more emotional than physical.

Beth had to stifle her chuckles as she read the current section of Dad's manuscript. She crept into the study and closed the door before releasing her laughter. It felt so good to laugh. Dad loved to laugh, but his sense of humor was a little warped, like that section she'd just read. In it he described feigning illness in middle school to get out of turning in an essay he hadn't finished. Unfortunately, his dad came home and offered him a trip behind the scenes at Disneyland. Since he wasn't sick, he'd reluctantly agreed getting out of the house might be good for him.

The guys working on adapting the new rides from the New York World's Fair were very nice to Dad and his dad, but their boss, Mr. Pierce, was a jerk. Since he knew nothing about the work, he offered Dad a drink from the vending machine when the others got into the details. By this time, he'd started to wonder if his illness was completely fake.

❧

Sunday, 8:50:18 p.m.

I cautiously select a ginger ale for my queasy stomach and ask Mr. Pierce, "Where are these Omni-movers going to be used here at the park?"

"They'll be on some new rides. The first one, Journey into Inner Space, makes you feel like you're shrinking to the size of an atom."

I take my first sip of the ginger ale while he goes on talking about a Haunted House ride that's also supposed to use these egg-shaped conveyances. I feel him warming to his topic. "These babies have significant advantages over the floatation, suspension, and track-based rides we've used to this point."

We walk back to where Dad's talking with the craftsmen. I can tell Dad's enjoying himself. He peppers the conversation with jokes and four-letter-words, getting howls of laughter from the guys and a frown from Mr. Pierce. At this moment, I feel those first sips of ginger ale reach my stomach, and pressure begins to build.

I remind Calla about an earlier memory we re-experienced together when I lost my two front baby teeth. "My thirteen-year-old self has a reminder of that collision. When the permanent teeth grew in, one overlapped the other, forming an angled gap one-eighth of an inch deep."

I'm about to throw up, for real this time. I want to maintain until we get outside. But Dad keeps telling stories, and the guys keep encouraging him. Holding everything down, I turn to Mr.

157

Pierce to ask where I can find a restroom. The bile in my stomach begins surging up my throat. I clamp down my teeth and lips to hold everything in.

It would have worked, too, except for that little gap between my two front teeth. The liquid spews out in a tight stream directly at Mr. Pierce's bushy eyebrows. It makes a graceful Disney arc but still strikes with great force.

Mr. Pierce makes a sound I never expected to hear from a man. His high-pitched shriek hurts my ears. I discover where the restroom is because he's running there. My thirteen-year-old self follows and completes the up-chuck in a toilet. My current self remains behind with Calla, jumping to the workers minds to explore the perceptions of those left behind.

Although they maintain straight faces, their thoughts betray them. I pick up a few from each man, including the floor manager Hal:

I love this kid. Great aim.

Pierce is such a wuss. He sounded like a fairy princess shrieking from a haunted castle.

The arrogant bastard. A perfect reward for the bullshit he's given us since he got here.

They've got to fire this putz.

"Bob, you can bring that talented son of yours here anytime," Hal says.

Calla and I jump to the restroom. I finish puking my guts out, while Mr. Pierce tears off his shirt and throws it in the trash. He's frantically shampooing his hair with hand soap when Dad comes in. "Peter, I can't tell you how sorry I am this happened."

Dad throws a mean look my way. I know I'm in for a severe tongue-lashing, or worse when we leave.

Mr. Pierce mumbles something that sounds like, "Take the specs and go." And we do.

But Dad doesn't yell at me when we get back to the car. He doesn't yell as we leave Disneyland or on the freeway going home, either.

He finally speaks when we pull into our driveway. "You can tell your mom you threw up but don't mention hitting anyone. Okay?"

Shocked and amazed, I manage to croak out, "Sure."

∼

BETH WAS STRUCK BY SOMETHING ELSE IN THIS section. Dad at Disneyland. he refused to go to Disneyland or Disney World with her and Mom. She'd even worked there for a while and could sign them in, but he never came. Dad loved the T-shirts she bought him with her employee discount and wore them everywhere with pride. One of his favorites had Goofy scratching his head with the caption, "Partly Confused, All of the Time!" But his favorite T-shirt by far was the one she brought him as a souvenir from Eric Idle's hilarious Broadway version of Monty Python, *Spamalot*. The shirt was totally black with the words "I'm not Dead Yet" on the front in white lettering.

He wore the shirt everywhere. Total strangers would walk up and say, "I love your shirt."

When asked for an explanation, he'd say, "I wear it to remind my daughter that she can't have the house yet."

Dad always got laughs with that. Now, Beth felt her own chuckles turn to sobs.

Laughing to crying in the span of ten seconds. *This must be what real grief is like.*

When she thought her heart would break, she heard her father's voice in her mind saying, "Damn good thing I wasn't wearing that T-shirt when I got shot. I refuse to wear factually incorrect clothing."

A perfect example of Dad's sense of humor.

I do miss you, Daddy.

Laughed and cried out, Beth returned to reading. She figured she might doze off like her mom when she finished a few more pages. But once she read the final lines of the next section, there was no way she could stop.

~

I TAKE CALLA A FEW MONTHS FORWARD. FOOTBALL season has begun and we're watching the quarterback for the Rams throw a bullet pass right into the receiver's hands.

The announcer says, "That's what I call pinpoint accuracy."

Dad looks at me and shakes his head. "No, that was just okay. Your toss at Mr. Pierce? That was pinpoint accuracy." Then he smiles and gives me a light punch in the shoulder.

I sense Calla smiling after we return.

"I was pleased to see you and your father bonding."

"All because of something that occurred at Disneyland. I had so many experiences there. By the time we watched that football game, I'd been to Disneyland over one hundred times. Disneyland was like a second home to me."

"I see why you wanted to share this with me, and I am glad you did. But you have something else we need to share, do you not?"

"No. I don't think so. I made it through high school and would like to move on to college and the army."

Calla waits a long time before replying.

"Robert, tell me the real reason you want to stop sharing. What happened the day after your father complimented you on your excellent aim?"

"I don't need to re-experience it."

"I think that you do. Take us forward one day." It's a command. And I comply. I feel cold inside. Fear claws at the edges of my mind. I can't let it in.

Chapter Thirty-Four

Angela's drive back down the hills beyond Wailuku was truly a breath of fresh air. The scent of eucalyptus filled her lungs as she looked down upon the busy harbor below.

She had a busy afternoon ahead of her and still hadn't found her shooter. Her first stop had been a posh mansion in the hills above Wailuku. The man who answered the door took her into a well-stocked library, where a man in a wheelchair methodically turned the pages of medical journals on an ornate wooden table.

The man in the wheelchair was Dr. Thomas Francis O'Rourke. A pair of glasses with huge, thick lenses covered half his face and a white cane leaned against his chair. Both of his legs ended in stumps.

The man seemed lucid though and explained his condition. "It's ironic really. My specialty was endocrinology. Somehow that didn't prevent me from developing the most severe complications of an endocrine disease, diabetes. Both legs had to be amputated due to complications from diabetic neuropathy. Diabetic retinopathy made me legally blind. But you wanted to talk with me about former colleague, didn't you, Sergeant . . ."

"Beyers, sir." Angela finished the sentence for him. This guy couldn't have fired the shot that killed Rob Lister, but he could've hired someone to do it. Nancy had told her that O'Rourke considered her husband a competitor. His scathing comments at a senior staff meeting had severely damaged Rob's chances of further advancement at the pharmaceutical company where they both worked.

"The colleague, Dr. Robert Lister. I understand you saw him as a competitor."

"Not just him, but a certain clique within the company threatened to focus us on protein products, rather than real drugs. He was just the spokesman."

"What did you do?"

"I took advantage of a conjunction of events to discredit him and his approach. He faded into insignificance, while my career blossomed. Tell me, why would I decide to kill him now?"

Angela had no answer. Nor was there any way for O'Rourke to know his old rival would be visiting the ʻĪao Needle that night. She recognized a dead end when she saw one.

She thanked him for his time and left. She only hoped that what Linda said she'd found in the manuscript's army section might suggest another suspect from Rob's past. Otherwise, she was down to two theories.

Now she was headed back to the ʻĪao Valley.

THE SMALL BLUE HERNANDEZ HOME, HALFWAY between Wailuku and the State Park, nestled against the steep valley walls. She knocked on the little white door and an attractive, middle-aged woman in an apron answered.

"May I help you?" the woman asked.

"Are you Mrs. Esther Kaleho Hernandez?"

"I am."

"I'm Sergeant Beyers." Angela displayed her badge. "We spoke on the phone."

"Oh yes, come in, come in. I expected a uniform. No problem. I just made us some mango iced tea." She walked into a small but tidy kitchen and returned with two iced glasses.

"What can I do for you, Sergeant?"

"I have a few questions, if you wouldn't mind."

"No. What about?"

Angela decided to get right to the point. "A shot was fired in the Valley on Sunday, up in the state park. Did you happen to hear about it?"

"No. There was nothing in the paper."

"The shooting hasn't been released to the press. We found a spent cartridge casing across the stream and multiple witnesses heard the shot."

"Why did that bring you here?" Mrs. Hernandez initial, warm welcome seemed to be fading.

"Based on the location of the cartridge casing, we think the shot may have been fired by accident. Based on the footprints we found near the casing, we think a youngster fired it. I guess you know it's a misdemeanor to have or discharge a firearm in that area."

"I also know there are a lot of youngsters who come to the valley. I ask you again. What brings you to our home?"

"The fingerprints on the spent casing. One was identified as belonging to your father. I believe the other may belong to the child who left the footprints."

"It could've been Manolo. He's my youngest. A good boy, but he always competes with his older brother to impress my dad. He's been acting weird since he came home Sunday night. I saw him sneak into his grandfather's bedroom, but he didn't know I was still awake."

"I see."

Esther's face hardened. "It's the old man's fault, like everything else. I was afraid something like this might happen. My dad's been taking my boys to the range to practice shooting his rifles. I told him to lock the damn things up, but he always kept one in a duffel bag in his bedroom. The boys both knew about it. Isn't it illegal to have a weapon in a home unless it's locked up?"

"I'm afraid it is. I'd like to see that duffel bag. Unless you have any objections?"

"My dad might, but it's not his house. I'll show you where the old fool keeps it." They walked into the bedroom.

"He keeps his other crap locked up in a footlocker, but I don't have the key to that, yet."

"This should be fine."

"Well, take the whole duffle bag with you and throw the book at my stupid father. I hope this teaches my son he shouldn't try so hard to be like his gramps." She handed the bag to Angela, who nodded and left.

Chapter Thirty-Five

Sunday, 8:50:18 p.m.

I'm back in my now fourteen-year-old body—the football game was after my birthday—lying on my bed asleep.

"You are frightened, my friend. I know why, but you need to do this. We arrive on a special day."

"Yes. Special and horrible." I'm helpless to prevent the re-experience from playing out.

My father comes into my room, as I know he will. "Good morning, Robbo."

"What time is it?" my groggy self manages to mumble.

"Nine o'clock." Dad looks so happy this morning.

"Hey, I've gotta get dressed. Tammy and Terry need to be at the church by nine thirty, don't they?"

"They do, but you don't. With them holding their dresses in the backseat, we can't all fit in the car. You can come later with your aunts. The ceremony doesn't start until noon, so go back to sleep for a little while. But make sure you have your tux on by eleven when Jane and Mary get here with your grandma." Dad gives me a hug and heads out the door.

I'm always grateful for a little more sleep. But after I hear the car back out, I'm anxious and can't sit still. I get up, take my shower, and head out to the kitchen for a banana. I take the banana back to my room and eat it while struggling into the monkey suit. I know there's a joke in there somewhere.

At least I only need to do this once.

I'm glad they agreed on the double wedding. Mom and Dad are glad too, given the cost difference between one double wedding and two single ones.

I try to remember what Dad told me about how to put on this black belt thingy. What did he call it? A cucumber bun?

I'm shocked to discover a tear creeping down my cheek. My sisters aren't going to live here anymore. Like any good little brother, I've dedicated much of my young life to embarrassing my sisters in front of their friends.

Despite such moments, my sisters always made time for their little bro. They taught me to play bridge when I was six, when they needed a fourth. They taught me the newest dances and spent hours helping me color or watercolor my many coloring books. They even took me to Disneyland without Mom and Dad. And, shock and awe, they let me go off on my own. I even think they selected the Disneyland Hotel as the site for their reception with me in mind. They agreed to let me go to the park if—no, when I got bored.

Dad would tell me to suck it up and wipe off this silly tear. A moment later someone bangs on our front door.

"Calla, I want to stop. Let's go back. Please."

Calla remains silent and the re-experience moves forward. I can't even close my other self's eyes or block his ears or keep him from opening the door.

My aunts' faces are covered with tears as I swing open the door. My Grandma must have stayed in the car for some reason. "You poor dear," Aunt Jane says.

"We wanted to be the ones to tell you," Aunt Mary adds.

They guide me to the living room and sit me down on the sectional we rarely use. Smashed between their large soft bodies, I'm horribly uncomfortable. I struggle to escape but am unable to move. They smell unusual. A sick-sweet, gardenia perfume overtone doesn't quite mask a more sinister aroma. They smell like smoke. I know they don't smoke. And this doesn't smell like burned tobacco.

"There's been an accident," Aunt Jane begins.

"It's so horrible," Aunt Mary adds.

"Your mother and father were killed instantly, but Tammy and Terry . . ." Aunt Jane can't control her sobs, so Mary continues for her.

"The car caught fire."

"Stop it. You're lying."

"Honey, we wouldn't lie to you. Theresa and Tamara were in the back seat with the wedding dresses between them. Those dresses were so lovely. Who could have known?"

I feel tears in my eyes and a catch in my throat. I manage to croak out a question. "Are they in the hospital? Are the burns bad?"

"They're gone, too. All gone." Her voice fades out and a full minute passes before she can continue. "By the time the fire trucks got there, nothing but ashes were left inside the car." Jane slumps down. She's conveyed the whole devastating story and is left completely spent.

"What about the jerk that hit them? Did they catch him? Is he dead?"

"Nobody hit them. They swerved to miss a child who ran into the road."

"Did the kid make it?"

"Yes. Your dad's quick thinking saved the girl's life, but the car hit a cinderblock wall."

"This isn't fair. God wouldn't let them die when they saved a little girl. He doesn't work that way. And where's Grandma? She knows God would never let this happen. Why didn't she come in with you?"

I can see from Mary's face that this burden has passed to her. "When we got the news, we drove straight to the crash site. When your grandma saw the horror at the scene, it was too much for her. The firemen came right over, but they couldn't save her."

Gone? Everybody gone?

Everyone that loved and protected me my whole life was wiped away in an instant. I'm left with these two weird sisters, whom even Mom could barely stand.

"Don't worry. We're here for you. You can come and live with us in Kansas," Mary says.

When she reaches over to hug me, I finally burst free. "Never. I hate you both."

"But we'll give you everything you need. We love you so much," Jane adds.

"Everything I need is gone."

I run to my room, slam the door, and flop on the bed. I close my eyes but can't block out the horrible image of my sisters wrapped in their burning wedding dresses, screaming. I feel the heat and imagine my own skin blistering. I try to scream and can't. I cry and cry and cry. Then I become completely numb. I've tuned out the physical world.

Calla allows us to return to the present.

I haven't returned to that memory for over fifty years. Whenever anyone asked about my parents, I'd just say, "They passed away."

I never elaborated. I never talked about my sisters to anyone but Nancy.

"My childhood was filled with fun and happiness, Calla. I was a funny kid who loved to joke and shared his emotions like you'd share a good story. I loved fantasy and saw Disneyland as the way the world should be."

"But the world is not Disneyland."

"I was never able to go there again. It held too many memories of the precious people I lost one Saturday in November, when I was fourteen."

"You were permanently changed."

"I became disillusioned with a world that could allow such horror to happen. It took years for that to change, even a little. I let in Nancy and Beth but few others."

"What about your aunts?"

"For the next five years, in Kansas, I kept to myself. I always kept a wall up with my aunts. On the surface, I was a model teenager. Inside, I was angry and hurt. I left as soon as I could to go to college back in California. I never went back, even for their funerals."

"Robert, you have most of your life to re-experience. But I believe you could use a change."

"Are there time-outs in purgatory?"

"Robert, has everything you experienced thus far taught you nothing?"

"I'm sorry. I keep trying to fit complex experiences into inadequate containers."

"During life, many attempt to describe the indescribable. But they can only approximate. You are beyond them now. Open your mind."

"I'll try."

"Back to my question. Are you up for a change?"

"Yes. Just so it's far away from where we just were."

"Quite far away, in both space and time."

"Let's go."

Beth read the last few lines through her tears, surprised she had any left.

Dad never told her how his family died. Now she understood why. It was horrible for him the first time. Making him re-experience it seemed heartless of Calla.

She laid the chapter beside her sleeping mother, retreated to the study, quietly closed the pocket door, and flopped on the bed. Until now, she found the sections about his childhood fun to read.

Now she understood why he was so protective once she learned to drive. He made her take that defensive driving class and minimize distractions while she drove. No cell phone, no loud music, and no more than one friend in the car.

Dad's story was no fantasy. This chapter confirmed it. He wouldn't have put himself through this. The story was real. Calla was real. She felt her father's presence in every word.

Chapter Thirty-Six

B ack at Keone's desk, Angela hoped she'd done the right thing. She hadn't told Esther that someone was seriously injured by the round that ballistics was now comparing to the rifle from the duffel bag. She hadn't had a warrant, but the mother was well within her rights in giving her the duffel bag. She'd have to discuss this with Lieutenant Alcala after she got the ballistics report.

Her cellphone rang. The display told her it was five p.m., and the caller was her informant Blue, not ballistics.

"He's coming," Blue said.

"Who's coming? Where?"

"Hopper Alavezos. He'll be at Brandy's Bar and Grill around five thirty."

"Are you sure?"

"He called and told me he'd be there if I needed anything. He sounded jumpy, though. I'll be outside to point him out when you get here. Gotta go." Blue ended the call.

Angela modified her outfit to blend in better at Brandy's. With luck, she could bring back an actual suspect for questioning. Lindsay had offered to back her up if she got a call from Blue, so she drove them over in her cruiser.

"I appreciate your help on this, Lindsay. I know you have your own work to do."

"No problem. You said this guy was an erratic driver, and the meet's right by the site of my hit-and-run. I'll say I was following up."

~

THE SHOOTER STOOD DIRECTLY ACROSS THE STREET AS Hopper Alavezos sauntered into Brandy's bar and grill. The shooter waited a few minutes to see if Hopper had a tail. A snitch named Blue emerged from a doorway a half block up from Brandy's. But Blue wasn't alone. A woman walked toward Brandy's with him and slipped Blue an envelope. Blue made a crisp about-face as the woman continued into Brandy's.

When she opened the door, the spray of light gave him a good look at her face. What he saw did not please him.

It's that lady cop from the crime scene.

He'd planned to offer Alavezos a few bucks to make himself scarce until the shooting investigation was over but couldn't do that now. That asshole better keep his mouth shut.

He watched the bar for ten minutes, then Hopper burst out the door and ran into the street. The numbskull didn't look first and was immediately struck by a passing car. Another woman, pistol drawn and waving a badge, jumped out of a parked cruiser, aimed her sidearm at Hopper and yelled, "Freeze."

The shooter found her command amusing. Hopper was writhing on the ground holding his left leg and screaming. He wasn't likely to jump up and run away.

Hopper started begging with the woman. "Okay, okay. I admit it. I hit that lady and drove off. You can lock me up but take me to the hospital first."

That dumbshit hit somebody with his crappy truck? When did that happen?

The first lady cop—the one from the crime scene—had caught up to them by now and must have wondered the same thing. "Hit what lady? When?"

"The lady here on South Main, last Sunday night. Please, please call me an ambulance."

"I guess that makes this your collar, Detective Kalani," the first lady cop said and called for the ambulance as her partner put the cuffs on Hopper.

The shooter didn't know whether to feel concerned or relieved.

When they ask Hopper about Sunday, he'll have no reason to mention me. He knows nothing about the shooting. Besides, they've got a suspect to investigate: the stupid kid.

THURSDAY, JULY 11, 6:15 A.M., SHIPS TIME (CEST) (Wednesday, July 10, 6:15 p.m. HST)

JULIE WOKE BEFORE KEONE. HER FACE GLOWED AS SHE recalled every tender moment of their first full night of love-making at sea. Their tender yet insistent touching and merging enhanced by the gentle back and forth of the ship. She'd marveled at the gentleness of her brawny husband, but his strength was always there, beneath the surface—like the vibrating force of an atomic chain reaction barely contained in a nuclear reactor. A warm wave flowed through her body.

She felt Keone stir and watched him roll on his side to face her. "*Aloha, nou no ka ʻiʻini.*"

"I love you and desire you, too, Keone. But if we're going to get our morning workout in before we leave for the shore excursion, we need to get moving."

"I guess we do have to see some of the old world, since we're all the way over here, but tonight you're mine."

Julie kissed him long and hard on the lips. "I'm always yours."

Before he could encircle her with his arms, she leapt from the bed and pulled on her workout clothes. "Later, Big Guy."

He reluctantly followed suit.

Chapter Thirty-Seven

Wednesday, July 10, 6:30 p.m. HST

Tony Alcala reviewed the day's reports from his detectives. He was pleased to see nothing had slipped through the cracks despite his limited resources. A knock on his door caused him to glance at the wall clock.

The evening shift's out in the field. Somebody's working late.

"Come in." He had a good idea who it was. Beyers had given him an update each day she'd been here and hadn't come by yet.

As he'd expected, Angela Beyers opened the door and leaned in. "Got a minute, boss?"

"Sure do. What have you got for me this evening?" he motioned her to the chair by his desk.

"Quite a bit, sir. I've obtained new information for all three tracks of the investigation."

"Better start by reminding me of your three tracks, okay?"

"Sorry, sir. Okay. Track one is Lister saw something he shouldn't have on the way to or after he reached the ʻĪao Valley and was killed to keep him quiet. Track two is someone from his life had a grievance against him and decided to take revenge. And track three is he was shot by accident."

"Since it makes the most sense, let's start with that second theory, where the shooter comes from Lister's past."

"I interviewed the last known suspect on that track, a Dr. O'Rourke. He admitted to sabotaging Lister's career back in the day at Rosen Pharmaceuticals. He saw him as a competitor then but claimed he hadn't given the man a thought since he retired. He also couldn't have been the shooter. Complications from diabetes cost him two legs and most of his vision. He could have hired someone, but it seems unlikely. No real motive. He succeeded in neutralizing Lister as a competitor years ago."

"Any other suspects from Lister's past?"

"I'm continuing to plow through his writings. I should be done by tomorrow. There could be something in Lister's military service. But that was almost forty years ago. End of the Vietnam War."

"Did he serve overseas?"

"No, only stateside."

"Okay, what about the first theory, he saw something he shouldn't have?"

"I thought we had someone there, a pot grower and dealer from the 'Īao Valley who had no alibi for Sunday night. I was about to interview him when he got nervous and ran out into traffic."

"Killed?" Tony asked.

"Broken leg, but he'll be okay. It turns out he has an alibi after all."

Alcala cocked his head. "What alibi?"

"He was the hit and run driver in Detective Kalani's case. His truck's been positively ID'ed. Lindsay backed me up during the interview and made the collar."

"Was there *any* connection to your case?"

"Yes. He admitted to sideswiping Rob's car on his way down with a truckload of pakalolo. Marks on his truck and Rob's car confirmed this. But when Lister was shot, he was on South Main Street hitting a pedestrian."

"Well, at least we nailed him for something. Have you widened your search to include any other possible candidates for theory two?"

"Yes. I'm following up on anyone who was apprehended within two miles of the park in the last year."

Alcala rubbed his chin. He doubted this would bear fruit, but agreed she needed to pursue it. "Okay. Do that."

Beyers looked as if she was going to say more but just stared at her notes.

"Come on, out with it. You found something on your flakey, third theory, didn't you?"

"Yes, sir. We have a viable suspect."

"Any evidence?"

"Yes, sir. But it could still point elsewhere."

"Do I have to pull this out one sentence at a time, Sergeant?"

"No, sir. The casing found across the ʻĪao Stream from the scene had fingerprints on it. CSI got a match to a Vietnam vet now living in the ʻĪao Valley with his daughter and her two sons. They found another print on the casing that didn't catch a hit."

"Go on." Alcala didn't like what he was hearing, but it sounded like a lead.

"I visited the home and talked to the mother. Her testimony suggested her younger boy may have borrowed his grandfather's rifle Sunday evening and returned well after the shot was fired. She gave me the gun for analysis. It fires twenty-two caliber rounds. Ballistics confirmed that it fired the shot that hit Dr. Lister. I'd like your permission to bring the boy in for questioning and possibly fingerprinting."

"You know you'll need a parent and Child Protective Services there, right?"

"Already communicated with them and an Assistant DA I know. But I didn't pull the trigger without your okay."

"You have it but watch your step. If the shooting was accidental, we don't want to be accused of being too hard on the kid."

"I will, sir. If he fired the shot, he did it by accident," Beyers said.

"If?"

"Well, there's still the grandfather and the older brother. Neither was home that evening, and both had access to the rifle. I'd like to get a little more information about them."

"Okay, but don't get distracted. Sometimes an accident is just an accident."

"Yes, sir."

"Good work so far. I'll be observing your interview with the boy and his mother. Don't screw it up."

"I won't, sir."

"Now, go home and get some rest."

"Yes, sir."

Chapter Thirty-Eight

Thursday, July 11, 7:00 a.m. ships time (CEST) (Wednesday, July 10, 7:00 p.m. HST)

A sweat-covered Keone headed to their cabin with a cucumber and mint smoothie, while Julie stayed behind to enjoy a special skin treatment he'd arranged for her in the spa. That gave him time before they had to assemble for their land package to the Amalfi Coast and Pompeii. He looked forward to a nice warm shower and a catnap.

His hopes were dashed when he saw a tanned, expensively dressed gentleman with a bushy mustache waiting for him outside their cabin door. Keone felt an annoying tingle at the base of his skull, a warning that something was about to change in his world. The man said nothing, put a finger to his lips with one hand, and flashed his Europol badge with the other.

Keone opened the cabin door. Once they were inside, Keone said, "I'm on vacation. You get that, yeah?"

"I understand." The man's accent was faint.

Keone waited.

"Detective Sergeant Boyd. We both know I have no authority over you, and you can just tell me to get . . . uh—"

"Lost," Keone finished for him.

"Yes. Quite correct. To get lost. And I will, but I must first ask for your help. I am here on a case that involves your tablemates."

"Tablemates? We blew off dinner last night. Haven't met them yet."

"An appropriate decision on the first night of your honeymoon cruise. But you will meet them, eventually. I would like you to keep an eye on them for me. Josephina Galliano, her husband Victor, and her friend Veronica Napoleoni will be on your shore excursion today. Madame Napoleoni's husband will not be joining them."

"Why do I think the table assignment wasn't an accident?"

"Madame Galliano and Madame Napoleoni are former Olympic athletes. They competed for the Canadian National Team in Athens a few years ago."

"Good for them."

"They were medalists."

"Even goodah fo' dem." Keone's use of pidgin reflected his impatience.

"Someone is killing medalists from those games. This person killed two on a cruise to Scandinavia three months ago. And two on a cruise in the Caribbean six months ago. I believe this murderer is aboard our ship."

"Why?"

"Because for him this is . . . what you call . . . a *jackspot*."

"Jackpot, Agent Calliopoulos." Keone always studied badges that were flashed at him.

The agent nodded at Keone's use of his title and last name. "Andreos, please. We are colleagues in law enforcement, are we not?"

"We'll see about that. Why is this ship a jackpot?"

"It is a reunion cruise presented by the cruise line to all nine remaining female Canadian medalists from those games."

"How did you arrange that?"

"Oh, I did not. I just take advantage of what is provided."

"Why is Ms. Napoleoni's husband skipping the excursion?"

"I do not know."

"Do you know his name?"

"I do not know that either. Veronica goes by her maiden name."

"The cruise line must have his name."

"They have *a* name, John Ferrino. But my investigations suggest it is an alias."

"Interesting. Tell me more about the killer . . . uh, serial killer."

Not many of those on Maui.

Andreos pulled some documents from his pocket and unfolded them.

"We received notes from someone claiming to be the killer after each of the first two killing sprees. He or she goes by the name Thanatos."

Keone took the offered documents and began to read. "This guy's crazy. Does he think he's some kind of god or something?" Keone joked.

"Actually, yes. Thanatos is the ancient Greek god of non-violent death."

"And how were these athletes—"

"Female athletes."

"All female. That's interesting. But my question is, how does he kill them non-violently?"

"He waves his hand over them, then they fall into a deep sleep, leave their bodies, and waken in the Elysian Fields."

"Wait, what?"

"Well, that's what he believes. The bodies each contained an unusual toxin. Our labs are working to produce an antidote."

"Seems violent to me."

"Please read on."

When he finished reading the letters, Keone folded them and returned them to the agent.

"So, you see Detective, Thanatos really believes he or she sent the victims to Elysium by divine touch alone."

"Keone."

The agent smiled. "We believe this individual is mentally ill. Will you help us stop this insanity?"

"I'll have to tell my wife."

"I prefer you do not. Our only hope to catch this beast is in the act. Why not let her enjoy her honeymoon."

Keone hated this idea but understood the logic. He would ask the same of a partner on a case like this. After considering every-thing, including his promise to Julie not to discuss work, he made the only logical decision. "How can I help?"

"Just do what you are already scheduled to do. Go on the shore excursion. Keep an eye on these people." He showed Keone pictures of the two couples on his smartphone.

"And be sure to eat dinner with them every night until we catch the killer," Keone added.

"If you would, please. Each murder took place while the ships were in port. Naples is next. I will contact you if I learn more."

"But our first port was Civitavecchia."

"Yes, they found a body there this morning. The body is being examined as we speak by the Italian police."

"Why didn't we return to port? Come to think of it, why did we leave port without a passenger? I thought there were rules about this?"

"On your second point, ships will leave their first port of departure if someone fails to check in. It happens all the time. During the cruise, when they don't return from a shore excursion, it is a very different matter."

"And my first point? A passenger was murdered."

"She was not officially a passenger, just a potential one, until she signed in."

"You're keeping this quiet."

"I am not anxious to throw away an opportunity such as this. I believe the killer is on board and plan to catch him before anyone else is harmed."

Keone stretched the rules a little on occasion himself, but the agent's secrecy made him uncomfortable. Before he could protest, his cabin phone rang.

The agent handed him a slip of paper and left.

Four p.m., Passport Bar.

Keone took his smoothie and the cordless handset onto their veranda and closed the sliding glass door to the cabin. Julie might not appreciate him taking a call on their honeymoon—not to mention agreeing to help with an international murder investigation on the ship.

Chapter Thirty-Nine

Wednesday, July 10, 7:30 p.m. HST

A familiar voice answered Angela's call. "Boyd." Angela was happy to hear Keone, even a dozen time zones away.

"Aloha, Keone. It's Angela Beyers. I'm sorry to interrupt your trip."

"Are you kidding? You're not interrupting anything. We finished our workout, and Julie hung around the spa for a special skin treatment. I'm sitting here on our veranda sipping a smoothie. Howzit back home?"

"Good. I've been working with your buddy Alcala this week."

"I got your text message. What are you working on?"

"The LT told me you aren't supposed to talk about work. He said Julie made that clear."

"Julie's not here and won't be for another half hour. Look, I'm going crazy here. You tell me what you're investigating, and I'll tell you what I am?"

"I knew it. I knew you'd get tangled up in something on that cruise. Okay let me bring you up to date on the shooting of Dr. Robert Lister, Ph.D."

"First tell me something. Did he happen to get shot in the ʻĪao Valley?" Keone asked.

How could he know that? "Did Alcala break his word to Julie?" Angela felt a little less guilty.

"I swear on my tutu, no one from Maui has contacted me since we left but you. It was just a hunch."

Angela knew how much his grandmother meant to Keone. *He must be telling the truth.* "Anyway, since you mentioned hunches let me tell you about how my hunches may be getting me into a butt-load of trouble on this case." This opened the floodgates, and Angela told Keone everything about the case, including the weird manuscript and her dream. Then she waited for Keone to laugh at her for taking those things seriously.

"Angela, you're kickin' it. You're doing exactly what I would do. Evidence is evidence, even that computer file. After the last case I worked on, I'm in no position to tell you anything's out of bounds. I followed up on leads from two total nutcases and they paid off."

"But you don't believe—"

"Our job isn't about what we believe. It's about following leads, wherever they take us. It's also about trusting our hunches. And what is a dream but our subconscious sharing our hunches with us when our brain isn't cluttered with sensory input. I had a dream about you and Tony, too, in our hotel room in Rome. It may mean nothing, but I'd like you both to be careful entering any rustic shacks in the jungle on this case, okay?" Keone's voice became very serious.

"Uh . . . sure, Big Guy."

"How do you feel about the accidental shooting theory panning out?"

"To be honest, I should be ecstatic, but I'm not. Alcala was never comfortable with that theory and now that he is, I'm not."

"Just keep following the evidence. Sure, it led you to the boy, and the boy led you to the gun. See where the gun leads you. What are your plans?"

"Keep ruling out other potential shooters but bring the boy in for an interview."

"What other suspects is your gut pointing you to?"

"I haven't ruled out the boy's grandfather, or his older brother."

"Good, keep working how and why. The grandfather sounds more likely to me."

"Me, too. But I'm not sure why." Angela was so happy to have someone to talk with about this with good instincts.

"Yes, you are, but you haven't admitted it to yourself yet. Let it out."

"He's much closer in age to Lister, more likely to have a beef with him."

"Good. Follow up on that. And Angela . . ."

"What?"

"Don't confuse Tony with what's in that file. Detectives are supposed to have confidential sources. Just don't tell him yours is . . . uh . . . sorta dead. Is there anything else in the manuscript that might help?"

"Linda wants me look at a section about when Lister was in the army."

"Hmm. I'm guessing Gramps was in the army about the same time as Lister. Did they cross paths?"

"That's what I've been wondering."

"How are you going to follow up? Military records?"

"Yeah. I just need a government contact who has access to those records. Any recommendations?"

"Ask Lindsay. I believe she has a boyfriend who can help."

Angela grinned. "He wouldn't be a certain DEA agent by any chance, would he?"

"I'll never tell."

"Say, before Julie gets back, what are you investigating, Big Guy?"

"Nothing yet, but I just ran into a Europol agent, who's after a serial killer who . . . uh . . . thinks he's a god. I thought I'd left all the crazies on Maui for you and Tony."

"What does he want you to do?" Angela asked.

"Wants me to keep track of two couples on our tour today and at dinner. They're also our tablemates. My new Greek friend from Europol believes the wives might be targets."

"Why does he suspect they're targets?"

"It seems the killer doesn't just think he's any god. He's the Greek god of non-violent death and feels obliged to send Olympic medal winners to Elysium as a reward."

"You're right. There is weirdness beyond Maui's shores," Angela said.

Another coincidence? Both of our cases have supernatural Greeks involved.

"Maybe we bring the weirdness with us, Ang."

"Maybe. Just don't let it mess up your honeymoon, Big Guy. Let everything else slide on by—like the waves."

"Now you sound like Julie. Good luck on your case. I know you'll do great. Aloha."

"Aloha aku no."

Chapter Forty

The shooter walked home from Wailuku with a lot on his mind. *What did that first lady cop want with Hopper? How did she know where to find him?*

Hopper wasn't there for the shooting, so he couldn't have left any evidence at the scene. *I'm missing something.*

When he walked into the house, that annoying woman shouted at him.

"We have to go to the police station tomorrow."

"Why?"

"Manolo may be in trouble."

"Good for him," the shooter said.

"You could come with us to show your support."

"I could, but I'm busy tomorrow."

"All day?"

He shrugged and went into his room. The time had come for the patsy to play his part.

~

AFTER ANGELA CHANGED INTO SHORTS AND A T-SHIRT, she came to the table and dipped a large spoon into her

Portuguese bean soup. Heaven.

"How'd it go today, girl? Catch some bad guys?" Linda asked.

"I did, but not the one I'm after. My two best leads fizzled out. I may be solving an accident, not a murder."

"I finished the manuscript and found another lead for you—if he's still alive. A guy from Rob's army days, who tried to kill him in his sleep. I've printed out the section that discusses it and put it in a folder by your bed."

"Thanks, Lin. I appreciate the help. By the way that license plate caught us a hit-and-run driver. The one that sideswiped Rob."

"Are you sure?"

"Yeah, but he hit a pedestrian later, in Wailuku, at the same time Lister was shot."

"And the license was for a truck?" Linda asked.

"Yeah. Everything matched the description in the manuscript. He even had paint from Rob's car on the side of his truck."

"He sure would have made sense as the shooter."

"I know, Lin. But I'm still checking on the kid's brother and grandfather. Keone thinks I may be on to something with him."

A funny look crossed Linda's face. "What?"

"Oh, I forgot to tell you. I called Keone before I came home. I just had to talk to him about the case."

"I'm glad you did. Did it help?"

"It really did. He said he likes the way I'm handling things."

"Good. Maybe you can get some sleep tonight. After dinner it's a hot bath and bed for you, Missy."

"Yes, ma'am."

"I want to look over another section in the manuscript. I may slip it into the folder for you, too."

"Want to tell me about it?"

"Not yet. May be nothing."

Angela went into her bedroom, saw the folder, and opted for the bath and bed. She'd have time to read tomorrow.

Part Three

The World of Yesterday—
Out of Order

"Life can only be understood backwards; but it must be lived forwards."

Soren Kierkegaard

Chapter Forty-One

Thursday, July 11, 10:00 a.m., CEST (Wednesday, July 10, 10:00 p.m. HST)

Trying to be an attentive new husband while looking after three strangers was a challenge, even for Keone. He quickly identified the tablemates they had failed to meet the night before from the pictures Andreos had shown him and wondered how he was going to justify staying close to them.

Without knowing Keone's quandary, Julie solved it for him.

By the time they boarded their tour bus, Julie had made friends with one of the women he needed to watch, Veronica Napoleoni. The two women hit it off instantly.

When Julie eventually got around to introducing Keone by name, they were seated across the center aisle from Veronica and her friend Josie.

Josie began to chuckle, and Veronica turned an interesting shade of red.

"What is it?" Julie asked.

"We know your names already, don't we, Roni?" Josie said.

"How?" Keone asked.

"We're the tablemates you stood up last night. I bet Roni you were newlyweds. The waiter confirmed my guess when he brought a bottle of champagne to the table for you." Josie grinned.

"They let us have the bottle when I promised to buy a magnum for you, if you ever decided to join us," Veronica added.

"I figured that settled your wager," a voice boomed from the seat behind Keone and Julie. "Hi, I'm Vic Galliano. The giggler on the left is my wife, Josie. How's the honeymoon going?"

Now it was time for Julie and Keone to turn red, which knocked down any remaining barriers. They spent the rest of the excursion together. The ladies even convinced Julie to sign up for the same excursion they were to take in Athens.

"Julie, you two must come with us in Athens," Veronica insisted. "The tour is reserved for us, our family, and our friends. We'll make sure the captain knows you're our friends."

"We wouldn't want to intrude," Julie said.

"Don't be silly. All the girls will love you guys," Josie said.

"What girls?" Julie asked.

"Seven other girls on this cruise, plus Veronica and I, won medals in the Athens Olympics. We come from all over Canada. Josie and I are the only two from Montreal. Anyway, our special tour visits the venues where we competed."

"Then there's a special performance at an ancient theater on the Acropolis. You've just got to come," Veronica added.

"How could we refuse?" Keone answered before Julie could react.

Surprised but pleased, Julie agreed.

This conversation took them to their first stop on the Amalfi Coast.

Although used to beautiful scenery, Keone found the Italian coastline breathtaking. From each tiny inlet, small boats made their way through multiple, beautiful shades of blue-green water to the rich blue of open sea. The towns Keone saw nestled in each inlet were as different from one another as they were picturesque, with ancient and modern blended seamlessly on their curved streets.

"This reminds me of Maui. All the roads go uphill," Keone whispered to Julie.

"They go downhill, too," she whispered back.

"Very funny, Mrs. Boyd." Keone switched to a normal voice. "Look at the terracing everywhere."

"The ancients knew how to use every inch of arable land," Vic Galliano replied. "I read about this area before the trip. Each level contains unique structures that span centuries. Look over there."

They followed Vic's direction to see that even the concrete vaults in the cemeteries mirrored the terraced layout of the houses below.

When they stopped in the next village for a lunch of local specialties, their Canadian companions surprised them, ordering in flawless Italian.

When Julie asked about this, Josie explained, "Vic's, Roni's, and my parents all emigrated from Italy as children after World War II."

"We were the first generation born in Canada. Our parents were very proud when we qualified for the Olympics," Veronica added.

"What events did you compete in?" Keone asked.

"Roni's a diver and I'm a kayaker," Josie said with a smile.

"And you won medals. How exciting," Julie said.

"Yes, neither of us won gold. But Canada did win three in our Olympics. We're so proud of our team," Veronica replied, looking as if she might cry.

Josie put her arm around her. "She's here in spirit, Roni." Turning to Keone and Julie she explained. "Roni was part of a synchronized diving team that won a silver medal. Her partner Helene died last year on vacation."

Veronica excused herself and Julie accompanied her to the restroom.

"What happened?" Keone asked Josie when they were alone.

"Some fluke accident during a cruise of the Caribbean. Helene had invited Veronica to go with her, but a burst appendix spoiled their plans."

And Thanatos's?

He'd check with Calliopoulos.

~

BY THE TIME THEY REACHED POMPEII A FEW HOURS later, they were in a much happier mood thanks to an extremely engaging young man from Southern California. He didn't have to tell them he was an entertainer. He had quips for each of the stops and even managed to crack up the tour guide a few times.

Once off the bus, Keone and Julie walked beside their new friend during the long, uphill walk to the ruins of ancient Pompeii. Keone kept Veronica and the Gallianos in sight, just ahead.

"Do you perform on our ship?" Julie asked.

"Guilty as charged. My name's Ron Morton. I'm a pretty good juggler and an adequate comic."

After keeping them in stitches all morning, Keone decided Ron was being modest.

"Is that your real name?" Josie asked, turning to walk backwards up the hill.

"Josie, that's rude," Veronica interrupted, mortified by her friend's question.

"No, no. It's all right. Many entertainers use stage names."

Ron's expression brought that familiar tingle to the base of Keone's skull.

"Why? Are they cursed with real names like Lipchitz or Hitler or something?" Josie asked.

"Generally, nothing that interesting. I have a juggler friend who was born with the same name as a well-known comedian. He changed his name to avoid confusion. He also does a little acting and Actor's Equity insists only one person use a specific name at a time."

Keone noticed Ron never actually answered Josie's question. To keep the conversation going, he said, "I've always been impressed by jugglers. You must have an amazing ability to focus."

Without missing a beat, the young man took a few oranges, apples, and a banana off a food cart by the entrance to Pompeii. Soon five pieces of fruit of different shapes and sizes were swirling in the air in front of Ron's face. He also kept up a constant stream of jokes about the ancient Romans the whole time.

The Italian fruit vendor gesticulated angrily. "No pay for *frutta.*"

Veronica soothed the vendor with a ten euro note, while their guide escorted them through the turnstile and up an even steeper hill. The dancing fruit entered the ancient site ahead of them.

At their first stop on the tour Ron tossed a piece of fruit to each of them and refrained from jokes when their guide described the tragedy that struck this large Roman port city in August, 79 AD.

She described a cascade of superheated ash that surrounded and suffocated people where they stood or crouched, destroyed the roofs of buildings, and buried everything. At their next stop, she pointed out plaster casts surrounding intact, human skeletons that were recovered from the ash. The flesh had decayed away but the void in the ash retained the shape of their bodies and clothing, as well as their skeletons. By injecting plaster, the archaeologists had restored the shapes of these doomed individuals, frozen in place while going about their daily lives.

Tears streamed down Veronica's face.

Keone, too, felt a special tie to these people. His homeland was shaped and often threatened by volcanic activity and tsunamis, both of which struck Pompeii. The geography had changed dramatically in the intervening centuries, leaving the remains of the city far inland. But, at one time it had been right on the coast like Lāhainā or Wailuku back home. He wiped away a tear of his own before anyone could see.

When they'd recovered from the immediacy of the tragedy, the guide lightened the mood. "For the rest of our visit we will focus on how this wonderful city lived and not how it died."

The open-air row of ancient, public toilets brought Ron back on form as did a penis-shaped paving stone.

The guide countered Ron's assertion that it was a guidepost for sailors new in town. "Some guides spread that awful story, but it is not true."

Keone couldn't help but notice that the phallus tip aimed directly at the next building they visited, which was indeed a brothel.

Hmm.

At the entrance, colorful frescos depicted every one of the services offered by the establishment, in vivid detail.

"Now I know where McDonald's got the idea for its picture menus," Ron said. Even the guide suppressed a laugh, though she must have heard such comments many times before. Ron's creative delivery made even trite lines seem fresh.

The individual sleeping chambers gave a glimpse of the reality romanticized in the frescos. The beds were J-shaped slabs of concrete. They looked less than five feet long and three feet wide. In his reading before the cruise, Keone had learned that hay was thrown on the slabs for a modest degree of cushioning. The plight of those women and young men who called this home turned Keone's stomach. He wondered how many citizens were making use of the brothel's services as the ash scorched them and froze them in position for archaeologists to discover two thousand years later.

The conversation that punctuated their long trek back down the hill to their bus was filled with comments about the size of the ruins. Pompeii had been a substantial city when Vesuvius covered it. Although never completely uncovered, the ruins spanned a vast area.

Veronica and Julie moved on to discuss plans for the evening. They would all attend the second show that evening, after dinner. Keone was pleased no one suspected the other motive behind his camaraderie with these virtual strangers, especially Julie.

He took his responsibility for their safety seriously. But they were making that more of a pleasure than a burden.

Just before they reached the bus back to the ship, Ron veered off toward a waiting taxi.

When the comedian noted Keone staring his way, he shouted, "I'll catch up with you back at the ship. I've got to go set up for my shows."

A crewman followed him to the cab.

"They always send some bunny to make sure I'm not late." He used his left hand to put rabbit-ears behind the unsuspecting crewman's head before they got into the cab.

This cracked everyone up.

When the crewman turned to find out what was so funny, Ron smiled innocently with his hands at his sides.

Chapter Forty-Two

Thursday, July 11, 3:45 p.m., CEST (Thursday, July 11, 3:45 a.m. HST)

The bus returned to the dock, after a brief stop at an Antique shop in Naples. Keone, wanting to make sure all the Olympians in his tour got back on board and document it for Calliopoulos, busied himself taking pictures of the harbor and the ship.

Tired of waiting, Julie said, "I'll head up to the cabin while you immortalize this place, okay?"

"Sure. I'll meet you in the Passport Bar whenever you're ready." He kissed her and continued taking pictures of the port.

The port of Naples bustled with activity, making it easy to pretend to be snapping pictures until the last Olympian trudged up the gangplank. His watch displayed three fifty p.m. Time to head for the bar and Agent Calliopoulos. Knowing Julie, Keone would have plenty of time to talk privately with Andreos before she arrived.

The agent was wearing cruise attire this time, with two Mai

Tai's on the bar in front of him. Handing one to Keone, he asked, "How was your day?"

"Happily uneventful, Andreos." Keone took a long sip from the fruity drink. "All the Olympians on our tour checked back in."

"The same is true for all the excursions," Andreos continued, pointing to an empty table.

"That's good." Keone placed his straw on the table and lifted the Mai Tai to his parched lips. "Where's home for you, Andreos?"

"I was born in a small town in Thessaly and educated in Athens. But I now reside in the Netherlands."

"That's right. Europol headquarters is in The Hague."

"I knew you were a great detective, *Agapite moi file.*"

"My Greek's a little rusty, Andreos, but I think you just called me your friend."

"Right again."

Keone watched Andreos stare at his own colorful, tropical concoction for a full minute without taking a sip. "Everyone's back safely and these beverages hit the spot. So, what's wrong?"

"One Olympian stayed on board."

"And."

"We cannot find her. Although the computer confirms that she never left the ship."

"You had her watched onboard?"

"Of course. Alternating crewmen. But—"

"They allowed themselves to be distracted."

"I am afraid so. I should have watched her myself, but Thanatos has always killed in port and never on the ship. So, I covered one of the other excursions."

"You can't be everywhere at once, Andreos. Who do you have looking for her?"

"The Naples police and customs agents on shore and ships security onboard. We're scheduled to leave in a few minutes, but I don't want to cause a disruption of the cruise only to find out she's in some new boyfriend's cabin. According to the ship's data, she's on board, so they will depart, unless I say something to the captain."

"And you'd have to report the death in Civitavecchia, too."

"Yes."

"Do you think the killer might have altered his MO and killed her on board?"

"I sincerely doubt it. I just hope she turns up."

"Alive, for your sake." Keone was becoming more and more uncomfortable with his role in Andreos's case. "Is there any information on that slip of paper by your elbow?"

"What?"

Keone could tell the Greek was surprised by the scrap of paper.

Andreos unfolded the note and read silently. His face fell. "From the killer."

"Are you sure?"

Andreos nodded. "He signed it."

Keone took the offered note from Andreos's hand.

My dear Agent Calliopoulos,

You may be suspecting that I changed my methods today, but I did not. A god is capable of transporting things, even people, with no one knowing. You will not find the one you seek on board. She is mine now.

Thanatos

Keone felt a mild tremor.

"Now, we leave port," Andreos observed.

"What's the plan?"

"The brochure promises a *Funday* at sea for tomorrow. I, however, will keep in touch with the police at the Port and in Naples, as well as the crew."

"But you won't tell the captain until we arrive in Athens."

"Unless I must or a crewman or security report my odd request to him. Thanatos has never murdered at sea."

Keone didn't find that comforting.

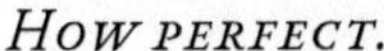

HOW PERFECT.

When one door closes, another opens.

All those tours with no opportunities. Then some dear soul suggests a lovely little shop to the child left on board.

I was so pleased to get her off the ship, with no record of her departure. The look of ecstasy on her face was not to be missed. I used my own hands once again. It's never as lovely when I work through a surrogate.

My power grows with each soul I send on, but more so when my own fingers touch them last.

Poor Agent Calliopoulos. He didn't know I spotted him when he boarded. He must have enlisted some helpers. No matter. I'll find them, too.

Now I get to enjoy the cruise and prepare for Piraeus and my homeland.

Chapter Forty-Three

Thursday, July 11, 6:30 p.m. ship's time (Thursday, July 11, 6:30 a.m. HST)

Keone emerged from the shower with new energy. He slipped on the lush, white bathrobe provided and wandered out onto the veranda to find Julie taking movies with her smartphone.

"Look at all of them, Keone. They've been following us since we left Naples."

Keone followed Julie's outstretched arm to observe a wake of seagulls in the darkening blue sky. They seemed a mirror image of the boat's wake, denser at the ship's stern and trailing away to the horizon in front of them. Julie's smile conveyed her child-like glee at the unexpected sight. One gull flew parallel to his wife, only a couple of feet separating their faces.

"He's my favorite. Been here since we left port. I think of him as our guardian." Julie held the rail and leaned back into Keone's arms. "This is perfect."

Keone wished this moment would last forever.

After ten minutes, Julie said, "My turn for the shower and one of those comfy robes." She rubbed the soft surface of Keone's wide collar. "If it makes a kanaka like you feel soft, think what it will do for me."

He reluctantly let her go to get ready for their first dinner with their new friends.

~

JULIE APPROACHED THE ELEGANTLY APPOINTED MAIN dining room of *The Argonaut*, glad she'd worn her best dress. The maître d' saw them to their table. Josie, Vic, Veronica, and her husband were already seated. A huge bottle of champagne dominated the table setting.

"A promise is a promise," Veronica said.

"Happy honeymoon, lovebirds," Josie added.

"Hello, you two. I'm John Ferrino. Sorry I didn't get to meet you earlier."

"John's not much for tours." Veronica laughed. "But he's going to be with us for the tour in Athens."

"I wouldn't dare miss it. What's your line of work, Keone?"

"Julie's is far more interesting than mine. She's a noted author. She writes under her maiden name, Julia Madison."

"You write the Hawaii Anna stories," Josie gushed. "My daughter has loved those since she was in primary school. She read them in French. I love them, too!"

"I wrote them in English, but I had a close friend on Maui, Madeleine, who translated them into French for me. When she read my stories aloud, they sounded like songs."

"What do you do, John?" Keone asked.

"I'm an actuary. It's all very boring. Just create tables of probabilities all day long. And Vic owns his own sporting goods stores. But you never told us what you do, Keone."

"Also boring, I'm afraid. I'm a civil servant. Now, sporting goods, that sounds—"

"Stop it, Keone. These are our new friends. Keone's a sergeant of detectives on our home island of Maui. And a very good one."

"Oh my, Roni. We should tell him about Gloria."

"Who's Gloria?" Julie asked.

"Gloria Arnault was a member of our team at the Olympics," Veronica began. "She missed the ship in Civitavecchia."

Julie saw Keone tense. *He knows something.*

"Have you checked with the purser?" Keone asked.

"She'll only confirm that Ms. Arnault never checked in. She advised me to check with the Italian authorities," Vic said, "which I did in Naples. They offered to investigate the matter and let us know if they discovered anything."

"Meanwhile, I checked with friends back home. They told me Gloria caught her flight to Rome, but no one has heard from her since." Josie looked about to cry.

"It's only been a few days. I can think of a dozen reasons why she could have missed the ship and been out of touch, none of which are any of our business. We're halfway around the world, after all." John tried to calm everyone.

"Keone, can't you help them out. Why don't you talk with the purser or even the captain? You're in law enforcement. They'd listen to you." Julie gave her husband an intense look.

"I'm way out of my jurisdiction here," Keone replied, sipping from his champagne glass.

"Well, tell them who can they contact?" Julie was getting impatient.

"I'd suggest Europol. They're kind of like a super police force for the EU." Keone wondered if he'd said too much. "But I'm sure John's right. Maybe, after she missed the ship, she decided to get the cruise line to get her on another cruise or fly her to Athens to join you. I hear that happens sometimes."

"You're right, Keone. If anything had happened to her, they'd have to halt the cruise and impound the ship," John said. "Isn't that part of the SOLAS Convention?"

"What's that?" Vic asked.

"The International Convention for the Safety of Life at Sea, or SOLAS, is an international treaty," John explained. "It sets safety standards for construction, equipment, and operation of commercial vessels. It operates in Hawaiian waters, too. Right, Keone?"

Julie noticed Keone become very interested in the varieties of bread in the basket on their table. *He does know something.* And why would John, an actuary, know so much about international treaties?

"Would this treaty cover someone who never boarded?" Vic asked.

"Probably, and they didn't hold our ship in Civitavecchia or Naples," John reasoned. "Anyway, could we discuss something less boring than maritime law?"

Keone spoke first. "How are we going to occupy ourselves during this supposed *Funday* at sea?"

Josie listed numerous contests and shows scheduled for the next day, including Ron Morton's main show. "When I told him we were coming to see the show tonight, Ron suggested we give it a miss. It mostly involves introducing the captain and crew. Some of the entertainers give previews of their shows, but he really wants us to see him tomorrow. Vic and I thought we might try the onboard Casino tonight."

"Why don't we join them, Julie?" Keone asked.

"Why? You feelin' lucky, big guy?" Julie replied with a head toss.

Their tablemates laughed, the somber mood dispelled.

Look at me. I told Keone not to discuss police work, and I'm seeing mysteries everywhere. Stop it.

Chapter Forty-Four

Thursday, July 11, 9:00 a.m.

Beth answered the phone on the first ring. "Hi, Beth. It's Angela Beyers. Am I calling at a bad time?"

"No. It's just . . . Mom's still asleep, and I didn't want to wake her."

"She needs her rest. I can tell you the reason for my call. We've made progress on the investigation into your father's shooting, and I think there's a good chance he was shot by accident."

"Was it that boy Dad described in the story?"

"I see you've been reading, too. We've found the weapon that fired the shot and a boy whose whereabouts were unknown Sunday night. I found them both in the same house. I don't want to get too far ahead of the evidence, but I think there's a good chance we'll have this wrapped up by tomorrow."

"You're coming on the boat, aren't you?"

"I'll try, but even if I can't make it in time to catch the boat, I'll touch base with you two tomorrow."

"Thanks for keeping us up to date. We're lucky to have you for a friend, Ange."

"I'm the lucky one. Aloha."

Beth peeked into her mother's bedroom to find her still asleep. With no hesitation she retired to the study and fired up her laptop.

A few minutes later the phone rang again. But before she could answer it, her mother did.

~

"HELLO," NANCY MUMBLED.

"Sorry if I woke you." Mike Butler sounded both embarrassed and excited at the same time.

"What time is it?"

"A little after nine."

"I should be up by now. Must have overslept. How are you, Mike?" Nancy climbed from the bed and threw on a light robe.

"I followed up with MPD and your insurance company. There's no question. Someone shot Rob from the other side of the 'Īao Stream. The insurance company will pay."

"That's reassuring news. I hope you understand why I'm a little paranoid right now."

"I understand completely. How about I take you and Beth out to dinner tonight so I can give you the details. And maybe you can lend me that mysterious manuscript to read, yeah?"

Nancy hesitated. "Uh . . . Okay, but only you. Promise me."

"Promise. I'll pick you up at five thirty. Aloha."

Nancy walked to the kitchen for more coffee, then to the sofa to continue reading from where she fell asleep. She'd slept over twelve hours. She could see Beth was in the study but decided not to disturb her. From the pile of pages her daughter left for her, she could tell Beth had stayed up long after she'd dozed off.

~

When Tony Alcala entered the viewing area for interrogation room one at the Wailuku headquarters, the boy Manolo, his mother, a public defender, and a woman from Family Services were already seated. The boy looked extremely nervous, and the mother was on her guard.

Angela Beyers entered, followed by an assistant DA with an audio recorder in his hand. "Good morning, everyone. I'm Sergeant Angela Beyers with the Maui Police Department."

"And I'm Fred Di Angelo with the Maui County District Attorney's office. We'll be recording this interview to assure that Manolo Likeke Hernandez receives every right entitled to a minor in such proceedings. With your permission I'll switch on the recording device."

Nods from everyone at the table.

"Good."

He cleared his throat and turned on the recorder. "For the record, present at this preliminary interview are Manolo Likeke Hernandez, his mother, Mrs. Esther Anuhea Kaleho Hernandez, counsel for the Hernandez family, Thomas Paul Hinkle, and the representative for Maui County Social Services, Ms. Lani Maria Ochoa. Also present from Maui County are Sergeant Angela Anelahokulani Beyers with the Maui Police Department and me, Federico Alphonse Di Angelo, Assistant District Attorney. Sergeant Beyers, has the suspect been advised of his rights?"

"Yes, sir."

"Do you understand the rights explained to you?"

Manolo nodded.

"Thank you, Manolo, for indicating yes with your nod. Normally that would be fine, but because we're audio taping I'll need you to respond orally."

Manolo looked to his mother who nodded. "Yes, sir."

"Sergeant Beyers, with counsel's agreement, you may begin questioning Master Hernandez."

Hinkle nodded, then caught himself and said, "Counsel for Master Hernandez agrees."

Alcala watched them go through the formalities. He, Beyers, Di Angelo, and the public defender had already discussed how this would go after they matched the boy's print to the one on the shell casing. Everyone was happy to avoid any unnecessary unpleasantness.

"Manolo, I'm interested in what happened last Sunday evening, July seventh in the ʻĪao Valley. Do you remember that evening?"

"Yes, ma'am."

"Did you go to the ʻĪao Valley that evening?"

"Yes, ma'am. I want shoot one bird an' prove to Gramps an' my lolo bruddah dat I can."

Angela smiled. "I have an older brother, too."

"He stupid?"

"Most of the time."

"Gramps take me to da range, but nevah let me go hunt wid dem. And I always hit somewhere on da target. Kāne miss dem a lot."

"I'm sure you're a good shot. Did you shoot a bird in the valley that night?"

"No. I trip over one stupid root and da shot go straight up."

"Do you know about what time that happened?"

"A li'l befo' seven. I check my watch when I run home."

"Why did you run?"

"I scared somebody hear dat shot and catch me."

"You know people aren't supposed to fire guns in the Valley, don't you?"

"Yeah, Mom told us, cuz a da law."

"Thank you, Manolo. I appreciate your honesty. What weapon did you fire?"

"Hunting rifle. Twenty-two."

"Does the rifle belong to you?"

"No. Gramps. Da one he let Kāne and me use sometime."

"Did your grandfather,"—Angela glanced at her notebook—"Mr. Koa Maleko Kaleho, know you had his rifle?"

"My client cannot read minds, Sergeant."

Alcala smiled. So Beyers was human after all. No biggy. He'd made that mistake himself a few times. Still did.

"I'm sorry. Let me rephrase that. Did your Gramps lend you his rifle to use on Sunday evening?"

"Uh . . . no. I took it outta him duffel."

"Did you tell anyone in your family that you had the rifle and were going off to shoot?"

"No. I don't tell nobody. Dey not let me."

"Was the duffel bag locked?"

"No."

"One last question, Manolo. Did you see where your shot landed?"

"No. I can't see. Too many bushes. I know it go up."

"From where you were, did it go up the Valley, down the Valley or across the stream toward the park?"

"It go up. I don' know which way 'cause I falling down."

"I see. Thank you, Manolo."

Di Angelo took over. "Manolo, I want to thank you for answering Sergeant Beyers's questions. You can go into the next room with Ms. Ochoa, while we talk with your mother and Mr. Hinkle."

They had what they needed, between the boy's testimony and the ballistics data. If the boy hit Lister, it had to be an accident. Although Tony saw no point in questioning the boy further, he wasn't completely satisfied. He felt a piece was missing but couldn't figure what.

After Manolo left, Di Angelo had Beyers lay out the evidence for Mrs. Hernandez and Hinkle. The case was solid. Di Angelo then excused Angela and discussed possible charges and pleas with Hinkle and Mrs. Hernandez. Tony guessed the D.A. would probably agree to an illegal firearm discharge count and a count of accidental homicide with probation. At the very least, the boy would have to spend a few days in the juvenile justice system.

~

ANGELA WASN'T SURPRISED WHEN ALCALA CALLED HER to his office shortly after the interview. He'd told her he'd be observing. She could kick herself for that one stupid question about what the grandfather knew—a rookie mistake.

"Have a seat, Sergeant Beyers. Looks like you managed to wrap up two cases this week. Not bad for a beginner. Are you ready for something new?"

"I'd like a day or two to finish the paperwork, sir."

"You have until tomorrow evening. There are plenty of other cases facing this office right now, and I think you've shown you're up to helping us."

"I blew that one question, sir."

"Yes, you did. But it's still your first week in CID. You recognized the mistake and learned from it. That's what you're supposed to do. Now get outta here and work on those reports. I expect them on my desk before you go home tomorrow." Alcala smiled. "But, tonight, go home on time. I don't want people to think I'm a slave driver."

Angela couldn't help but return his smile. She did plan to get on those reports, but she also wanted to finish reading the manuscript sections Linda had given her. She felt a little guilty that Alcala believed she solved the cases without help. Rob Lister had helped her with both.

Walking past the ballistics lab, she had the feeling she was forgetting something. Something important. She went back over the case in her mind until something leapt out at her. The rifle. She'd never had Manolo identify the rifle. Now that she thought about it, the mother had never identified the rifle either. She'd just given her the zipped-up duffel bag.

What had Keone said? *Just keep following the evidence. Sure, it led you to the boy, and the boy led you to the gun. See where the gun leads you.*

As she stood with her hand on the door to the lab, an officer brought Manolo by on the way to juvenile holding.

"Tommy, could you hold up a second. I need to show Manolo something."

"Sure, where do you want him?"

"Could you take him back to interrogation room one?"

"On our way."

As Angela signed out the weapon, a sense of dread threatened to overcome her. *What if . . . ?*

She carried the rifle, wrapped in green plastic, into the interrogation room.

"Sergeant, my mom said to thank you fo' understand I nevah wanna hurt nobody. I din't know. It da kine impossible ting it hit dat man. I'm so, so sorry." He looked like he was about to cry.

"The shooting was an accident."

"I nevah touch a gun again, evah."

Angela switched on the recorder, concerned that Manolo's mom and attorney weren't here but needing the tape to show Alcala she'd followed up on her own initiative. "Manolo, I need you to look at this rifle. Is this the weapon you took from your grandfather's duffel bag and fired in the ʻĪao Valley last Sunday, July seventh?"

Manolo picked up the bag and looked at the weapon for a moment before his eyes went wide, and he slowly shook his head.

"What's wrong?" Angela asked, hoping his reaction was the reality of his crime hitting home.

"Dat's not da gun. Dat's my gramps' special sniper rifle. He nevah let us touch it. I shot da other one. Da brown one."

"Are you sure?"

"Yeah. I nevah touch dis gun in my life. Gramps, he keep it locked up in one footlocker in da carport."

"Thank you, Manolo. You've been helpful again."

As they took Manolo away, Angela felt as if she'd been punched in the gut. Her solved shooting looked a lot less solved.

Suddenly, she was extremely anxious to read the manuscript sections Linda had pointed out to her about Rob's time in the army.

Chapter Forty-Five

Sunday, 8:50:18 p.m.

Calla hesitated before responding to my *Let's go.* "What is it, Calla. Is something wrong?"

"Before I suggest our next destination, I want to share some words from the great philosopher, Soren Kierkegaard. He wrote, 'Life can only be understood backwards; but it must be lived forwards.'"

"Are you suggesting that I start re-experiencing backwards? I don't think I could understand my life on rewind." I imagine the crazy sights and sounds of a video played in reverse.

"You misunderstand. I am not suggesting that you re-experience backward. I am suggesting that you no longer need to choose your re-experiences in chronological order. The actual memories will be re-experienced in the forward direction," Calla explained.

"Why'd you have me begin in chronological order?"

"You can answer that."

"Because I had to learn how to perceive this new existence in

"

the same way a child learns to perceive his. By beginning as a child, I progressed in parallel with my living self."

"Precisely. But once you lived through the death of your family, you were no longer a child."

"I'm still confused. But I'm game. Do you want me to start when we were living in New Jersey and go up to my untimely demise?"

"No. I suggest you begin in your twenty-first year. I believe you joined the military after you graduated from college."

I feel Calla challenging me to try something I would never have come up with on my own. "Aren't you breaking the rules a little by suggesting this?"

"Of what rules do you speak?"

"You know, the rules. The ones you operate under. The guide rules."

"Oh, I make those up as I go along. But I always follow them. Earlier you complained that I wasn't providing you with answers. Do you remember what I replied?"

"You said, 'I am a guide, not a teacher. You must learn your own answers to the important questions.'"

"And now?"

"Now, you're helping me discover new questions. No wonder you Greeks laid the foundations for logical discourse. You have devious little minds. Okay, Calla, see you in a few years or so —for me."

~

I HAVE A LOT TO SHARE WITH CALLA WHEN I RETURN, but he speaks first.

"I thought you were a soldier. Why did you wear a symbol for the Greek god of medicine on your uniform?"

"I was a soldier and a medic. And we call that symbol a caduceus. Stop reading my mind before I get a chance to share."

"Are you asking me to join you?"

"Sure. You'll love it. Come on."

We enter a hospital corridor in my twenty-two-year-old body. We're re-experiencing the first time I saw Maddie Murphy on the Pediatric ward. A closed door mutes the gentle crying from within. Then the door opens, and I glimpse a form huddled under the bed covers before the door snaps closed.

On Maddie's second day on the ward, I'm assigned the task of bringing her lunch. I'm on the swing shift for a change, not my usual night shift.

She makes no sound as I enter.

I say, "Lunchtime."

The muffled response could have been, "Not hungry," or "Pot fungus." I decide it's the former.

"I see. So do you want to play with it or throw it at me?"

"What? What did you say to me?" She emerges slightly from the blanket. Her grey eyes are quite lovely—though she's twisted her mouth into a truly unattractive shape.

"Your name's Maddie, right?"

"Madeleine. Only my good friends call me Maddie." She emerges completely from the blanket and brings her entire nine-year-old presence to bear upon me.

"Well, Madeleine. I believe you have had the requisite twenty-four hours of feeling sorry for yourself and suspect you might want to get on with living. In that case, eating would be a good habit to reacquire." I hate having to say this to children with lethal diseases but know from experience they need it.

"Who or what are you and how come you get to talk to me like this? That lady doctor from the Philo Beans told me I've got something bad, something that can kill me. I might die. Why shouldn't I cry?"

"She's from the Philippines, and I didn't say you shouldn't cry. Heck, I'll cry with you if you want. I said you should finish up with feeling sorry for yourself, so you can start having fun again."

"Fun? I'm in a hospital. There's nothing fun here."

"Have you ever played wheelchair polo? It makes the nurses furious."

"No."

I wait while she thinks this over.

"Could you teach me?"

"Sure. First, there's the small matter of lunch. Let's split this hamburger and tell them you ate it. It'll mess with their minds. I love doing that."

"Okay. So, what's your job here?" She perches on the edge of the bed, ready to eat.

"I'm a Clinical Specialist—that's army-talk for Good Guy."

"If you're in the army, do you have a rifle?"

"Nope. Clinical Specialists carry scissors." With this, I whip out my angled bandage scissors and twirl them around my index finger, gunslinger style. "They prefer no rifles in the hospital."

"I can see why," Maddie says with a serious expression.

"I did have guard duty once when I was in training down in San Antonio. The whole experience was weird, though."

"Why?"

"They were too smart to give us weapons, so they gave us each a heavy flashlight and a white helmet. I guess they expected us to flash the bad guys to death."

A smile. She takes a small bite of the hamburger.

"Anyway, my task was to guard a Coke machine. I must have done a fine job because, as I was relieved, I noted the Coke machine hadn't moved an inch."

A giggle makes her drop the potato chip bag on the bed.

"I thought very little about this stimulating night until I was called into the company office a few weeks later. My captain told me I wouldn't be going to San Francisco as planned after my Christmas leave. I was ordered to remain at Fort Sam Houston— as a witness."

A serious expression, as she sips her juice.

"Although generally hesitant to ask a regular army officer any questions, I managed to croak out, 'A witness to what, sir?'"

More giggles.

"'I cain't tell ya, son,' the captain said." I lay on a phony southern accent.

Another laugh.

"Three weeks after I returned from leave, I was ushered into an attorney's office. He asked me the critical question, 'Did you see a car turn at the corner of X Street and Y Avenue?' It's too long ago to remember the names." I use a phony New York accent for the attorney, which makes him sound like a cab driver.

"He pointed out the two streets on the post map that had been enlarged and placed on an easel. 'Sir, would this little square on the map be my Coke machine?' I asked. 'Yes. That's right.'"

I gave Maddie the same strange look that I'd given him. "'Sir, I couldn't see that intersection from where I was standing. The training building was in the way.'

"'I see,' he said. 'But did you see a car turn there?'

"'No, sir. I couldn't see the there you're pointing to, so I couldn't possibly have seen a car turn there.'"

Real laughter this time.

"'Thank you, Specialist. We'll call you when we need your testimony.' My testimony? My testimony? The illuminating information that I didn't see a car turn on a street that I couldn't see, on a night I guarded a Coke machine with a flashlight, Madeline. Obviously, key evidence that guaranteed a conviction."

By this time, Maddie is curled up laughing. When she catches her breath, she says, "The army is a silly place."

"Indubitably," I respond in my best Dick van Dyke voice, which makes her laugh again.

"What's your name, Mr. Cynical Species List?"

I smile for the first time. "My name's Robert."

"I shall call you Roberto." After a long pause she adds, "And you may call me Maddie."

I leave her room at this point and notice my roommate, Allen Foreman, waiting for me to go to lunch. He'd been listening in.

"You never told me that story. Is it true?" Allen asks, as we walk down to the cafeteria.

"Oh, yeah. But the story turned a lot darker than I wanted to share with her. Let's get lunch, and I'll tell you about it."

The food in the cafeteria at Letterman Army Medical Center smells surprisingly good. Allen and I carry trays bearing juicy, Reuben sandwiches and freshly made seasoned fries to an empty table.

I savor my first bite with the homemade Russian dressing saturating the perfectly spiced corned beef and can't help but smile.

Allen decides I'm putting off telling the story. "All right, all right, back to San Antonio, if you please."

"Oh, you still want to hear about that. Okay, here's the rest of the story." I do my exceptional Paul Harvey imitation. Allen appreciates this, as much as I do his excellent Jack Benny.

"Due to our situation as holdovers, no conventional barracks could be used to house the unlucky guards from that fateful night. They did have one extra building for people in transition, so that's where we wound up. In addition to our band of one-time guards whose last names began with L, the building housed some guys just back from Nam, waiting to be discharged."

Allen looked like he was about to explode, so I said. "Do you have a question?"

"Yes. Did you ever find out what crime you were held as witnesses for?"

"Not until much later. There was a firebombing the night we were on guard duty. It was some officer's house. He and his family were killed."

"Jesus."

"May I continue now?"

Allen nods.

"Both groups in the barracks kept to themselves and didn't have any trouble until one unfortunate day. I needed a shower, so I went into the proper location in the barracks for such activities, also the location most frequently used for smoking pot. I found the pungent smell repulsive, especially when I was striving to clean off the smell of the army."

Allen nodded in empathy.

"Some guys were gathered around a joint, and one offered me a hit. I said, 'Thanks anyway.' I didn't want to make anyone angry, but I never enjoyed marijuana. The tall, muscular fellow who offered me the joint gave a shrug as if to say 'Your loss', so I went in, took my shower, dressed, and headed over to the mess hall for dinner."

"When I got back, I read for a while and fell asleep. Around one a.m. I woke to find my airway completely blocked. My arms were pinned, so I opened my eyes to see an inverted face. The face belonged to the guy who had offered me the joint. He kneeled at the head of my bed and twisted something around my throat. I couldn't breathe, much less make a sound. Rapidly losing consciousness, my last lucid thought was, 'I've gotta wake up Lopez.' I swung my legs up and kicked the bunk above me."

Allen's no longer eating.

"To my joy, Pasqual jumped right down and yelled, 'What the fuck are you doing?' This woke several other guys, which spooked the fellow choking me. My attacker bolted out the door, and I never saw him again."

"Did you report it?"

"Yeah. That provided an opportunity to move off-post when I was freed from my witness responsibilities. I figured the Coke machine must have talked."

This finally gets a chuckle from Allen.

"A month later, I started my training in San Antonio, not San Francisco. After fifty weeks of training, I was pleased to find my permanent duty station was to be here at the lovely Presidio of San Francisco. As you know, I was assigned to pediatrics. I'd been working there for a couple months when a new guy was assigned to the ICU unit next door. This was about a month before you became my roommate."

"Oh, the pre-historic era."

"Anyway, he came over to me the first day and asked if I remembered him. I worked through the various compartments in my memory. High school—no. College—no. Basic Training—no. I finally gave up and spoke:

You do look familiar. But I can't remember from where.

Name's Lazaro. I was a Coke machine guard that night in Texas.

Oh, yeah. You were in the bunk across from Lopez and me.

That's right. Hey, you remember the night that guy tried to kill you?

I looked at Allen. "You know, I'd completely blocked out this memory until his question released it."

Oh, uh, yeah, sort of, I guess.

You ever wonder what happened to that guy?

I know he ran out after Lopez jumped down.

He ran all right, into town, and damn near killed two prostitutes.

How?

Strangled them.

"At those words, I felt an electric charge shoot through my body. He would have done it. I could easily have been killed right then and there. Thank God for Pasqual Lopez."

"Amen," Allen adds.

"Funny, but they never called me as a witness for that guy's trial. I could have presented relevant testimony for that one. I think Maddie's right. The army is silly."

Calla pauses the re-experience. "You know who that man was now don't you, Robert?"

"Yes, I saw him in the truck that side-swiped me the night that I . . ."

"Proceed."

Chapter Forty-Six

Thursday, July 11, 5:30 p.m.

Nancy shared the bathroom mirror with her daughter as they applied make-up for their dinner out.

"What did Mike say when he called?" Beth asked.

"He's talked to the police and insurance company and there's no danger of them thinking Rob caused his own death. But I want to hear the details. Oh, and he wants to read the manuscript. I printed a new copy and left it on the table for him." Nancy dabbed Chanel behind her ears and offered some to Beth.

"No way. I hate that perfume. Good about the manuscript though."

The doorbell chimed.

Mike ducked his lanky, six-foot-two-inch frame through the doorway to give them each a kiss on the cheek. "I'm starving. Let's eat." While he said this, his hand smoothly plucked the waiting manuscript off the dining room table.

Mike made a production of opening the doors of his Cadillac

XLR roadster for the ladies. "How do you like my Ferrari for the big and tall?"

Nancy took the back seat. Beth preferred shotgun. Soon they were through Lāhainā and headed to the Pali. As he drove, Mike asked, "Did you know someone sideswiped Rob's car on his way to the Valley?"

"They haven't released the car to us yet," Nancy answered, reflecting on the near-miss Rob described.

"The other vehicle was in the wrong. They have the driver in custody, and he's admitted responsibility."

"Could that guy have been involved in the shooting?" Beth asked.

"They thought so at first, but he was somewhere else when the shot was fired."

"What about the shooting?" Nancy was impatient.

"The police have shown that the shot was fired from clear across the ʻĪao Stream from where Rob was standing. They've also shown that the shot was fired from a rifle and that it struck Rob at the base of his skull. No weapon was found near the body. The weapon that fired the shot was found in a house on the road to the ʻĪao Valley. Besides, it's physically impossible to shoot yourself in the back of the head with a rifle and create the wound they found."

"What about the insurance company?" Beth asked.

Nancy appreciated her daughter asking about what mattered most to them.

"That's who I got most of information from. The cops just shared the basics. Your insurance company is more than satisfied with the evidence. They've authorized payment in full."

Nancy's sigh was audible. "Thank you, Mike. We knew he didn't shoot himself, but insurance companies can try to avoid paying if there's even the slightest question."

"There's no question." Mike glanced back at Nancy and patted Beth's hand.

"Enough about that. Let's talk about happier matters," Beth said.

"Well, if this little parcel's any good," Mike patted the manuscript that lay between them, "there should be no problem publishing it. You were vague on the phone. What do you think?"

"Well, we're only about three-fourths of the way through—" Nancy said from the backseat.

"It's amazing," Beth interrupted, "and by far the most moving piece he's ever written."

"And you're not biased because your dad wrote it?" Mike asked.

"Wait 'til you read it. It'll knock your socks off. If you're wearing any."

The trade winds blew at their gentle best as they strolled past the beach and into Mama's Fish House. The aromas of gourmet cuisine mingled with those of sunscreen-slathered diners. After they each ordered the chef's special, Mike resumed their conversation.

"So, what's this book about?"

"It's about a man who comes to his senses to find he hasn't got any," Beth replied with a straight face.

"Huh?"

"He eventually discovers he's dead," Nancy clarified.

"Who's the man?"

"A retired scientist, who's now a writer. You may know him. His name is Dr. Robert Lister." Nancy sensed Beth was on a roll.

"What?"

"We'll discuss it, once you've read as much as we have," Nancy said to refocus the discussion. "I'm trusting you to do nothing more until we *all* finish reading the entire manuscript."

"Naturally. You'll have final say on anything we do with this." Mike appeared shocked at Nancy's concern.

"Now, I'm looking forward to a nice dinner and discussing the weather, sports, and the latest movies, okay?" Nancy's eyes remained on Mike until he nodded.

"Okay?" She re-directed her look to Beth.

"Sure, Mom. I'm hungry."

"After that fantastic lunch you made us?"

"That was hours ago."

"All right. By the way, I believe we deserve champagne tonight. Beth received some wonderful career news today—completely unrelated to Rob's story. Tell Mike about your upcoming debut."

"Oh, Mom. I was saving that for later. Okay. My play is moving to Broadway from off, off. And, Mike, I've been asked to direct."

Chapter Forty-Seven

Friday, July 12, 8:00 a.m. ship's time (Thursday, July 11, 8:00 p.m. HST)

Keone was trying his best to circumnavigate a small swimming pool on the Lido deck of *The Argonaut*, balancing a water balloon on a ping pong paddle. He was one foot from Julie's outstretched paddle, when the clumsy oaf next to him fell over and knocked the balloon off Keone's paddle.

"So close. We almost won," Julie said.

"I had it balanced perfectly, until . . . Not my fault," Keone replied.

Ron, who was emcee for the contest, said over the microphone, "I think that guy may get a nice Hawaiian punch for knocking that balloon off Mr. Boyd's paddle."

Keone smiled and said, "No harm no foul. It was an accident."

The oaf smiled back at Keone, clearly relieved the man twice his size had decided to forgive him.

Out of the pool Keone and Julie dried off and joined their

new friends at a table near the Lido Bar. Josie and Vic had been eliminated from the balloon balancing contest long before Julie and Keone, but Veronica couldn't get John to even try. John was sprawled on a lounge chair next to their table fiddling with his laptop. He kept it angled away from everyone, but Keone had caught a glimpse while he was toweling off. The documents were property of the Canadian government. He wondered if the computer was as well. He'd have to ask Andreos more about Mr. Ferrino when they met later. He planned to beg off when the group went to play bingo this afternoon and meet with the agent again in the Passport Bar.

~

ANDREOS WAS SEATED AT A SECLUDED TABLE WHEN Keone entered the Passport Bar to discuss plans for tomorrow's arrival in Piraeus and Keone's group's excursion around various Olympic sites from Piraeus to Athens.

Andreos greeted him with, "*Kalo apogevma,* how is your *Funday* at sea going?"

"Good afternoon to you, as well. It's been surprisingly entertaining. I really enjoy our new Canadian friends and so does Julie."

"I am pleased. I hope this makes my imposition on you less annoying."

"Well, I wish it was over, but I'm as invested in their safety now as you are." Keone paused. "But before we get into our plans for tomorrow, I wondered if you could tell me a little about your family and what it was like to grow up in Greece."

"Well, my last name is Calliopoulos. I was born in the port city of Piraeus, as were multiple generations of my family. We were fishermen, for the most part. There is a legend that my earliest ancestor, a fisherman, would take any fish he couldn't sell at the agora and sell them for a cut rate price to the guards at the prison in Athens."

"When was this?" Keone asked.

"In the time of Socrates. The legend goes on to say that my ancestor, his name was Calla, provided Socrates his last meal and spoke to him shortly before he drank the hemlock that ended his life."

"What did they talk about?" Keone was enthralled with the story. He'd studied Socrates when he studied Greek and Roman history and languages at UCI. His death scene was immortalized by Plato in his *Dialogues*.

"They talked about death and what followed. My ancestor believed in an afterlife and Socrates doubted everything. But at the end, when he took his poison, Socrates said to my ancestor, 'I am about to find out if you are right. You will find out another time.'"

"What a great story, but I feel like there's got to more," Keone said.

"And you are right. Our family name comes from him. *Opoulos* means son of or family of. Calliopoulos means family, or descendants of Calla. Now about tomorrow."

"Okay," Keone said, realizing he wasn't going to get any more personal information from Andreos. "But I'll be honest with you, something about tomorrow troubles me."

"What is that, my friend?"

"My wife Julie's going to be with us all day tomorrow and doesn't realize her proximity to potential violence. If I could warn her, she might agree to stay on the ship."

Keone waited as Andreos pondered this. "I cannot ask you to put your wife in danger, nor can I assure you that there is none, even though Thanatos has only gone after female Olympians thus far. But I can assure you that, if you do not take the tour, your friends will be in even greater danger than they are now."

"What if we don't catch him tomorrow?"

"If we do not, this ship will not leave port again and all the Canadians and their families will be sent home at the cruise line's expense. That will happen even if we do catch him."

Before Keone could ask why, Andreos continued, "I was summoned to the captain's office this morning. We never located the woman onboard—alive or dead—who supposedly never left the ship. And, although the police in Naples haven't found a body yet, it is only a matter of time."

"You just hope it happens after the shore tours have departed, right? Andreos, you are taking a great risk. It could backfire on you—and me."

"I have arranged for you and your wife to transfer to another ship to continue your cruise of the Greek islands, after a couple extra days in Athens, at Europol's expense. Consider it our thank you for your help and discomfort. But I assure you tomorrow is the final risk we are prepared to take with these people's lives and the final twenty-four hours that I will request your silence on the matter."

Now it was Keone's turn to think. After a few minutes he sighed. "Tell me everything I need to do tomorrow from the moment our tour departs until we return to the ship. And I want every single detail about every Olympian, crewperson, and Italian law enforcement agent involved. Do you understand me, Andreos?"

"I do. And I will share absolutely everything with you, including what I discovered about Mr. Ferrino."

"I've been wondering about him." Keone said. "He seems to know a lot about international treaties. He also has official Canadian government documents on his computer."

"He should. He works for the Canadian government. I could only find out so much, but I believe he is employed in a profession similar to ours. Most importantly, he is not the killer."

"Good to know."

"Now, I will share everything else with you, including these." Andreos waved his hand toward a waiter approaching with two tall schooners of beer. "I took the liberty of ordering us two beverages called Longboard Lagers. The waiter told me this delicacy comes from your islands. I hope it is satisfactory."

"Andreos, you chose wisely," Keone said, despite his concerns.

~

"LADIES AND GENTLEMEN," RON MORTON SAID AT THE midpoint in his show. "I need an assistant for my next trick. Which one of you is brave enough to volunteer?"

Veronica raised Josie's hand and waved it around.

"Ah, we have our volunteer," Ron responded. "Come on up here, Josie. Ladies and gentlemen. Let's have a big *Argonaut* welcome for Mrs. Josephina Galliano."

During the applause, Julie leaned over to Keone. "Are you having a good time?"

"I really am, Julie. Ron's a fantastic juggler, but it's his jokes that get to me. He's hilarious."

Julie was proud of her husband for being such a good sport during the games today. Well, mostly. Keone had begged off at four p.m., when the group decided to play bingo. She wondered how he'd spent those two hours. Sure, he'd been lying on their bed in the room with his eyes closed when she returned from bingo, but she could tell he hadn't been sleeping. The bed was barely mussed, and Keone moved around when he slept—a lot.

Still, tonight they were with friends, and he was clearly enjoying a great performance.

Back on stage, Ron had taught Josie to juggle three nerf balls. As she proudly tossed them, Ron secretly swirled five sabers in the air behind her, generating a thunderous round of applause she believed was for her.

Veronica doubled over laughing.

After the show, Ron joined them for cocktails and shared pictures of his wife and two children in California and how much he missed them. Julie made a fuss over the pictures. These were the kind of fond memories of their honeymoon cruise Julie'd hoped for. But she couldn't shake the feeling that Keone was keeping something from her.

Had Tony found some way to check in with Keone and involve him in what was going on at home? Had Keone found some criminal activity on the ship to investigate? What about that friend of Veronica and Josie's? She hadn't shown up in Naples.

I could just ask him. But no. She had to trust he would tell her as soon as he could. Her husband had spent his life as a very private person—he couldn't change overnight. She'd already pushed him out of his comfort zone. Time to ease off a little.

Chapter Forty-Eight

Friday, July 12, 9:15 a.m. HST

Nancy Lister had emerged from denial. Five days ago, she couldn't accept what had happened. Four days ago, when she drove to Wailuku to see Rob, she refused to believe the doctor. Tuesday evening, with the help of Rob's story, she allowed in the truth. Wednesday, she grieved and said goodbye. And today they'd give him the final rest he wanted.

The number of people who made the trip to Maui for the celebration of Rob's life pleased and astounded Nancy. She saw his childhood friends, college chums, work associates, and newer, Maui friends—a testament to how many lives he'd touched in his life.

Mike's yacht sliced through the waves with ease to reach the point midway between Lana'i and Moloka'i Rob selected. Once he dropped anchor, she and Beth had one last act to perform.

The white-capped sea roiled with four-foot swells as Nancy removed the lid from the small container that held the physical remains of her husband of thirty-five years. Even in Mike's forty-foot sloop, the waves made standing by the rail a challenge. Beth helped her tip the box-like urn over the side, and together they watched Rob's ashes gust onto the cresting waves.

Nancy remembered how Rob used to kid her when she got mad at him. "Is it time for me to take that little swim to Moloka`i?" Whenever Rob said this, it diffused her anger and triggered a smile. If only she'd known how soon he'd be taking that swim.

While she stared out towards Moloka'i, Mike's left arm wrapped around her waist, his right around Beth's. The three stood there for a long time, silently gazing at the swells.

Returning to the ship's cabin, family and friends surrounded them. As Rob requested, there would be no service. He wanted them to share a few bottles of champagne and some stories.

Rob hated funerals.

One of the last to speak was Jim Horne, Rob's friend from both his biotech and pharma days. "Rob was at his best in that little biotech company, Pro-Test, where we tried to create a cure for colon cancer. We managed to do the impossible there and created a protein molecule that passed all the animal models and was ready for the clinic. Then we ran out of money. We both took the jobs we were offered at the pharma partner, but Rob kept trying to get somebody to test our drug in patients, right up until they turned off the freezers and threw away the cells that made our protein.

"He knew the odds were against it working, but he felt short-changed, when it was never tested in the clinic. He didn't stop working though. He was a role model for all the young scientists in the department he ran at Rosen Pharmaceuticals, and some of those folks went on to develop effective treatments for various cancers. When he retired, I told him he was the greatest mentor any of us had ever known." He raised his glass. "To Rob."

"To Rob," everyone responded.

Nancy was glad the voyage ended with recognition of her husband's accomplishments. Rob would have been pleased.

Angela Beyers entered the forensics' lab with a duffle and a new rifle for examination. "Harry, could you check this one to see if it matches the cartridge and shell we checked against the other rifle? I'm also hoping there might be prints on this or on some of the other stuff in the bag." She paused. "I'm afraid it's a rush."

"Good timing. We can get right on it."

"I owe you. Mahalo."

Angela walked back to the room that held the detective's cubicles, but before she reached Keone's, Lindsay Kalani called out from hers. "Got it!"

When Angela leaned into Lindsay's cube, her friend plopped a file in her hand.

"It wasn't easy, but I've got everything the military has on Special Forces Sergeant Koa Maleko Kaleho. I got a little help from a friend in the government." Lindsay smiled.

"That friend wouldn't be a certain DEA agent you met during the Walden case, would it?" Angela asked

Lindsay ignored the question. "Sergeant Kaleho was involved in multiple combat missions in Nam and received commendations for his exploits as a Special Forces sniper. He spent long stretches inserted behind enemy lines, and his CO said he never missed a target. The record after he got back makes interesting reading for other reasons. That's why they made it tough to get. The military doesn't like to share its mistakes. I've stuck Lister's military record in there, too. You can see if they were ever at the same post at the same time."

"I will. You're really something, Lindsay."

"I also have everything I could get on the older grandson. Looks like he worships his grandfather and wants to become a military sniper, too. He's only fourteen but has a sheet. Mostly pot use and some dealing. He's been linked with several growers, including our friend Hopper Alavezos."

"Could you check with Hopper about both of them? I still think there's a connection there."

"Sure," Lindsay said and changed gears. "How'd it go with Mrs. Hernandez?"

"Once I told her about Manolo's contention that the gun we have isn't the one he fired, she took me into the carport and opened her father's army footlocker. The gun we found inside was the one her dad let the boys use and not his sniper rifle."

"Looks like Gramps has some explaining to do."

"The footlocker also contained a duffel with a noise suppressor and a sniper scope. I gave everything to forensics."

"That should be an interesting report. I hope you get it soon."

"Mahalo Lindsay. I mean that. And thank Agent Freeman for me, too. I plan on reading every word in here—twice." She tapped the folder, walked to Keone's cubicle, and sat down at the desk to read.

She found the link she needed in a brief scan of Rob's and Gramps's military files. Both were on-post at the same time at Fort Sam Houston, San Antonio, Texas. Gramps looked more and more like their shooter with every page she read. He had the skills, the criminal record, and the temper. But she still struggled with motive, after all these years.

If he didn't pan out, she could follow up on the other grandson, but he seemed less likely. Murder would be a big jump for him. And what motive could he have?

She looked at the clock in Keone's cubicle and realized Nancy and Beth should be heading back to Māʻalaea Harbor about now. She needed to tell them Rob's shooting was looking less and less like an accident.

Chapter Forty-Nine

Nancy collected appetizers and decorations from the cabin while Mike escorted everyone else off his boat. Nancy's arms were filled with flowers and Beth's with bags of leftovers when he returned. Nancy watched as Beth kissed Mike's cheek before walking to the dock. But when Nancy started to follow her daughter, Mike enveloped her in a bear hug. Nancy returned the embrace, then and pulled away to leave, but Mike kept hold of her hand.

"Is there something else?" she asked.

"That story. Nancy, it's the finest book Rob ever wrote. Please let me share it with his publisher. I know he's going to want to publish it."

"How much have you read?"

"I finished reading the part where he lost his immediate family in that car crash. I want your permission to share at least up to there. Fred's literally salivating to see this manuscript."

Nancy hesitated. "I'm probably gonna regret this, but . . . oh, all right, go ahead and share it with Rob's publisher. His last name's Zimmerman, yeah?" She wished she'd talked this over with Beth first but felt Rob would want her to trust Mike.

"Yeah. Fred Zimmerman. Only him. I promise."

"Okay, but nothing more until we've finished reading it. I mean it, Mike. Promise me."

"I promise."

Mike finally let her hand go, and she hurried off the boat and over to their rental car. Beth had already started the engine, but before Nancy could get into the car, Angela Beyers rushed up, out of breath.

~

BETH LEANED OUT OF THE DRIVER'S SIDE WINDOW AND said, "Hey Ange, take a sec to catch your breath. We're in no rush to get home."

"I'm sorry I couldn't sail with you today to say goodbye to Rob," Angela said between breaths. "But new developments in the case kept me at the station."

"We understand, Ange. You're doing an important job and we're grateful," Beth replied. Her mom made Angela sit down on a bench before saying any more.

"Beth, did you share everything I told you about the accidental shooting with your mom?"

Her mother answered before she could. "Yes, she did. And I'd be happy to recommend a light sentence for the boy. I'm glad Rob wasn't shot on purpose."

Beth saw Angela flinch at her mother's words.

"I'm afraid I was wrong. The boy's shot missed Rob."

"What?" Beth understood the implication.

"The gun that fired the shot that hit Rob wasn't the one he fired. I'm having ballistics run the second gun now. I'm pursuing a theory that a Vietnam Vet had a forty-year-old grievance with Rob. I have a lot more to read in his file, but I think Rob mentioned him in the manuscript. Have you read the part about Rob's army years yet?"

"Not yet," Beth replied. "We finished the part where Calla

suggests they change their approach and that Rob re-experience those years."

"Then Mike took us dinner, and with the memorial this morning that's as far as we got," her mother added.

"We're planning on finishing the book before I take off on Sunday morning," Beth finished.

"Do that and . . . uh . . . hang around your home for me, would you?"

"Are we in danger?" Mom asked.

"I doubt it. From what I've read, the suspect was only focused on Rob. But I've assigned an officer to keep an eye on you two." Angela pointed to a black-and-white unit in the parking lot next to her unmarked car.

"I promise we won't leave the house until you tell us it's safe," Beth said. She'd make sure Mom concentrated on the manuscript until Angela caught the bastard.

Chapter Fifty

Sunday, 8:50:18 p.m.

Calla and I move to another time in the hospital where I met Maddie. We're back in my younger body, enjoying one of those too-rare, sparkling autumn days that cheers Letterman Army Medical Center like a smile from heaven. This close to the Golden Gate, overcast weather or even fog would often linger throughout the day. But today the entire hospital glows. I'm filling in on the morning shift. After the morning ablutions are complete, Maddie finds me making her bed with her lying in it hilarious for some reason. But she's too tired from her treatments to make it difficult for me.

"Roberto, you should be Dr. Lister," Maddie says, her voice hoarse from the previous day's vomiting.

I'm a bit surprised by this and suspect a prank. "You like how that sounds do you, Madame Murphy?"

"No, I'm serious. I think you should be a doctor." She does sound serious.

"While I'm honored to work with the fine physicians here, I

241

once applied to medical school, but they found candidates more to their liking. You see, at the time I applied, many intelligent young men decided going to medical school, which provided a deferment, was far better than going to business school or law school, which didn't."

"What's a detourment?" she asks.

I marvel at the aptness of her malapropism. "Well, a deferment means you can't get drafted into the army so you can avoid the unpleasantness of getting shot at or blown up."

"Oh. I don't mean the kind of doctor that gives you shots. I mean the kind who thinks stuff up."

"A scientist? A guy who works in a lab and makes discoveries?"

"Yeah, that kind. They're the ones who help find medicines and other ways to make us better. You need to be that."

I've considered applying to graduate school, among other possibilities, when I exit the army next year. I have the G.I. Bill to pay my way but haven't investigated it seriously yet. "I might have to pass a test first."

"Promise me you will, Roberto. You need to do everything you can to make people better who have cancer. I mean it."

"I promise, sweetie."

She rolls over and ends the conversation.

"Calla, that Christmas, on leave, I contacted a professor from my university and asked him what I needed to do to apply for graduate school. He said, 'First, you need to take the Graduate Record Exam. See if you can achieve scores that would qualify you for consideration. Send me your results and we'll talk.'

"I discovered the test was being offered that Saturday at Chapman University in Orange. I took it with no preparation after two years away from college. I took it for Maddie and found it surprisingly fun. Even more surprisingly, my scores were solid. I performed better than I did three years earlier on the Medical College Admissions Test, which I'd prepared for night and day."

"You did better because you felt less pressure," Calla suggests.

"Knowing I hadn't prepared, I relaxed and played it like a trivia game."

"Did you tell Maddie?"

"I told her I took the test, but . . . by the time I got the scores, she was gone."

"I see."

"I have one more experience I need to share."

"Proceed."

"From the day I first saw Maddie, the day after her ninth birthday, until what I'm going to share with you next, she never had a good remission. But she never cried again. She told her parents if they didn't stop moping around, she was going to have me carry them bodily from her room. She said, and I quote, 'I may only have six months, but I'm not gonna waste it with a bunch of mopes.'"

She had eight.

We enter my younger body again, but I have little time to enjoy the sensation. I'm coming on duty, working my usual night shift. We didn't call it the graveyard shift for obvious reasons, but we could have. Over sixty percent of our deaths on the ward occurred during this shift. I lean into the office to hear the nurse's report in progress: "It happened five minutes before report. Dr. L. pronounced her, and Specialist Webbley should be packing her now." Kate's voice sounds official and nurse-like. But I know she's feeling it.

Then it hits me. A child died on our ward, a girl child. But which one?

I run down the hall to Maddie's room. I see Webbley next to the tiny, still form of my dear Maddie. "Out!" I shout at him.

"Just doing my job, Rob. You aren't on duty yet. I need the practice. I've never packed a little girl before."

I clamp my hand on the back of Webbley's neck and escort him from the room to the desk where Kate's waiting.

"I'm going to prepare Maddie. Any problem, ma'am?" I say evenly.

"No. I think you should. Webbley, come with me. Johnston in twenty-five needs an enema."

I could kiss Lieutenant Kate Charles, R.N. at this moment, despite the court martial that would follow. Instead, I quickly return to Maddie's room.

I undo Webbley's half-assed work, get fresh materials, and start from scratch. I clean her small worn-out body gently and thoroughly. I know she can't feel anything anymore. Yet it seems right. I cross her hands and tie them firmly, then tie her feet. I slip the chinstrap on, and my lips brush her forehead. I apply the plastic shroud. Kate, looking quietly from the doorway, sees I'm tucking Maddie in more than wrapping her up. I check the tags and tie them in place. As I tie the tag to her big toe, I can't help but remember the last time I tied her shoes. She was leaving to visit Disneyland with the Make*a*Wish Foundation. I'm glad her last time away from the hospital was so much fun. She looked so happy and didn't seem to mind the crummy, synthetic wig on her bald head. The head cover was for others' sensitivities, not hers.

I lay the final sheet over her and lift her gently onto the specially designed gurney for her trip downstairs. Patients and visitors don't like any reminders that people are dying around them. The gurney looks a lot like a laundry hamper from the outside, with the body gently cradled within. I take it down the hall and ring for the elevator. During the elevator ride, the tears and sobs come. After nine years, I'm losing another sister. My white uniform smock still displays teardrops when I reach the basement. No one's there to see it or the tears still flowing down my cheeks. I straighten my smock, and my posture, to take Maddie to the morgue. No, not Maddie—Maddie's body. My Maddie's somewhere else. Somewhere beautiful.

"You loved her and could not save her," Calla says, as we return to our point in space.

"Yes. Her memory never left me. Our failure to help her fired my interest in research. Maddie made cancer personal for me. I ended up dedicating my thesis to her."

"And, to an exceptional degree, your life," Calla adds.

"I guess, for all the good it did."

"She was not quite ten when she died, and you were not quite thirteen when you lost your entire family. Did you ever feel a resonance?"

"Look. I came a long way emotionally, working on the pediatrics unit. I allowed myself to care for people again in a way I hadn't been able to since my family died. If I learned anything from Maddie, I learned to listen to my own advice. Enjoy life for as long as you can. I'm glad I helped her to do that."

"So am I."

I realize I'm finally clear about something. The answer to why I could never move on from my failure to get the drug we designed tested in humans. I felt I owed it to Maddie. Even though the molecule was for another form of cancer, I saw it as my one chance to justify her faith in me.

"You know she is here, in this existence. You could commune with her now."

"And tell her what? Tell her I did what she wanted me to do, got my Ph.D., and even worked on a cure for a really nasty cancer?"

"Yes."

"No, she doesn't need to hear that." My thoughts make it clear to Calla. This discussion's closed.

Chapter Fifty-One

Nancy was pleasantly surprised when Beth offered to make dinner so she could complete Rob's Army section.

She gave her daughter a big hug before clearing the table. "Thanks for making dinner, so I could catch up to you, kiddo. You make a mean Spanish omelet."

"No problem. I thought we should wait a day before attacking the leftovers. What do you think about the army section?"

"This must be the section that sent Angela after that boy's grandfather."

"For sure," Beth said. "But how did the grandfather know Rob would be standing alone in the ʻĪao Valley Sunday evening? How did he know his grandson would be up there as well and fire a wild shot? There's a piece missing."

"I agree, honey. Besides, that strangling episode in the Army was just a misunderstanding. Your dad was never a narc, in the army or anywhere else. He was a medic, a nurse really. I hope Angela manages to catch that old man and get some answers from him."

Beth decided to change the subject. "He never told me about Maddie. It must have broken his heart when that little girl died."

"He lost many patients while he was in the army. But hers was the only funeral he attended."

"So, it's true."

"Yes, I'm sure it is. He told me the whole story one Christmas, when we were at our college friends' annual Christmas party. It was many years after it happened. He'd just passed his oral exam during his doctoral research. I could tell he'd made some decision that night when he decided to open himself up to me. The next month we went on our first date since college—almost eight years after we graduated and twelve years after we first met."

"And you got married that September. Well, once you got together things moved fast. Did Dad ever get over his feeling of failure at not getting his drug tested in patients?"

"Your dad hid it well, but his melancholy occasionally broke the surface before he could push it back down. The failure to get that drug tested in patients represented a key unanswered question in his life. If it had failed in testing, he would have understood and moved on. But that question remains unanswered and always will."

"I felt his sorrow sometimes, too. Something was always hiding beneath that happy, retired-guy mask, but I only caught glimpses. Whether he resolves this through the story or through his afterlife, which I happen to think this is, it's still important." The smirk was a formality.

"Beth, I'm beginning to—" Nancy's cell phone interrupted.

She recognized Mike's voice through a lot of background noise. "Hi, Nancy. I'm in San Francisco."

"What?"

"Yeah, I'm on my way to New York. I faxed Fred the first section of the manuscript before I left. We both read while I was flying."

"Fred? Rob's publisher? What's the time there?"

"A little after nine p.m. I figured you two would be home, and . . . anyway, Fred likes what he's read and wants to talk with you tomorrow via a conference call."

"Mike, we haven't even finished reading the manuscript. You're moving too fast."

"Don't worry. We're talking preliminary discussions here. But I don't want to dampen Fred's enthusiasm. He wants to read the rest before we talk. Please let me send it to him and agree to talk with us tomorrow morning, okay?"

"Okay. But try to remember the time difference."

"You're a sweetheart. Gotta plane to catch. Aloha."

Nancy turned to Beth, knowing she'd overheard Mike's loud comments. "I forgot to tell you. When we got off the boat Mike asked if he could share what he'd read of your dad's manuscript with Rob's publisher. I was so emotional I said yes without asking you first. I'm sorry."

"No prob, Mom. I want to see it published, too."

"Thank you, honey. I like what Rob's written, but I'm surprised Fred's so excited."

"Maybe there's something juicy in the industry part. Could it be something from Dad's years at Rosen? Were they into shady drug marketing or something?"

"Rob always complimented them on their integrity. Especially their conservative approach to drug marketing. He didn't agree with every decision, but he understood their vetting process."

"Could it be something from his years at that biotech, Pro-Test? Rosen did sell them to that other company, Test Ticklers."

"The name was Test-Tacklers. But they did have a test for prostate cancer, so . . . Anyway, Rob didn't know much about them. They were more interested in the diagnostic tests than the therapeutic proteins your dad worked on. We'll need to keep reading."

"Mom, thank you."

"For what?"

"For asking me to read this with you. I've always loved Dad, but for the first time I'm beginning to understand him."

"He would have been happy to hear that."

"He knows." With that, they each picked up their remaining piles and started reading.

Chapter Fifty-Two

Tony Alcala kept Sergeant Beyers waiting outside his office. He was pleased she was ready to meet at five thirty this time, not after seven like their previous meetings. He moved some files off his desk to make room for her final report. Ready, he called his secretary and told her to show Beyers in.

The temporary detective looked uncomfortable as his secretary closed the door behind her. Tony hadn't expected nerves at this point but pointed her to a chair.

"Good timing. I cleared my desk so we can discuss your final report on the Lister case."

Beyers held the folders she'd carried into the office tightly to her chest and showed no sign she wished to hand them over. He decided to let her proceed at her own pace.

"Sir, there have been some new developments in the case."

Tony couldn't hide his frown. "Go on."

"After we talked yesterday evening, I completed the last step in my investigation of the Hernandez boy. I brought the rifle to him and asked him to identify it."

"Makes sense."

"He identified the weapon as his grandfather's but not as the rifle he used that night."

Tony leaned forward in his chair. "What? Was he sure?"

"Yes, sir. I recovered the other weapon this morning from the home. It seems either someone switched their locations before my first visit to the home, or the boy's lying."

"He seemed forthcoming during the interview. Do you think he's lying?"

"No, sir."

"On what do you base this opinion, Sergeant?"

"On evidence obtained during my interviews with the mother, ballistics and other forensics evidence from the two guns, and a review of the grandfather's service record."

"Service record?"

"Yes, sir. Mr. Kaleho served during the Vietnam War as a Special Forces sniper. He specialized in targeted assassinations behind enemy lines. But I'd like to discuss what I learned from Mrs. Hernandez first to follow the order in which the evidence was obtained."

"Continue."

"Mrs. Hernandez was surprised when I told her what Manolo said about the weapon that I'd found in the duffel bag. She said her father always kept a simpler weapon in the bag. He kept his sniper rifle, sniper scope, and noise suppressor in a locked foot-locker in another portion of the house, the carport."

"Did you inspect the footlocker on this visit?"

"Yes, sir. Mrs. Hernandez agreed to unlock the trunk for me with a key she'd obtained from her father."

For obtained, Tony substituted stolen, but said, "We need to be sensitive to chain of evidence, Sergeant. What happened next?"

"Mrs. Hernandez was surprised by which rifle we found there."

"Just surprised."

"She seemed shocked to me, sir. It wasn't the sniper rifle, but the weapon Mr. Kaleho let the boys use. Still, the sniper scope and noise suppressor were there, in the footlocker, along with ammunition. I took it all to forensics."

"Would one of those be their report?" Tony gestured to the files Beyers was clutching.

"Yes, sir." Beyers handed one of the folders to him.

"Both weapons fired twenty-two caliber rounds like the one the doctors removed from Dr. Lister and the cartridge case from the far side of the stream," Tony read aloud from the report. "Based on rifling on the shell, they confirmed the round in Dr. Lister's head was fired from the first rifle, the special sniper rifle. However, the casing found where the boy fired his shot was ejected from the second rifle and never held the bullet found in Dr. Lister's head." Beyers had his full attention now. "How did they figure that out?"

"The hammer from the rifle the boys used hit the cartridge slightly off-center, while the sniper rifle was perfectly aligned to strike dead center. The second rifle had fingerprints from both boys and the grandfather, while the sniper rifle did not. The grandfather's rifle was wiped clean in a professional manner. Finally, the shell that hit Lister passed through the noise suppressor, which only fit on the sniper rifle."

"Sounds like Gramps pulled a switch. I'm impressed, Sergeant. But can we prove the switch was after the boy borrowed the rifle?"

"Both weapons were last fired on Sunday, July seventh at approximately the time Dr. Lister was killed. But there's more." She handed over the second folder.

The military records. Tony was again impressed and again read aloud from the file. "Sergeant Koa Maleko Kaleho was a highly decorated combatant who had serious problems when he returned from the war. He was eventually sent to Fort Sam Houston for disciplinary infractions and to await a general discharge. During this period, he shared a barracks with Specialist Four Robert Lister. During this period, he went AWOL and committed two attempted homicides. The record also shows he once tried to strangle a young medic." Tony glanced up. "Lister?"

Beyers nodded.

"That can't be a coincidence," Tony said.

"I agree, sir. I believe Kaleho's our shooter and that the shooting was no accident."

"We need to bring him in."

"I've already arranged that, sir. The mother convinced him to come in tomorrow morning to speak as a character witness for his grandson."

Tony smiled. "I think that's a perfect opportunity for you to have a little chat with Mr. Kaleho, don't you?"

"I do, sir. I wish I'd talked to him earlier."

"Beyers, you may have made some assumptions after everything pointed to the kid. We both did. But, if Gramps is the shooter, your willingness to explore the accidental shooting scenario was critical. If you hadn't done that, we would never have found the casing with Gramps' fingerprints on it and associated him with the shooting."

"But I spent a lot of time on the boy when I could have focused on Gramps."

"In this division, our job isn't about how fast we clear cases, it's about bringing criminals to justice. When you took the murder weapon to the kid for confirmation, after the case seemed wrapped up, you proved that you see your job that way, too."

"Thank you, sir."

"This next step will be tricky. I could interview Kaleho, but I think it's best that you do. Can you guess why?"

"Because if the head of CID interviewed him, he'd suspect we know something about his involvement in the shooting."

"Right. But you need to play it cool during the interview. Let him say whatever he wants about the grandson. He'll probably damn him with faint praise. He believes he's got the perfect patsy to take the fall for him. And we want him to keep believing that. While he's spinning his tale, try to get the guy talking about his time in Special Forces. I'll be watching through the one-way glass and can take over at any point if you encounter a problem. Am I clear?"

"Yes, sir."

"Questions?"

"No, sir."

Chapter Fifty-Three

Nancy laid down the pages she'd just finished reading. "He loved working at Pro-Test. He was so happy there."

"I wish I could remember more about his time at the biotech company, but I was so young."

"You were another reason your dad was so happy during those years. We both were."

"I'm ready to get back to reading," Beth said, then stared at the pages. "It looks like the next part won't be so much fun."

"Some of it won't. But it'll help you understand your dad more than anything you've read so far." For once she was grateful that her daughter was the faster reader. Nancy still had a few pages before she would confront the hardest period in Rob's career.

~

Sunday, 8:50:18 p.m.

WE'RE IN NEWARK, NEW JERSEY AT THE CORPORATE headquarters of Rosen Pharmaceuticals. I'm about to give a presentation to the leading scientists at the company about our project.

"Calla, we'll be jumping around quite a bit to highlight key portions of this re-experience. If you get lost let me know."

"I will stop you if I become confused."

I'm surprisingly calm, considering what's at stake. It's strange, but when I'm about to speak I always see myself as a teacher, not an advocate. I need to lay the background out very clearly. I can't assume anything.

My friend Woody Branch, an Executive Director in the Oncology Group, finishes his introduction as I enter the richly appointed conference room, which resembles a small theater. Woody's my closest friend at Rosen. We've collaborated on a dozen projects since Rosen acquired Pro-Test seven years ago. He's someone who believes in our approach to treating cancer and lets everyone know it.

"Hello, I'm Rob Lister and I'm a Pro-Tester."

Mild laughter.

"As you know, we Pro-Test folk believe proteins are excellent models for the design of novel drugs. Yes, they're a lot bigger than those petite and powerful organic molecules you folks have created such fabulous treatments with, but they have some properties that merit your attention for cancer therapy. They can't cross the blood-brain barrier, but human-derived proteins are as invisible to the host immune system as those tiny molecules you use. They also have the ability to carry out multiple functions in a patient that smaller molecules cannot."

I have their attention.

"Let's face it. Colon cancer's a bitch. The only solution is to somehow distinguish the cancer cells from their normal siblings as quickly as possible and destroy them. The most effective therapies manage to kill the cancer cells without wiping out too many healthy cells nearby by exploiting the rapid replication rates of these aberrant cells. But in colon cancer, the adjacent healthy cells replicate rapidly, too. The harsh environment in which they live forces cells in the gut lining to turn over constantly. An effective treatment for colon cancer must kill abnormal cells in the gut, liver, and other secondary sites, like lymph nodes, without damaging the healthy cells next door."

Time to cut to the chase.

"Our colorectal cancer treatment causes less collateral damage because we pre-localize a non-toxic selective binder then administer a small toxic molecule that is rapidly cleared from the body unless our selective binder captures it.

"What's this magic binding agent? It's an engineered human antibody. More accurately, it's a hybrid antibody combining the key components from two engineered human antibodies. One arm of the molecule binds with 99% specificity to colon cancer cells and the other with 100% specificity to a small toxic molecule. The latter clears the body so quickly after injection that if it isn't stuck to something, it causes virtually no damage. In animal models, we've not only arrested cancer growth, but also caused significant regression of established tumors with no negative side effects. No other agent has achieved comparable results in these models, including those already on the market and in clinical trials."

All eyes are on me now.

"We're here today to get your support to continue this work long enough to prove our assertion in the clinic. I'll turn the presentation over to Dr. Jim Horne to share the molecular details with you."

"We have moved again," Calla says.

"Not far. We've completed our presentation, and I've been asked to have lunch with the president of Rosen's research division."

"Let me get this straight. You killed your own imaging project because you realized the molecule had to be changed for the therapeutic application?" Dr. Jack Lydersen seems surprised.

"Imaging was an offshoot of our real goal, dosimetry. As you know, calculating the correct dosage when you're giving agents that are potentially toxic allows us to walk the fine line between efficacy and toxicity. If we couldn't use the same molecule for dosimetry, the data would never be accurate enough to assure we didn't overdose a patient."

"But if you wait to re-engineer the imaging product, you'll delay the launch by months."

"The imaging agent was flawed. The loss of a glycosylation site sent the agent to the kidneys too often for removal and obscured any metastases there. I know they're rarer than those in the liver and lung, but we don't have to lose them. It goes without saying that kidney localization would be catastrophic for the therapeutic application."

"Don't get me wrong," Dr. Lydersen says. "I think your decision was right. But few people around here would have had the balls to kill their own project when it could have made it to launch. Especially if problems wouldn't crop up until well after they'd moved on to another project."

"I'm a scientist, not a businessman. I know we can validate the new imaging/dosimetry agent in two months and have it in the clinic in six. We only have to do equivalency studies and make cosmetic changes to the CRAs, and the IRBs will approve them. That will give us the chance to complete the animal studies and get the dosimetry and therapeutic trials in place at the same time we would have anyway. Our breakthrough product has always been the therapeutic. Help us get it into the clinic. Please."

It all came down to this. As president of the research division, Dr. Lydersen could provide the funding we needed to get the molecule into the clinic. And Pro-Test was willing to let Rosen have it, even if they sold everything else.

"You have three years. Use them wisely," Lydersen says and offers his hand.

I shake it vigorously and say, "You won't be disappointed, sir."

"I was following along pretty well, but those two abbreviations were unfamiliar to me," Calla says.

"I'm sorry. CRAs are clinical research agreements. They

define what will be done in a clinical trial. IRBs are institutional review boards, the folks at the hospitals that determine if the clinical trial makes sense."

"We've jumped again."

"Sorry, Calla, but I have a lot to show you. We are now in a conference room at Pro-Test."

I'm at the front and begin to speak. "Hello, everybody. I know some rumors have been circulating, so I decided to tell you exactly what happened back in lovely, icy Newark, New Jersey. Your colleagues, our lead scientists, presented a compelling case to the Rosen scientific leadership. Before we left, Dr. Jack Lydersen, president of the Rosen research group, assured me that he would personally provide funding for our effort for three more years. In short, our molecule has a job to do, and so do we."

"This had to be a great moment for you," Calla says

"One of the greatest in my life. But we need to visit one more re-experience before we discuss this."

After we jump, Calla notes our situation. "We have moved again, Robert, but only in time."

"Yes. We're in the same conference room two weeks later. I'm about to present the most terrible news that I've ever had to relay to people I care about."

Chapter Fifty-Four

Saturday, July 13, 7:30 a.m. ship's time (Friday, July 12, 7:30 p.m. HST)

Keone woke to hear Julie moving around the cabin. When he looked up, she disappeared into the bathroom. He assumed she wanted to look her best for their excursion with the Olympians. Keone swung his feet over the bed, walked onto their balcony, and saw Piraeus, the main port for Athens, glowing in the morning sun. Their ship edged ever closer to an open berth on the passenger dock.

Keone was glad Ron would be entertaining tonight at the celebration for the Olympians. But he worried about Julie being there. He knew she could take care of herself but didn't want to be distracted at a critical moment.

Julie joined him on the balcony. After a few minutes, he decided to tell her the truth. But before he could speak, Julie grabbed his arm—hard.

"What's wrong, sweetheart?" He wondered if she might be dizzy.

"I didn't want to tell you, but I haven't been able to keep anything down all morning. I don't think I'll be able to join everyone on the excursion today."

Thousands of thoughts bombarded Keone. Had Thanatos done this? Had Andreos, to keep her away? What could he say to Julie that made any sense about why he still needed to go?

"I know how much you were looking forward to seeing the Olympic venues today. You're going, and I'm not listening to any arguments," Julie said before he could respond.

Keone managed to look unconvinced. "You're going to the ship's doctor with me right now. Then we'll see if I'm going anywhere."

The doctor spent a lot of time with Julie and took blood and urine samples to be processed on shore. When Julie emerged, she said, "The doctor told me there's nothing to worry about, but I should stay on board today."

"I'll take good care of her, Mr. Boyd," the doctor said, then leaned into Keone's ear. "Please take that tour, or she'll kill me. She'll be fine by the time you get back."

Keone was almost convinced. "You have to promise to stay in our cabin and use room service until I get back."

"I can have ship's security keep an eye on the door to make sure she isn't disturbed," the doctor offered.

What an odd thing for the doctor to suggest. "Wouldn't it be easier if I just stayed?" Keone asked. He wanted Julie to know he cared.

"No. I like to be alone when I'm puking my guts out. You'd be a pain in the ass." Julie knew how to make a point.

"Okay, I'll go. But you need to let me take my cell so you can call me if anything changes. That goes for you too, Doc."

Julie took Keone's phone from her purse and handed it to him. "It was silly of me to take this. I need to learn to trust my husband."

When he leaned in to kiss her on the lips, she re-directed him to her cheek. *Oh, right, dumbass. She's been puking.*

On the way to join the excursion, Keone passed Andreos.

"Where's your lovely wife?"

"Sick. Not coming."

Andreos seemed to consider that for a moment.

"The doctor said he'd have ship's security make sure she wasn't disturbed. I accepted, but thought it was an odd thing for him to say."

Andreos just stared at Keone.

Of course, the agent had looped in the doctor. Smart guy, this Greek. "What about the missing girl?" Keone asked softly.

Andreos looked down. "Still missing. They will thoroughly search the ship one last time today, while most of the passengers are ashore. My money is on the Naples police, though. He must have hidden this body better than the first one. But now, you must join your tour."

Keone hurried off to his tour bus. When he caught sight of Veronica, Josie, and their husbands waiting to board the bus, he joined them at the rear of the line and told them about Julie.

Veronica and Josie were both concerned.

"Poor Julie," Josie said. "We'll miss her today."

Veronica pointed to her husband. "Even John's going on this one. You must take dozens of pictures for her, Keone."

"I will. Let's start with one of everyone." This new responsibility could help keep him close to everyone he needed to protect.

THE TOUR GUIDE SPOKE INTO A MICROPHONE BEFORE their bus pulled away from the dock. "Please switch on the audio devices you were given as you boarded the bus. We guides love these devices because they save wear and tear on our throats. They also allow you to spread out as we walk around and still hear everything."

Not such a good thing for someone who needs to keep an eye on everyone, Keone thought.

"On this tour we will visit most of the venues from the Athens Olympic Games. I must warn you in advance that some sites are better preserved than others. The recent financial situation in Greece forced the government to prioritize renovation and repair projects. But your memories remain. We hope that revisiting these places of your triumphs, whatever their outward appearance, will bring you joy."

The venues were scattered in and around the city and suburbs, including in their port city of Piraeus. While some looked much as they had during the Olympics, others were just examples of modern ruins. Keone shared the athletes' sense of loss. How quickly modern structures could fall into decay without constant maintenance.

Chapter Fifty-Five

Sunday, 8:50:18 p.m.

"Hello, again, everyone. Once again, there have been rumors. And, once again, I wanted to talk with you together to relay the accurate information you need."

I pause, steeling my resolve.

"Dr. Jack Lydersen called me last night and relayed the following decision to me. Despite his desire to fund our group, financial and legal issues related to Rosen Pharmaceutical's impending sale of Pro-Test prevent their research group from funding our project."

The groans are audible.

"As their group recognizes the excellent work we've done and the exceptional talent in our group, they're offering each of you the opportunity to interview for positions at the corporate head-quarters in Newark, New Jersey. I apologize that the information I shared with you two weeks ago no longer applies. But I want you to know that when I told you we were to be funded in place for

264

three years, I was accurately relaying what I was told. I'll answer any questions now."

I see despair on the faces in front of me. It takes every ounce of control I can muster to avoid breaking down.

"If we agree to go back to that hellhole, pardon my French, will we at least be able to keep working on our molecule?" Cathy Newsome asks.

I dreaded answering this question more than giving the announcement. The fact that it comes from Cathy, who worked her butt off on the project from the beginning, makes it unbearable.

I manage to force the next distasteful reality past the huge lump in my throat. "Rosen can't pick up the project due to the terms of its pending sale of Pro-Test to Test Tacklers. And, before you ask, Test Tacklers hasn't decided what to do with our therapeutic effort, yet. I . . . I'm truly sorry."

When Calla and I return to our point in space, I'm as disgusted and ashamed as I was standing in the conference room.

"Did they give you any explanation?" Calla asks.

"Yes. Dr. Lydersen was blindsided by the Rosen financial group. Unknown to him, they had determined Rosen couldn't keep any Pro-Test intellectual property due to some profit-sharing agreements Pro-Test had enacted before the acquisition."

"Did anyone from your group remain?"

"Test Tacklers were only interested in the diagnostic assets and kept some folks from that division of Pro-Test. But no one from our group was offered anything but a severance package. This didn't tempt anyone to enlighten Test Tacklers about what was hiding in their newly acquired freezers."

"How many went back to Rosen Pharmaceuticals for interviews?"

"Seven of twenty-five, including me. They offered us good jobs, but only four of us accepted."

"Did you ever find a way to do anything about your project?"

"In a way, yes. But you'll see this in the last re-experience."

"Proceed."

~

"Why are we back at Pro-Test?" Calla asks.

"Technically, we're at the former site of Pro-Test. Two years have passed since the last re-experience and Test Tacklers has moved everything they wanted to their own facility in Fremont, California. Jim and I are here to see if we can use any of the equipment they're auctioning off."

I'm standing in what was once our lab space. Only equipment remains, no people. Jim's writing up sealed bids for items we bought new a few years ago. I'm wandering around, remembering.

"I'm done," Jim says, when he catches up to me in the area where we kept all the ultra-low temperature freezers. Then he notices the tears in my eyes. "What is it?"

"They're unplugged. I hope Test-Tacklers sold the therapeutic assets to someone and didn't just unplug the freezers and throw away the cells that made our molecules." That's what I hoped, but not what I feared.

When Calla and I return from these re-experiences, I say, "Now you can see what a failure I truly was. All that great research by so many wonderful scientists, but I couldn't save it."

"But in an earlier re-experience, when you retired, you accepted that you had made significant accomplishments."

"Oh, I did. But that was later. After my nervous breakdown. After I lost the group I'd led at Rosen. I was given a new job that was considered useless by the big shots. But, as with the group I was given earlier, I made this position relevant to working scientists. Soon even those who questioned my stability were seeking my help to find break-through technologies. And I found them. This laid the foundation for the company I would help start and lead for my final three years with Rosen."

"Then you succeeded."

"I succeeded in pushing my failures from the front of my mind, by immersing myself in challenging work. But after I retired, those ghosts were still waiting in the shadows, and they looked a lot like a nine-year-old girl in a hospital bed."

~

Friday, July 12, 11:00 p.m.

BETH LAID THE PAGES SHE'D READ ON THE COFFEE table, walked into the study, and closed the pocket door. Her mother had gone to bed hours ago, but she'd needed to finish the Pro-Test story.

She settled into Dad's recliner next to the sofa bed in the study. Sitting in his chair, she was still emotionally drained by what she'd read in the final Pro-Test sections.

A mere two weeks separated the best and worst days in her father's scientific life. He was responsible for the first but had no control over the second. He did what he had to do and did it nobly, but it tore him apart inside.

As a confident young professional, who attained success quickly in her own career, she realized—possibly for the first time—she had yet to face a challenge like her dad's. He'd prepared her for disappointment but always instilled confidence in her abilities. She applied the same approach with her cast and crew in the tenuous world of theatrical production, and it worked. But she'd never had to tell them a show's run had been cancelled, that they had to look for new jobs. Those days would come. She only hoped she'd handle them as bravely as her father had.

Beth saw her father in a new and different light after reading these sections. She now understood his strength and courage but also his vulnerability. She also knew what little girl he was talking about at the end. Maddie, the one he'd made a promise to so many years before Beth was even born.

Too exhausted to read anymore, she rolled onto the sofa bed and nodded off.

Chapter Fifty-Six

Saturday, July 13, 1:00 p.m. Athens time (Saturday, July 13, 12:00 a.m. HST)

Their final stop before the Parthenon was beautiful. The Olympic track stadium was in perfect shape bearing the five linked circles and looking ready for another competition. The athletes wandered around the stadium recalling moments and getting into the spirit of the day. Normally they would have gone from here to the Plaka for some shopping, but Andreos had nixed that stop. They headed directly to the Acropolis.

Their tour through the ruins was extensive. Keone was as fascinated as the Olympians at this massive expression of ancient Greek construction and modern Greek restoration.

"Look at the size of those blocks they're putting back in place," Veronica's husband said, pointing to the Parthenon.

"I read about this," Vic Galliano said. "They are involved in a restoration project that will take decades longer than the original construction. As in similar reconstructions, they are duplicating missing elements in a different color of stone to distinguish ancient from modern."

"Vic loves this stuff," Josie added. "Before he decided to build his own sporting goods stores, Vic was a stone mason and worked on large governmental structures. When you two visit us in Montreal, I'll show Julie everything he's worked on. They're so beautiful."

Keone thought he caught a slight reddening of Vic's face.

Wait. Julie. I haven't called to check on her. Great husband I am. Keone pulled out his cell.

THE OLYMPIANS AND THEIR FAMILIES CONGREGATED A few hours later, after a box lunch amid the ruins, at a small theater on the side of the Acropolis. Completely restored, the ancient structure hosted modern concerts as well as classic Greek tragedies and comedies. With Ron in charge, Keone expected comedy tonight.

Force of habit caused Keone to locate each of the Olympians in the theater. He saw all of them except Lily Du Champ, a swimmer. He spotted her husband on the far side of the seating area. But Lily wasn't with him. Just as Keone was about to make an excuse to go look for her, he saw Lily enter the stadium with a crewman guiding her towards her seat. Keone decided to keep Lily in sight until she reached her husband.

Veronica tapped his shoulder.

He turned, a reflex.

"How's Julie feeling?"

"Much better. I missed a call from her when we were at the Olympic stadium, but I called back during our lunch on the Acropolis. She'd had some soup and was keeping it down."

When he turned back, he could no longer find Lily. He glanced over to see that her husband was anxiously searching for her, too. Lily and the crewman had disappeared.

Why did Veronica have to pick that moment to tap my shoulder?

Keone saw Andreos spring from his seat on the other side of the theater and run out the nearest exit. He took off after him and saw Andreos jogging back down the hill to check the path up to the Theater. Keone went the opposite direction back up toward the Parthenon.

The Parthenon, now empty of tourists, glowed a warm golden-brown in the lingering rays of the setting sun. Keone saw no sign of the crewman or Lily.

Then a movement in front of the porch of the Caryatids caught Keone's eye. In a space filled with broken stones, he spotted Lily sprawled over a large flat stone with the crewman bent over her. The rosy light glinted off of his two out-stretched fingers.

"Hands off her!" Keone shouted.

The crewman leapt away from the woman and bolted toward a small border of trees.

Keone sprinted around broken stones to the woman's side. "Lily?" No response. "Lily!" He touched her neck and found a weak pulse but saw no evidence of breathing. He was about to begin CPR when Andreos appeared at his side.

"Go after him, Keone. I have her."

He turned at the agent's voice.

"You cannot help her, but I might. Go after him. And try not to kill him. Only he can help us solve the riddle of Thanatos." Andreos pointed along the line of trees.

Keone didn't argue and took off. He spotted the crewman weaving his way back toward the theater through the trees.

Why would he go back there?

Keone wound his way behind the stage's proscenium and saw the crewman stretch out his arm to climb the ancient stones. Keone had no choice but to follow.

As he climbed, Keone heard the crowd laughing at Ron's jokes. Leaning around the proscenium, fifteen feet above the stage, he saw Ron nonchalantly tossing six Indian Clubs in the air. He was gaining on the crewman when the man swung around to the front of the proscenium, directly above the spinning clubs.

Keone tried waving at Ron from his perch on the side of the proscenium. He only succeeded in getting the crewman's attention. The crewman removed a pistol. Keone watched the weapon rise toward his face.

~

FROM HER SEAT, VERONICA NAPOLEONI SPOTTED THE crewman climbing around a stone wall above the stage and pointed to him. "Josie, do you think that man on the wall is part of the show?"

"Isn't that Keone trying to catch him?" Josie responded. Then they both watched Keone gesturing wildly to get Ron's attention. "He's got a gun," Josie said to Veronica, then shouted, "Turn around, Ron!"

Startled, Ron spun with a single club in his hand and let the rest fall to the stage with a loud clatter. Seeing a gun in the crewman's free hand, Ron seemed to realize what was playing out on the proscenium was serious. As the crewman raised his gun toward Keone, the big Hawaiian motioned to Ron to toss the club. He did, straight at the crewman.

The club was far from lethal, but it struck the crewman's left hand—the only thing holding him to the stone facing. Veronica saw the man's shocked face the moment before he plummeted to the stage, his gun discharging aimlessly into the orange sky.

The stone floor of the stage, by contrast, was quite lethal. The killer landed with a loud thump at Ron's feet, jerked once, then lay completely still. A scarlet pool of blood spread around his shattered skull.

Veronica watched Ron Morton's eyes roll up in his head before he tipped forward onto the body at his feet.

Part Four

The Worlds of Fantasy and Tomorrow

"Fantasy, if it is really convincing, can't become dated, for the simple reason that it represents a flight into a dimension that lies beyond the reach of time."

Walt Disney

Chapter Fifty-Seven

Saturday, July 13, 6:10 a.m.

Nancy woke to the jangling of the home phone. The walk to the kitchen gave her time to clear her head before answering. Beth emerged from the study as Nancy lifted the receiver.

"Hello?"

"Hi, Nancy. It's Mike. I'm in Fred's office."

"Huh? Oh, your call from the airport. It's still early here, Mike."

"Fred was anxious, and I didn't want to disappoint him. Can I put you on speaker?"

"Okay, I'll do the same so Beth can hear."

"Great," Mike said as Nancy heard a loud click, then Fred's voice.

"Can you hear us?" Fred said.

"Yes," she and Beth replied in unison.

"I've finished reading Rob's manuscript," Fred continued. "And I want this book. I'll give you a fifty-thousand-dollar advance and the established publication terms we've used with

Rob in the past. Mike will bring the documents out to you. We're letting him hitch a ride on the corporate jet as far as Honolulu with a group we're sending out there for the Pacific Rim eBook conference."

Nancy thought Fred sounded unusually pumped for a jaded New Yorker.

"Fred, it's a generous offer. But we haven't finished reading the manuscript yet. Besides, we aren't quite sure what this is." Nancy stopped there, reluctant to disclose Beth's suspicions about the book.

"I'll tell you what it is," Fred continued, undeterred. "It's a fabulous fantasy with legs in the real world. This could be a great, final tribute to Rob's writing ability. This story will move people. Look, Nancy, I know you need to finish reading the book before you can sign anything, but Mike won't get to Maui until tomorrow evening, your time. You can certainly finish by then. I'm willing to consider any reasonable conditions for publication."

"What if it's real?" Nancy couldn't believe she'd said this out loud.

"Are you crazy? Real? No way. Mike told me how you found it. That can add some hype to the P.R. But we can't seriously suggest it's real. We'd be laughed out of the bookstores." Here was the hard-nosed businessman she recognized.

"I'm going to write a section or two about our finding and reading the manuscript," Beth said.

Fred paused at this. "I'll need editorial control over that. And you'll need to use a ghostwriter who can write it as third-person past tense. We need to break up this first-person, present narrative, anyway. You can tell the truth. But you can't claim it's real. We can . . . uh . . . leave it up to the reader."

Nancy looked at Beth. Her daughter was scowling.

"Fred, I'm not sure—"

Beth hit the mute button. "I don't like it either, but it may be the only way we can get it published."

Nancy disengaged the mute button. "All I can promise for now is that we'll seriously consider your proposal. I want the terms I suggested put in writing, but Beth doesn't need a damn ghostwriter. She's an experienced author." She winked at Beth.

"And I'm flying back to New York tomorrow morning to take the play I wrote to Broadway. Mom has asked me to manage things on that end." Beth looked at Nancy.

"Yes, that, too," Nancy said.

"I'll have my secretary schedule a meeting for us on Tuesday, Beth." Fred sounded resigned to working with the young woman. "Will that work for you?"

"For now," Beth said.

"Got that, Mike? Don't bother showing up tomorrow night unless there's wording in there about the chapters we're writing and about Beth being our representative in New York," Nancy added.

"Got it. I'll see you tomorrow evening, Nancy. You ladies are doing something important. Rob would be proud of you. Aloha."

"Aloha, you two," Fred added.

"Aloha." Nancy ended the call.

Nancy whipped up a quick breakfast while Beth pondered the conference call.

"Do you think Mike and Fred see a scandal here involving a pharmaceutical company?"

"I don't think that's it. Rob didn't blame Rosen. He even wrote about it." She picked *Failure to Lead, Leading to Failure* off the pile of documents and read from the back cover:

The best decision for a corporation, with responsibilities to its shareholders, is often not the one a scientist might make. But a scientist isn't responsible to shareholders, only good science.

"Even in the manuscript he blames himself and poor timing, not the decision makers. He couldn't get his drug tested in the clinic and that's what gnawed at him. If it had failed, he could have handled it. But not knowing was unbearable."

"I wonder if Rosen might have some problems with this being published," Beth said.

"I doubt it. Mike and Fred think it's a fantasy, so they probably figure they can change a few names and avoid any flack. They do this every day."

"On the phone you sounded like you're starting to believe this isn't just a story."

Nancy wanted to change the subject, but Beth beat her to it.

"We still need to decide if we're going to let them publish this as a . . . *a fantasy with legs in the real world.* Wasn't that what Fred called it?"

"Yes. You said something about leaving tomorrow morning?"

"They want me there for the Off-off-Broadway wrap party. It's a theatre tradition."

"Then we'd better get back to reading."

"You're sure it's okay for me to go tomorrow?"

"I'm sure. We're very close to the end of the manuscript. Besides we can't leave the house until Angela catches the shooter."

~

Angela had never seen Koa Kaleho until he entered the interrogation room at eight a.m. Saturday morning. Fred Di Angelo was seated at her side, but they'd agreed she'd lead the interview.

Kaleho was a tall, thin man in clean work clothes. His posture was casual, but his eyes seemed to look far off into the distance at something no one else could see. Angela had seen that look before in vets. Part of this man was still in Vietnam and would never leave.

"Mahalo for coming in this morning, Mr. Kaleho. Please, have a seat. We appreciate your willingness to talk with us about your grandson, Manolo," Angela began.

Kaleho nodded.

"I understand you took your grandsons to the firing range by Hali'imaile a few times."

"Yeah. I think the older boy might make a good soldier someday."

"What about Manolo?"

"Oh, he can hit what he aims at . . . sometimes. But he's too jumpy to be a good sniper."

Angela opened the file in front of her and read a few lines from the man's military record. "I see here that you were decorated for your contributions during the Vietnam War. You obviously know what it takes to be a good sniper."

"I did my job. Everyone did." He couldn't hide the pride on his face

"I know, but you were Special Forces. In Vietnam, you guys were the best of the best."

"Don't say that to a Navy Seal." He grinned. "I gotta give 'em credit. Those squids had it rough, too. A lot of their missions were at least as dangerous as ours, but more tactical. You know, in and out. But we had to stay inserted for weeks at a time behind enemy lines. We used to joke with them that they even f— uh, did other things that way."

Angela saw Di Angelo suppress a chuckle, but she moved on. "We should get back to Manolo."

"Sure. My daughter thinks the world of that boy."

"And you?"

"He's okay. He's a little too artsy to make a good soldier. He reads that fantasy crap and . . . what do you call those Jap comic books?"

"Manga?"

"Yeah. What a pile of horseshit. Why couldn't he read about Batman or Superman or some real American heroes?"

Wasn't Superman from Krypton? she thought, but said, "Like you and your brothers in Nam. People who did what had to be done despite the risks and with little hope of reward."

"That's for damn sure."

Time to move into more dangerous territory. "My dad told me what a rotten environment those Vietnam vets returned to. It must've been hell."

"I got out right after I got back. Couldn't stand the pansy way the military was giving in to the damn hippies. They even had gooks for officers at Fort Sam."

"That's right. I read a second lieutenant with Vietnamese grandparents got snuffed at Fort Sam when you were there."

"I don't know nothing about that. I was just there waiting for my discharge." His face lost color.

A lie.

"Oh. I thought they named you as a subject of interest. Let me see." She flipped through the file.

"Oh, that shit. I remember now. They didn't have nothin' on me. What does this have to do with my grandson?"

She'd pushed too hard.

"I'm sorry, Sergeant Kaleho. I was just surprised by how they treated you after you'd served your country so honorably. Didn't they realize you had PTSD?"

"They didn't even know what the hell that was back then. Years later I got some help, but I was already in stir by then. Thanks to some goddam narc."

Bingo. She had what she needed. The look on Kaleho's face told her he was afraid he'd said too much. Time to change gears. "I think Manolo and his brother are lucky to have a role model like you. It's hard being *hapa* here sometimes."

"What you mean hapa?"

"Well, you're pure Hawaiian, but your daughter married a Filipino, didn't she?"

"Her mistake, not mine. They're separated now, thank God. I straightened her out when I got back home."

"That was a year ago, right?"

"Nine months."

Angela had the date he was released from the last of the military prisons where he'd been detained in the file in front of her, along with the list of violent crimes he'd committed after he returned from Vietnam. But she wanted to hear him say it. Too bad they didn't have enough evidence to nail him for the fire-bombing, too.

"And in those nine months, you've had a chance to get acquainted with your grandsons. I bet that was rewarding."

"Sure. Yeah. The older boy could pass for Hawaiian. He's learned a lot about his culture from me. Manolo's too much like his pussy father. Filipino to the core."

Angela suppressed a smile. Kaleho had no idea her own father was half-Filipino. Bigotry and stupidity travelled together, no matter what the race.

Fred Di Angelo spoke for the first time. "Is there anything else you'd like to tell us about Manolo?"

"When they told me he stole my rifle, I couldn't believe it. He never breaks any rules. Made me wonder if he might have some balls after all."

"He was helpful during the interview," Di Angelo added.

"Yeah. I heard he couldn't wait to cop a plea. Well, that's not my fault either. I told you the kid's a pussy."

"Once again, thank you, Sergeant Kaleho, for coming in. And thank you for your service to this country." Angela waited until he rose from the chair before asking her last question, a long shot. But she needed to put him at the crime scene. "Hey, do you know Efren Alavezos? I think he was in Nam, too."

Kahelo's face lost its color as he struggled to stay unfazed. "No. I don't know Ho— who that is."

He almost said Hopper before he caught himself.

Kaleho left the room without another word. She was glad Alcala had been watching.

He'll put a tail on Gramps.

Meanwhile, she'd have a little chat with Efren Alavezos.

This case was getting more interesting by the minute.

Chapter Fifty-Eight

Saturday, July 13, 2013, 11:30 p.m. Athens' time (10:30 a.m. Hawaiian Standard Time)

Detective Sergeant Keone Boyd hesitated outside the hotel room Andreos Calliopoulos had arranged for them at the Hotel Grande Bretagne. He knew Julie was waiting for him inside. He also knew he had a great deal to explain to her. What he said in the next few minutes might well determine the future of their lives together.

Open the door, you coward.

Julie was seated on an exquisite antique sofa surrounded by their luggage from the ship as he slowly opened the door. She stared at him and challenged him to utter the first word.

"I'm glad to see they brought you here from the ship. How are you feeling?"

"Wrong! Try again." Julie's monotone conveyed more peril than a shout ever could.

Keone thought long and hard about what he would say next.

"I'm sorry. What I did was unforgivable. I promise with all my heart to never do it again."

"Better. But I need to know that you understand the one thing that you did that was worse than all the rest."

Keone stared at his wife of eleven days, who waited patiently as he struggled to select the precisely correct words for his next sentence. The only words that had any chance of saving their marriage.

"I kept a secret from you."

Tears crept from their eyes.

"You bet your big, handsome Hawaiian ass you did." The words exploded from Julie's mouth. "Do it again and—"

"I won't. Not even on a technicality or to save you from pain. What I did was wrong."

Neither one moved for what felt like an eternity to Keone.

Then they rushed together in an embrace that allowed Keone to hope again.

"You will now tell me every facet of that secret from the moment you started keeping it from me to the present and you will say or do nothing else until you're finished. Promise me."

"I promise."

Julie was impressed with the precision with which her husband recounted all the relevant information about the case he had pursued during their honeymoon:

"It started when we arrived in Naples. When I returned from our visit to the spa, a very polite gentleman with an accent was waiting for me at our cabin door. He showed me a badge and we went inside . . .

. . . the killer landed at Ron's feet, jerked once, then lay completely still. Ron passed out on the body."

He'd spoken non-stop for thirty minutes by the time he reached the end.

"So, you caught this Thanatos."

"We caught someone. A crewman named Janos Pratt."

"Was Andreos satisfied?"

"The authorities discovered that Pratt, like Andreos, was on all of the cruises where Olympians were murdered."

"You didn't answer my question."

"Andreos was pulled off the case. His superiors and the cruise line were convinced they had their man. We were questioned separately about the events on the Acropolis. They let me go, but Andreos was kept longer."

"Did you tell them about the first murder and the missing woman?"

"They didn't ask. I'm pretty sure Andreos kept me out of all that."

"Did you see Andreos again?"

"No."

"What about the woman the killer tried to poison?"

"The authorities informed me that she died. The antidote Andreos carried kept her alive for a couple more hours but failed to reverse the toxin's effects."

"Were you satisfied?"

"I was surprised Thanatos would be so sloppy. I also doubted the crewman was smart enough to write those letters. But he could have had an accomplice."

"Or been the accomplice." Julie understood what her husband was really saying.

"What did they tell you on the ship?" Keone asked.

"The ships doctor came and got me after they made the announcement about the end of the cruise and brought me here. He told me a very nice man had made further arrangements for my husband and me and that you would meet me here this evening."

"What did they tell the other passengers?"

"They told them that due to suspicious criminal activities

ashore, the police needed to impound the ship, then offered to compensate the passengers for the missed portion of their cruise. I guess that means Ron is out of a job."

"I'm sure he'll find something. He really is talented. I never even got to thank him for saving my life."

"What about the rest of the Olympians?"

"The cruise line flew them all home and promised them a future cruise at the line's expense. I didn't get to thank Josie for getting Ron's attention, either."

"You believe the killer's still out here, don't you?"

"No."

"No?"

"Well, I'm not sure. If Pratt was the accomplice, Thanatos is still alive. If so, I'm sure he's not done."

Julie paused. "What do we do now?"

"First, I tell you the rest of my secrets. I really have learned my lesson."

"There's more?"

"I had two communications from Maui since the one I got at the airport in Chicago, when you quarantined my phone. The first was my conversation with Janet. I didn't share everything we discussed with you before."

"Oh?"

"I talked with her about something that happened before we left on our honeymoon. I hadn't shared it with you because I thought it was nothing."

Keone explained everything that happened when he met with Sam Loftus in the hospital, including the assertion Hasselbach made about him being clean shaven the day before. "Janet confirmed what Hasselbach said. That means I still have some follow-up to do on Sam's case, but I promised myself to do nothing more about it until we get home."

"I appreciate that."

"I don't think Sam's going anywhere before we get back."

"Okay what was the second communication from Maui?"

"That one wasn't completely my fault. Right after I met Andreos our cabin phone rang. It was Angela calling to tell me about the case she was working on with Tony. I couldn't just blow her off, so I helped her narrow down the suspects."

Julie frowned.

"I'm sorry, but I will always be a police officer and have to be available to help my colleagues."

"Look, Keone. I realize now I should never have forced you to make that silly promise. I just wanted us to focus on each other these few weeks. But when I married you, I knew what I was getting into. I know there are secrets you have to keep inside the department. But if I ask about something like that, please have the courtesy to tell me you can't talk about it because of your job. Keep the secret but let me know you're keeping a secret. Do you get what I'm saying?" Tears filled Julies eyes.

"I do. That's what I should have told you about helping Europol after Andreos asked me to keep it a secret. I wanted to tell you about it so badly. I hope you can forgive me."

"Only if that was the last secret. Tell me now if there is anything else I need to know," Julie said.

"I can't think of anything else right now. But if I do, I promise to tell you, okay?"

"Okay."

"Julie, we do need to decide about something else, though. The cruise line has offered us an executive suite on a Greek Islands cruise that leaves Athens next week—or we could just go home with the promise of a future cruise."

"This may surprise you, but I just want to go home. On the condition that you can't go anywhere near work for two more weeks. Agreed?"

"Agreed."

"And you can keep your damn cellphone. Let's just leave the luggage here for now and go to bed. We can book our flight home in the morning."

"But I don't have any pajamas."

"I know." She leered at him. "I have a little secret of my own to tell you. And, since it's partly your fault, you don't get to hide behind clothes."

Chapter Fifty-Nine

Saturday, July 13, 12:30 p.m.

Angela headed for a different interrogation room, knowing Alcala wouldn't be watching this time. As she'd waited for them to collect Efren "Hopper" Alavezos, she'd checked in with Lindsay, who backed her one hundred percent, and re-read a few key lines in the manuscript on her computer. During the interview with Kaleho, something had clicked in the back of her mind. That was why she'd asked about Hopper. When she got back to her desk, she re-read the section in Rob's manuscript where he first described driving up to the ʻĪao Valley. The lines jumped out at her:

"As the truck slows, the driver, his passenger, and I exchange surprised stares. Something about one man's expression—fear, recognition, I don't know, something—commands my attention before I shake it off and hurry on to the ʻĪao Valley . . ."

Then she jumped to the section about Rob's time in the Army, and what he said to Calla about the guy who tried to strangle him:

"Funny, Calla, but they never called me as a witness for that guy's trial. I could have presented relevant testimony for that one . . ."

Calla pauses the re-experience. "You know who that man was now, don't you, Robert?"

"Yes, I saw him in the truck that side-swiped me the night that I . . ."

But there were two people in that truck. Rob had recognized the passenger, not the driver, not Hopper. This was the itch in her subconscious that caused her to ask Kaleho that last question. Is that what makes a good detective, the ability to use your subconscious mind? Is this what Keone was trying to tell her when he told her *weird* is part of the job?

The policeman who brought Hopper over cuffed him to the table and left the room when Angela arrived.

"What's up, Sarge? I thought you were working another case."

"I am, Hopper. But you never told me who your passenger was Sunday night."

"I was alone when I hit that lady."

"I know you were. But I'm interested in something that happened earlier. Do you remember the guy you sideswiped in the ʻĪao Valley? He told me you weren't alone when you grazed his VW. We can check your truck for paint, but I'm guessing we'll find it." She'd already matched the paint and Rob had never told her anything, except through the manuscript.

"Okay, okay. Damn, nobody reports a little scratch like that here. Da guy must be anal."

Good guess. "Tell me what happened."

"Like you said, we was coming down from the Valley with a truckload of pakalolo and we sideswiped this guy. There's usually no one coming up that road that late."

We.

"What time were you taking the marijuana down the hill?"

"Aftah six. Six thirty?"

"And who's we?"

Gramps or Kāne? she wondered.

"I don't want to get the guy in trouble. I was driving. He got out after the sideswipe, called me a crazy driver, and decided to walk."

"Withholding evidence in a murder investigation won't help when you face trial on the hit and run, Hopper."

"Murder? Shit, what dat crazy bastard do?"

Angela settled back in her chair and just stared at Hopper.

"Okay, okay. Koa Kaleho."

Gramps.

Angela switched on the small recorder in the room. "To clarify, you are identifying Koa Maleko Kaleho as the second person in the truck when you sideswiped the VW last Sunday evening, July seventh."

"Yes. And I don't know where the hell dat buggah go aftah that." Hopper was now earning his nickname. He'd reverted to pidgin and looked like he was about to hop out of his skin.

"When he left the truck, did he take anything with him?"

"He took dis duffel bag wid his guns. He was riding shotgun fo' me."

"What guns?"

"He had a couple handguns and dis special kine rifle. He showed it to me once, da kine you could hook tings onto. He modified it to handle a standard twenty-two load but packed his own shells so dey'd tumble."

"What was he doing when you last saw him?"

"You know, dat's funny. He was walking back up da road."

"Why's that funny?"

"His daughter's house was da udah way."

Chapter Sixty

Angela saw Manolo's mother, Esther, waiting outside the Hernandez home. The boy and his mother rushed together in a crushing embrace. When the mother finally released her son, Manolo ran into the house.

Esther turned to Angela, tears streaming down her face and embraced her. "Thank you for showing Manolo didn't shoot that man. You've made a real difference in his life."

Angela gently extricated herself from Esther's embrace. She wanted to leave but had questions that needed answers. "Esther, your dad moved in with you last year, right?"

"He came straight from prison, nine months ago. I didn't have the heart to turn him away. For the first month, everything was okay. Then he started ragging on my husband, whose grandfather was from the Philippines. Even though Elvin's grandmother and mother are Hawaiian, my dad refused to accept him. Called him a girl-man and worse. Elvin got fed up and moved to O'ahu. His company has an office there. He said he wouldn't be back until I sorted out my father."

"I'm sorry. I didn't know."

"The past eight months have been hell. We went to O'ahu as soon as school ended to give the kids time with their dad. My dad stayed here and got involved in some shady deals. The boys loved him, though, and wanted him to love them. He told them about his adventures as a Green Beret but omitted what happened after. I didn't tell them, either."

"Did he ever mention anything about the people he met in the Army or looking up old friends?"

"About a month ago, we went to Lāhainā. The boys like to snorkel at Airport Beach. While we were in town, we went into a used bookstore that the Maui Friends of the Library runs in the Wharf Center. I thought he might like the old books about the war that they have in there. We were leaving when he spotted a book by a local author and asked the owner about it. He ended up buying the stupid book. When I asked him why, he said a guy he knew in the Army wrote it."

"Do you still have the book?"

"We might. Let me check Dad's room." She ran into the house and emerged a few minutes later with a copy of *Failing to Lead, Leading to Failure* by Dr. Robert Thomas Lister, Jr. She handed the book to Angela who flipped it over. Rob's face smiled up at her from the back cover, with a brief bio stating he lived on Maui. The final piece fell into place.

"Mahalo, Esther. This helps fill in some gaps."

Angela watched Esther's face fill with understanding and her body stiffen. It may have filled in some gaps for her, too.

"He was here," Esther said.

"Who?" Angela asked.

"Dad. He didn't see me. Just rushed in and grabbed a backpack from his bedroom. But I heard him talking on his cell."

"Go on."

"He was talking to a pilot friend. He arranged for the guy to take him to Tahiti. I don't know the guy's name, but he's got an old cargo plane that he modified to hold extra tanks. Flies out of a strip near Hana but lives in Haiku."

"I think I know that guy." Angela hoped he hadn't moved recently.

Esther pulled a scrap of paper from her housedress and read from it. "Dad said he'd meet him at the strip, and they'd leave at nine thirty tonight."

"Thank you for your help."

"No. Mahalo nui loa for giving me back my son. And if you see him, tell my father he has no place here anymore—ever."

"ALCALA." TONY ANSWERED HIS PHONE ON THE FIRST ring and immediately jumped from his chair.

"You what? How?"

His mouth twisted, as he listened to a contrite police officer explain how he'd lost a seventy-year-old grandfather on a motorcycle.

"Did you at least put out an APB?"

"Yes, sir."

"Good. That's one thing you didn't screw up today. We need to find that son of a bitch—now." He slammed the phone down on his desk. But before he could sit back down his cell rang.

What else can go wrong?

This time the voice on the other end of the line was calm and in command. It was also female.

"Beyers. I'm glad you called. There's a problem."

"Let me guess. Gramps gave your boy the slip."

"There's an APB out now. We'll catch him. The officer that let him slip will be getting some tough love from his CO."

"I know where Kaleho's headed, and I'm on the six of the guy who's meeting him there."

"Oh? May I ask where he's headed?"

"I'm sending you the coordinates now, sir. He's in a blue hummer." This was the first time she said sir in the conversation.

He deserved that.

"He's heading to an old WW II landing strip in Hana. I've made a couple busts there. Name's Randy Opaka, a pilot in the pakalolo air force. He's planning to take Gramps out tonight in an old cargo plane he rebuilt. He's also the person I'm tailing. There is no way I'll lose him on the road to Hana. Besides I know where the strip is."

"Good work, Beyers."

At least one person around here knows what the hell she's doing.

"The tip came from the boy's mother. She also filled in the remaining blanks. Gramps is the shooter. No question."

"I'll look forward to hearing the details when I meet you at the landing strip."

"Uh . . . you're coming to Hana?"

"I'm getting in my car now. You have point on this, but I'll send some uniforms to the airstrip to back you up. Don't make a move until I get there."

"Yes, sir. Uh . . . may I suggest we send the back up from the Hana division. I know those guys. They know where the strip is, how to get there fast, and how to avoid being seen."

"Good. You call them and set it up. And stay in touch while we're on the road."

Chapter Sixty-One

Saturday, July 13, 6:30 p.m.

Nancy and Beth stopped reading long enough to order a pizza delivery. The last section they read described a point in Rob's life when he almost ended it. He'd been in San Francisco on business.

~

"YOU HAVE LEFT OUT ONE RE-EXPERIENCE, HAVEN'T you?" Calla says.

"I've suppressed that memory for fifteen years. I couldn't bear to re-experience it on my own."

"I know. That is why I will join you for this one."

"Thank you."

"Proceed."

I find myself in my living body, sitting on a bed at the Fairmont Hotel in San Francisco. I've returned to my life's darkest moment. No wonder I skipped over it in my re-experiences. I'd done everything I could to block out this memory. I succeeded until now.

My cell phone rings.

"Hello."

"Hi, boss." Jim's voice seems subdued.

"Hey, Jim, what's up?"

"I hate to have to be the one to tell you this." I hear him clear his throat. "I just confirmed what we guessed when we were out at Pro-Test for the auction. Test Tacklers did empty the freezers and tossed all the stocks into biohazard waste, including ours. It's over."

"Thanks for the call. How are you holding up?"

"I'm fine. I came to terms with it two years ago. How about you?"

"Fine. See you when I get back." But I'm not fine. I realize I'd always held out a faint hope that I was wrong and that someone, anyone had seen the value of our work and saved those stocks from the freezers. But they hadn't.

I end the call and throw my cellphone at my reflection in a mirror. The mirror shatters and I don't bother to clean up the mess. I decide it's time to get shit-faced and leave my room for the bar.

Four hours and too many drinks later, I stand at a spot on the Presidio of San Francisco near where I used to eat lunch sometimes. This overlook offers views of the south entrance to the Golden Gate Bridge from the ocean side. The lights stream over the hump at the bridge's center and pour down towards the city. Directly beneath me, the crashing surf pummels the ancient rocks that struggle to maintain the peninsula. A ten-foot, chain-link fence separates me from the cliff's crumbling edge. Its prominent sign warns, RESTRICTED AREA – UNSAFE FOOTING.

On this same Presidio, a short distance away, I once sat on a hospital bed and made a promise to a nine-year-old girl. A promise I committed my career to. Those cells that produced our molecule were my last hope for keeping this promise—and they threw them away.

I place my toe in a chain link in the fence's base and gradually start to climb. Despite my intoxication, I'm still able to take the next step up the face of the fence, before I'm bathed in a bright white light. I turn to face the brilliance and see a small form emerging from the light. It appears to be a young girl, and she's speaking to me.

"Roberto, did you keep your promise? I counted on you."

"Who are you?" I ask but know the answer.

"It's me, Maddie." Her name echoes in the night air, swirling at me from every direction.

I can't bear this. She knows I failed her. She's here to torture me.

I sense an abrupt change in my perceptions.

Calla and I are no longer moving forward through the re-experience in my younger body. I hear a new voice in my mind. A lovely, sweet voice that I haven't heard in over thirty years. "That girl's not me, Roberto. I'm right here."

My mind floods with joy and sorrow. "My sweet Maddie."

"Why are you so sad, Roberto?"

"I didn't keep my promise."

"What promise?"

"To cure a cancer for you."

"That's not what you promised. Come with me."

I find myself back by her bed that fateful day.

"*Oh. I don't mean that kind of doctor. I mean the kind who thinks stuff up, not the kind that gives you shots.*"

"*A research scientist? A guy who works in a lab and makes discoveries?*"

"*Yeah, that kind. They're the ones who help find medicines and other ways to make us better. You need to be that . . .*"

"*Promise me you will, Roberto. You need to do everything you can to make people better who have cancer. I mean it.*"

"*I promise, sweetie.*"

Then I'm back with Maddie and Calla by the bridge.

"I think you did what you promised," Maddie says.

"No, sweetie. I did help make a drug, but people never got it. I failed."

"What about your friend Jim? And those other scientists you helped? Their drugs help people with cancer, even some with the same cancer I had."

"I know, but I didn't work directly on that one."

"Who cares? Would it exist without you? Did you try your best?"

This throws me. I realize, at last, what I've truly regretted through the years. "But I couldn't save you. I couldn't take away your pain."

"But you did. Come with me."

We're in Maddie's tiny nine-year-old body. It's her first day in the hospital and Dr. Estella Rodriguez tells Maddie she has cancer. For the next eight months, Calla and I experience everything Maddie saw, heard, felt, and worried about up until the moment she died. Every needle prick, every bout of nausea, every moment of despair, every fever, every chill, every ache, every loss of strength—even her last painful breath.

When we return, I'm whole. I realize I've done something I needed to do. I shared her pain.

"See, Roberto. You did ease my pain. Every day. That's why I love you."

"I guess I did. I loved you, too, from the moment I first glimpsed you through that door."

"Now you need to love yourself. Promise me you will, Roberto."

"I promise, sweetie."

"Come and see me sometime but finish what you need to do first. There's no hurry."

"I will." My heart is too full to say more.

Calla and I are again alone.

"May we complete this re-experience, now?" Calla asks.

"I think we should."

I continue to climb over the top of the fence, and the image of Maddie continues saying her name, a name that represents my total failure. I can't take this anymore. I'm ready to jump to the waiting rocks and crashing surf. I'm done. Then the sound seems to morph into something far less threatening.

"Daddy. Daddy." I hear my own nine-year-old daughter's voice. "Look at me. You can't do this. I need you. I need you. I need you."

As I turn to look, I see my Beth, standing there looking at me as only a nine-year-old can. She puts one hand on her hip and shakes her finger at me, saying, "Oh, no, you don't. I still need you. I still need you. Please. Please."

At this moment, I know I can't jump. I feel a presence beside me calming me, soothing me, like a mother soothing a child.

I look back at the approaching form. It comes right up to where I hang perched at the top of the fence. I realize it isn't Maddie or Beth.

A small female MP stands with one hand on her unbuttoned holster and gestures to me with the other. "Please, sir, I need you to come down from there. You can't be here. You're in a restricted area. Please, climb down slowly and keep your hands higher than your head."

I only hang there for another moment before retracing my steps down the chain links. The woman snaps the leather flap over the gun at her hip. This tiny, young woman helps me down from the fence with strong, gentle hands. I think of my mother's hands. She smells the alcohol on my breath and asks, "Where's your convention, which hotel?"

I manage to get the word Fairmont out semi-audibly, and she leads me to her jeep.

∿

Nancy decides to break the silence after dinner. "Look, Beth, you'll be gone when Mike comes by tomorrow. We need to agree on what I need to do and say."

"I know. I've been thinking about that phone call. They won't publish it as a true story. And I understand their reasons. But we can't let them come out and call it a fantasy." Beth looked directly into her eyes. "After what we've finished reading, what do you believe?"

"I believe every word in it is true." For the first time Nancy had no doubts. "But we can never prove it to their satisfaction. We've got them to agree to insert some sections about how we found the manuscript and our thoughts on reading it. I plan to hold out for one last concession."

"What?"

"If they won't let us say Rob's story is true, we'll make them agree not to say it's fiction. That way the readers can decide for themselves."

She watched her daughter mull this for a full minute, before Beth said, "Let's do it."

Before they could finish the final section of the manuscript, the home phone rang.

"Hello?" Nancy got there first this time.

"Hey, Nance. It's Ange. We're close. We've got the grandfather dead to rights. He's on the run, but I know where he's going. We'll catch him tonight. Please stay at home until I call back."

"Ange, you're the best. Thank you from both of us. It'll be such a relief to have closure. We'll get together next week to cross the rest of the t's . . ." Her throat tightened up.

"And dot the rest of the i's. Rob's story helped us catch his killer. I hope you plan on getting it published."

She looked at Beth before answering. "We do. But we've got a few more pages to finish before Rob's agent arrives with the contracts tomorrow. Mahalo, my friend."

"See you soon. Aloha."

Chapter Sixty-Two

"Beyers to Alcala. Over."

Tony reached for his mic. "Go ahead. Over."

"I'm still on Opaka's six and just entered Hana. Two of my guys from Hana are at the strip and report Gramps hasn't arrived, yet."

"Are there any structures at the site?"

"Yes, sir. There's an old shack with a tin roof. My guys checked it. It's clear. No people and no weapons."

"Good. Have them stay hidden until you arrive. If you get the slightest hint that Opaka's made you, pull off and take backroads the rest of the way. Hmm. Are there any—"

"Hold one, sir. I just spotted one of my guys from Hana who'll take him in from here. I can beat him to the strip by at least fifteen minutes if I break off now."

"Do it."

"I'll make contact again when I check in with my guys at the strip. How far out are you, sir?"

"I should be there by nine. Out."

Tony Alcala was pleased with Beyers. No question. But he still hadn't seen her under fire. He suspected that might change at the airstrip. Gramps wasn't the type to go down without a fight.

Angela parked her car far enough away from the deserted landing strip that she couldn't be seen or heard. A bird whistle, a couple dozen yards to her left, confirmed that her colleagues from Hana division were on-site and watching for her. Following the whistle, she encountered Officer Billy Mahoe.

Mahoe briefed her as they walked closer to the site. "Pilot's not here yet. Nate's keeping the watch."

She knew Nate was Officer Nathan Sapiandante. She couldn't have asked for two better guys for this assignment.

"Hey, Nate," Angela whispered, as they arrived at a point with a clear view of the field and the small shack.

"Hi, Sarge. How goes the detecting?"

"We'll see. Lieutenant Alcala's on his way." She looked over her shoulder toward the road. "I hope he gets here before the shooter."

"What did the jerk do?" Mahoe asked.

"He shot my friend's husband and tried to pin it on his ten-year-old grandson."

"What a sweetheart. I sure hope he gives us an excuse for a little payback."

"Billy, the LT needs to talk with him. We don't want any question hanging over the kid."

"Gotcha."

Angela heard a vehicle approaching and headed back towards the road she expected both Opaka and Gramps to take to the airport. As soon as she recognized the pilot's blue Hummer, she got an idea and punched her speed dial.

"Alcala."

"I'm on site at the strip, sir."

"Have the pilot or Gramps arrived yet?"

"The pilot just showed up, but no sign of Gramps yet."

"It'll take him a while to get the plane ready for takeoff. Hang tight until I get there."

"Yes, sir. If he gets the plane ready before Gramps arrives, I have an idea that will give us much better control of the situation. Do I have your okay to implement?"

"As long as you don't approach Gramps before I get there, you may assess the situation on the ground and take any necessary actions. I'll be there in less than thirty minutes."

Angela appreciated Alcala's faith in her. She wouldn't let him down.

Chapter Sixty-Three

Saturday, July 13, 9:00 p.m. HST

Angela waited as Alcala quietly pulled up and parked his unit next to hers away from the landing strip. When he started to walk toward the site, she intercepted him.

"What's our status, Sergeant?"

"The suspect hasn't arrived yet, and I've taken measures to improve our control of the situation." They crept closer to the vantage point.

"Is the plane ready for departure?"

"Yes. As soon as Opaka got it prepped, he went inside the shack to use the john. Then he brought a sandwich back and sat down outside."

Angela saw Alcala glance over at the pilot working on one of the engines with his back to them. "He's not by the shack, now. Explain, Beyers."

"I didn't like the idea of two loose cannons in the mix, one of whom could jump in a plane and take off when it got dicey," Angela said.

"I share your concern. But what did you do?"

Officer Sapiandante walked up beside them. "I've got him secured in my unit with a gag in his mouth, Sarge."

"Sergeant? I'm waiting."

"We took the pilot into custody and replaced him with Officer Billy Mahoe. Billy's the same height, build, and complexion as Opaka and will keep his back to the old man."

"What? I told you—"

"Sir, you told me not to approach Koa Kaleho. You never said anything about the pilot. Besides, Mahoe's a licensed pilot and was a flight engineer in the Gulf War. He's disabling the plane as we speak."

Before Alcala had a chance to object, Sapiandante gave a hand signal that told them, coupled with the sound of a badly tuned motorcycle engine, Gramps had arrived.

"We'll talk about this later, Sergeant," Alcala said. "What's your plan now that the suspect's here? I hope you made sure your guys know I want to talk with him—alive."

"Yes, sir. I'm guessing that after a long drive on a vibrating vehicle, Gramps will need to use the facilities. Once he goes into the shack, Mahoe will back off and we'll rush it. Our body armor should give us time to pick a non-lethal shot—if he's armed and decides to shoot it out. We'll take him alive, sir. And you can ask him anything you want."

"There are more holes in this plan than I can name, but I don't have anything better. Let's hope his bladder's about to burst, and he doesn't decide to have a chat with the pilot."

"Well, he is old, sir." Angela grinned.

All talking ceased as the motorcycle pulled to the side of the shack and Koa Kaleho jumped off, yelling at the pilot's back, "Get her ready, Randy. I've got to pee like a racehorse."

Mahoe gave the man a thumbs-up without turning around or speaking. Gramps rushed into the cabin.

So far, so good.

Angela gave him a minute to get into the head, then waved Mahoe back.

She saw Billy give a quick twist with a wrench before heading over.

"Nobody's going anywhere in that plane," Mahoe whispered in Angela's ear.

She whispered back, "Thanks, Billy. Now get to Nate's unit and make sure Randy keeps quiet."

Angela turned to Alcala. "Are we go?"

"Do it."

Alcala approached with them as far as the plane, then crouched behind the wheel assembly, waving them up.

In perfect precision, Angela and Nate approached the shack. They'd done this together many times before. Angela raised one finger and Nate kicked in the door.

Angela burst inside, her heart pounding but her weapon leveled and ready.

Chapter Sixty-Four

Sunday, 8:50:18 p.m.

"My dear friend, now that you have completed your re-experiences, how do you feel?"

"I've found comfort and acceptance."

"Robert, I see that you have left every door open to me. I know what this means and am grateful."

I feel Calla's love and return it fully. He's opened all his experiences to me as well. He knows I'll explore them. But I have something to do first.

"I'm ready to move forward in time and space. Will you join me on my first trip?"

"I agree you are ready and would be honored to travel with you. But I must make sure that you understand two more aspects unique to travelling forward before you take this journey. Can you tell me what they are?"

I think before replying. "When I moved backward in time, I couldn't be perceived in any way, even when I switched from re-experiencing my own thoughts to experiencing everyone else's."

"Yes, keep going."

"It isn't the same moving forward. When I move forward, some individuals, in some situations, will perceive me. I won't be seen or heard but felt, inside their minds. Is this the other half?"

"You do not disappoint. Do you see the danger?"

I pause for a long time. I recall another movie, *A Beautiful Mind*. "Schizophrenia, or something like it. If too many souls are perceived too often by a living soul, the person's mind could become overloaded. I must communicate rarely and be certain no other soul is doing the same. You mentioned a second aspect."

"When you move forward, you must make certain to stop frequently and reflect. Remember, this is not like your trips to the past."

"I need to be careful of fast forwarding without thinking it through. Once I fast forward past a time, I can still go back and visit it, but I can no longer impact it. Right?"

"Yes."

That means Calla has never experienced this time either or he couldn't impact me. How long did he take to move all the way from his death in ancient Greece to my present? My mind struggles with the concept.

"Robert, the time has come. Take us forward."

I allow my consciousness to move forward five seconds and stop, cutting the distance to earth in half. "How did I do?"

"Five seconds forward and a clean stop. You will need to do this repeatedly as we get closer to Earth. You can probably move forward by halving the distance with each move. Do you understand why we must move forward in time as we move forward in space?"

"I believe the reason was evident when you brought me closer to Earth before. The perception when moving with time contains that dynamic quality you mentioned before. The unfinished nature of the experience."

"Why are you able to do this now? You failed the first time you returned to earth on your own."

"I wasn't ready then. I hadn't accepted who I was and where I was. Since I didn't truly believe I was here, I couldn't move forward in this reality, unless I entered someone else's mind."

"You have learned well. I am proud, my student."

We move in deliberate steps. I'm astounded to find the next step closer, which would have overwhelmed me before my re-experiences, quite manageable. I perceive every wavelength of electromagnetic energy at first. Then I gradually tune out wavelengths unimportant to this visit. Filtering out radio and television signals proves especially helpful. At this distance, I experience the life force of the planet, not each individual soul.

As we move closer, I'm able to enjoy, then filter out, sentient entities and geographical regions I don't wish to focus on. I'm focused on the Hawaiian Islands and can feel Nancy, Beth, and our friends on the island. I find it strange and wonderful to be one with a vital, moving time stream. I feel closer to being alive than I have at any time since I died.

A plan forms in my mind to comfort Beth and Nancy and accomplish something more.

Chapter Sixty-Five

The first thing Angela Beyers saw when she burst through the door to the shack with her weapon drawn was Koa Kaleho seated on a toilet. He must have had to do more than *pee* like a racehorse.

The old man raised his hands as Nate moved over to check him and the area around him for weapons. "Had a pistol and knife in his pants, otherwise he's clean."

"I will be once you let me wipe my ass," Kaleho snarled back.

While Nate watched the old man, Angela walked to the door and waved Alcala up.

"We have your suspect, sir. Nate checked him for weapons and is reading him his rights while he finishes, uh . . ."

"Wiping his ass. I heard. Nice arrest, Sergeant."

Angela hoped it was nice enough to help Alcala forgive her for replacing the pilot on her own initiative. But her concern about that couldn't dampen her joy at solving the case and catching the shooter.

She wondered what remaining questions Alcala had for the guy. They had him cold for shooting Lister.

~

ALCALA ENTERED THE GRIMY SHACK. HE WAS PLEASED the officer had allowed Kaleho to pull up his boxers before placing him on the filthy bed against the far wall of the shack. All the bedding lay scattered on the floor, so the old man sat on a bare mattress in his boxers and a sleeveless undershirt. Tony was reminded of how his own grandfather used to walk around their house in Mānoa dressed in a similar manner.

Tony wasn't surprised the officer had cuffed the suspect with his hands in front of his body. He must've cuffed him while he was still on the john. The smell in the shack was overpowering.

"Do you understand the rights explained to you by Officer . . ." Tony glanced at the young man's nametag. "Sapiandante, Mr. Kaleho?"

"Yeah. I know the drill," Gramps snapped.

"Then you probably also know we have you cold for the Lister killing."

"Yeah. This bitch wouldn't let it go."

Tony slapped Gramps across the face. "No one calls one of my officers names in my presence."

Tony saw Angela flinch. Sapiandante had left to take the man's clothing, weapons, and backpack outside to perform a more thorough search.

"We know you were in the 'Īao Valley Sunday night."

"How?"

"Hopper rolled on you. When we told him about the murder, he told us how you left his truck with your duffel and what was in it. He also told us you walked back toward the Valley."

"Bastard."

"We know which rifle fired the lethal shot and which one fired the miss from down by the stream. We know you hated Rob Lister and why. I'd like you to tell us the rest."

"Why the hell not? I'm old and got nothin' to look forward to anymore. I don't care about anyone, and nobody cares about me. I wanted that damn narc dead, and he is."

"You met Lister at Ft. Sam, right?"

"The little pissant wouldn't even share a joint with me. I could tell he was a narc from the way he looked and the way he smelled. I would have greased him that night if that damn Mexican hadn't woken up the whole stinkin' barracks."

"Then you bravely ran off post."

Gramps smug smile didn't waver. "I ended up by the Alamo, where the hookers congregate. And guess what happened? Two damn gook hookers chatted me up. I took them back to their place and gave 'em a happy ending."

"You strangled them."

"Yeah. Their necks were so small, I did 'em at the same time. One with each hand."

"They weren't Vietnamese, you know. They were Korean."

"So?"

"And the EMT's revived them which is why you're still alive."

"Not my fault."

"And Rob Lister was never a narc. He was a medic. But you knew that, didn't you?"

Gramps's smile slipped at this.

"Come on, Sergeant Kaleho. It doesn't matter anymore. Tell me the real reason you killed him."

Angela's face revealed her surprise at this question.

"He was guarding a damn Coke machine the night I took out that gook lieutenant and his family."

Alcala had figured this part out on his own. Once Angela identified Kaleho as a viable suspect, he contacted his own friends in military intelligence.

"But Lister told the investigators he couldn't see the street the car went down and was never called to testify in the case," Tony added.

"No, he couldn't see me when I drove by and tossed the Molotovs. But he saw me when I walked back. Some smart lawyer would've eventually helped him remember, and I'd have been screwed. When I saw him in the barracks, he had to die."

"But why now? Surely, he'd never be asked to testify now."

"Through my whole tour in Nam, I never muffed an assassination. Everything that happened after that was Lister's fault. Even the hookers. When I saw his face smiling up at me from that book and read that he lived on Maui, I saw a chance to complete my mission. And I did."

"Three more questions."

"Sure. I don't have anywhere to be." The smug grin was back.

"Seeing him on the road in ʻĪao Valley was a fluke, right?"

"Yeah, I happened to be riding shotgun for Hopper that night, and Lister just appeared out of nowhere."

"Where did you build your sniper's nest? We never found it."

"You forgot to look up. There was this palm tree up above the other treetops."

"You're seventy years old, right?"

"In a month."

"How the hell did a seventy-year-old man get from the place Hopper sideswiped Lister to the top of that palm tree before Lister left the park?"

"I may be old, but I'm still fast. I was in top shape in Nam and ran every day in the joint. One good thing about military prisons, they keep you in shape."

"But the palm tree?"

"I had palm spikes and a climbing strap in my backpack along with everything else. Before I went in the army, I made my living trimming palm trees. It's like riding a bike. You never forget how. When I saw him going to the Valley, I knew exactly where I could go to take him out. I'd found that palm tree a month ago, was gonna show it to my grandson as part of his sniper training."

"And your other grandson being in the Valley that night?"

"The greatest stroke of luck I could've hoped for. Once I heard that wild shot and saw him stumble out from the bushes, I knew I had the perfect patsy. Would've worked, too, except for her."

Kaleho glared at Angela. She smiled back sweetly. Alcala loved it. "Let's take this slime in, Sergeant."

"It would be a pleasure, sir," Angela replied.

Tony grabbed Kaleho's left arm and lifted him from the bed. The suspect's feet seemed to tangle in the filthy bedclothes, and he went down, almost pulling Tony with him. By the time Tony wrestled Gramps back to his feet, there was a pistol in his hand. He hadn't taken his other handgun into the toilet, but he hadn't left it in the backpack either. He'd hidden it in the bedding, and no one had searched through it.

Tony backed away with his hands raised, but Gramps had the gun leveled at Alcala's chest. He wished at this moment he'd worn some of that body armor.

Before Gramps could fire, a blur passed between them, and a loud bang resonated through the shack. Tony's ears rang as he stared at the space previously occupied by Koa Kaleho. With all the echoing, Tony couldn't be certain if he'd heard one shot or two. Kaleho's body lay flat on its back with a small dark hole between the eyes.

Realizing the blur must have been Angela, Tony looked around. There at his feet was Sergeant Angela Beyers, blood pouring from her scalp.

Damn, Two shots.

Chapter Sixty-Six

Sunday, 9:05:00 p.m.

We arrive at my beach. I know we are moving through time
because the waves are breaking.

"Calla, I used to walk here every day."

"What do they call this lovely place?"

"People here call it by different names: Airport Beach, North
Kā'anapali Beach, or North Beach for short. The little beach park
here is named for King Kahekili, so some people call it Kahekili
Beach."

I savor this verdant, palm-tree-stippled swathe of grass. Succu-
lent plants separate the lawn from the beige sand that embraces
each gently breaking wave.

The beach has few inhabitants after eight p.m. But with my
new perceptions, the park's lush vitality stands out as clearly to
me as its bright green leaves do in the daylight. I also perceive each
humuhumunukunukuapuā'a (reef triggerfish) and *honu* (green sea
turtle) swimming amidst the coral that dominates this stretch of
Kā'anapali Beach.

"I love the ocean, my friend. I was a fisherman when I was still alive in Hellas. I'd catch my fish in Piraeus and run them up to the agora in Athens for sale."

"Is that what your name means in Greek? Fisherman?"

"No. Fisherman is *psoras*. *Calla* means beautiful, which I was not. But the word was derived from the color of a flower. Do you know of the Calla Lily?"

"I do. But aren't they white?"

"They are now, but in ancient days they were a pale teal color. Unlike my competitors, I went way out into the water to cast my nets. I couldn't swim any better than them, but I tied a rope around my middle so I could pull myself back to shore. My father, who fished with me in our secret spot until he died, called me Calla for the color of my pale chest in the teal water."

I could tell Calla was smiling, inside. "Thank you for sharing that with me. When we're done here, I look forward to sharing some re-experiences with you."

"Are we not done?"

"Not quite. I'm going to stop moving forward through time and space for a bit. But I'll be right back."

"You will return the moment you left as far as my perception goes. We have now moved forward to 9:05:00 p.m. Proceed."

I travel first to our condominium and find my computer. I perceive its electronic memory's essence and the files carefully protected there. I understand what I must do but need a bit more knowledge before I can accomplish my task.

I return with the knowledge required, start moving through time again, and begin my task.

"Please tell me what you are doing," Calla says.

"I'm transferring my memories from the moment I left my body onto my computer. The process proved a little tougher than I expected. I must turn thoughts into words then translate them into computer code before transferring them as electromagnetic energy into the computer. I also need to edit, so I don't overwhelm the reader. But to anyone reading the file, it will look like any other."

I explain this with one portion of my mind while the rest busily transfers data. "My last trip sent me to the High-Performance Computing Center at the University of California, San Diego. I joined Dr. Kerry Harlow's mind. He's the center's director and used to work with me in Newark at Rosen. I experienced his exploration of direct energy transfer between distant sources and computer chips. His experience provided the key to transferring the energy comprising my memories into the computer's memory."

"I see."

Calla and I are back at my beach, moving forward in time once again as I transfer my thoughts to the computer. We don't speak for a few minutes, before Calla asks a question I've dreaded.

"Robert," Calla asks, "what are your thoughts about your molecule now?"

Overwhelmed by all that I've experienced, I'm at a loss for words. "I . . . I don't know."

"I could show you what would have happened if it had been tested in the clinic."

"No. It doesn't matter anymore."

"Because of what little Maddie showed you?"

"That was the missing piece. She showed me that it's not always about saving someone's life. Sometimes it's about making the life they have better. But it took everything I re-experienced to get there. Thank you, Calla. Now, I have one last question for you."

"Ask it."

"Is everything written, Calla?"

"No. Your future and that of every soul is yet to be written. Hope is a wonderful quality. Some may even start their journey by reading that manuscript you so ingeniously created on your computer after your mortal life was over. Because it can help others, it will remain on the computer, where your wife can find it. But this download must end when you take your next step. You may share no more about your continuing adventure by this method. You have much growing to do."

"I know, Calla. I know."

"May I ask where you plan to go next?"

"Yes, but only if you ask in precisely the right way."

"I see." Calla mulls this over for a few moments then speaks.

"Dr. Robert Lister. You've just re-experienced your entire life, laid to rest your demons, left your family an impossible message, and found peace. What are you going to do now?"

"I'm going to Disneyland—with an old acquaintance who was called Walt. Want to come?"

The time is 9:11:15 p.m. on Sunday, July 7th, 2013.

~

SATURDAY, JULY 13, 9:30 P.M.

BETH LISTER'S MOTHER LAID DOWN THE FINAL PAGE OF Rob's manuscript and said, "It's all true."

Beth could tell her mother meant it. "You were worried during the last part, weren't you? I could see it in your eyes."

"I wasn't sure what Rob planned. But what he did was perfect. Everything each of us did was right. In the end, he found a peace I never thought possible. And so did I."

"What about the book?"

"I think we're doing the right thing with that, too. If we try to tell people it's true, they'll think we're weirdoes and never read it. This way they'll make up their own minds."

"You still want me to go back to New York tomorrow morning?"

"More than ever. I know you'll defend our interests with Fred and Mike. I can't believe it's been only six days and a few minutes since Rob put the manuscript on the computer."

"Me, too." Beth walked over to the screen door and looked out. "Hey, that cop's leaving. They must have caught the old man."

"Funny. Angela hasn't called us back."

As if on command, Beth's cell phone rang. But the ID said unknown caller.

Chapter Sixty-Seven

Date: Unknown, Time: Unknown

Angela Beyers' consciousness returned to no sights or sounds. Her thoughts were clear though. She remembered firing her weapon and the shock of feeling the pain in her head.

I was shot.

"Yes, you were." The voice in her head was comforting and familiar. She sensed an accent, European.

"Oh, hell. You're Calla."

"I have been called that."

"Am I dead? Like Rob?"

"What do you think?"

"I can't see or hear, but . . . damn my head hurts like hell."

"The anesthetic must be wearing off, little angel. Open your eyes."

~

Sunday July 14, 8:00 a.m.

. . .

ANGELA WAS RELIEVED TO SEE HER ROOMMATE LINDA'S face hovering over her. "About damn time you woke up. You scared the shit out of us."

Us?

Turning her head slightly, she saw Linda wasn't alone at her bedside. Alcala was there, too.

"Welcome back, Detective."

"Are you real?"

Linda pinched Angela's arm. "Hell, yes, we're real. Even those two Listers over there."

Angela turned her head to see Nancy and Beth looking relieved.

"They risked missing Beth's flight to make sure you were okay," Alcala said.

Linda eased the women away from Angela when she felt they'd hugged long enough. "Now, beat it you two. Don't miss Beth's plane. Ange is gonna be fine. It's just like Tony and the doctors told us. Scalp wounds bleed like a mother, but the bullet just creased her skull."

"Did I get the shooter?"

"Right between the eyes," Alcala said.

"Hey, wait a minute. Did you call me detective?"

Alcala handed her a golden shield.

Epilogue

Sunday, July 14, 2013, 7:30 p.m. HST

Detective Sergeant Angela Beyers was finally alone with her thoughts, having forcefully ejected her housemate from her hospital room when Linda couldn't keep her eyelids from drooping.

From the way Lin held her hand all day, she guessed their relationship may have just evolved, but they could deal with that when she was back home. The thoughts this prompted were quite intriguing, but a buzz from her cellphone redirected her focus.

"Beyers," she said into the phone.

"Hello, Detective. I hear I'm going to have a new partner when I get home and you get out of that hospital." Keone Boyd's voice was loud and clear over the phone.

"Where did you hear that? Nobody's said anything to me about a partner."

"All new detectives get assigned a partner for their first twelve months. And it was a little bird named Tony who told me I was assigned when I called to check in."

"Julie gave you back your phone? Where are you? Is the honeymoon over?"

"Not quite. We're in Athens. But we've decided to spend the rest our time ashore. From here we go to Venice for a few days, and after that—"

Julie's voice broke in. "After that is nobody's business. How are you feeling, Angela? We heard you took a bullet."

"Aside from a terrible headache, I made it through pretty well, considering. And the stuff they're giving me through this IV is starting to make that headache go away, too," Angela said.

"You do everything they tell you to. And take better care of yourself than Keone does, okay? Here he is."

"She was really worried about you. So was I," Keone said.

"I guess we messed up a little at the end, but the rest of my detective work was good enough for Lieutenant Alcala to keep me around." Angela was still embarrassed they hadn't found that gun in the bedding before waving Alcala forward. Nate probably thought she'd checked them while he was checking Gramps.

"Well. We all keep learning lessons, but you should have listened to my warning about going into that shack. I'm psychic you know." Keone laughed.

"I guess I should be glad you're going to be my partner for a while."

"You know it."

"We can talk more about how to deal with the weirdness attached to cases here on Maui. Hey, how did your case turn out?" she asked.

"Not great. Let's just say I dodged my bullet only slightly better than you did, but I had help from a juggler and two Olympic medalists."

"You're pulling my leg."

"Nope, I swear. I was up to my ass in weird, too. We'll compare cases when I get back. No secrets. The one person I need to trust almost as much as my wife is my partner."

"I can't wait to tell you about my ancient Greek fisherman."

"Wait. What?" Keone's voice sounded so confused that she decided to leave him hanging for a change.

"His name was Calla. Aloha, partner." Angela ended the call.

Acknowledgments

I've been blessed with a multitude of wonderful people who read and commented on this book during its various incarnations. Ken Andrus, R. J. Johnson, Elaine Gallant, Deyna Puckett, Lara Bernhardt, Doug McLellan, and Christy and Jennifer Ludwig plowed through the current version of this book and provided valuable feedback. Detective Lieutenant Audra M. Sellers, Maui Police Department provided valuable input on Maui Police Department structure and law enforcement procedures.

Any errors that remain are mine.

Thanks to the great authors in Maui Writers, Ink for valuable input and especially Marti Wukelic for getting us started. I also thank my colleagues in William Bernhardt's writing seminars, whose talent inspires and encourages me every day.

The Maui, Hawai'i, Aloha Writers, Rose State, Red Sneakers, and WriterCon Conferences have provided me the opportunity to meet and learn from several authors, editors, and agents.

I began this novel in 2013, and the Maui it describes is the one I experienced at that time. I recently rewrote the entire novel from portions of two others, but I decided to keep it set when it was written, because this was the Maui I experienced at the time. The cane fields are gone now, as are a few of the restaurants, but the spirit of this blessed island remains the same.

I'm forever indebted to William Bernhardt, a fantastic writer, teacher, mentor, and friend, who has taught me more about writing than anyone deserves to learn. His recommendation that I completely rework the self-published version of this novel and submit it to Babylon Books was a godsend. How often do you get a second chance to do something right?

My family of Christy, Jennifer, and Jonathan teach me something new every day.

About the Author

James Richard (Rick) Ludwig, Ph.D. spent forty years in the academic, health care, biotechnology, and pharmaceutical disciplines. Rick also maintained a writer's journal since his junior year in high school and populated it with short stories, poetry, and essays throughout his career.

Although a published author of multiple scientific papers and textbook chapters between 1975 and 2008, writing for a popular audience presented a unique challenge. Rick spent the first year of his retirement converting all his writings, including his original writer's journal (1967-2008), to digital format. Since then, he has written full-time and completed multiple manuscripts. *Voice of the Victim* is the second novel in the Maui Mystery Series published by Babylon Books. The first was *Eyes of the Beholder* (2022). The third book in the series, *Pele's Fire,* was initially published in 2019 by Babylon Books, but Rick is currently rewriting this book to bring it into alignment with the first two books.

Rick participated in the 2009 Hawai'i Writers Conference in Honolulu, Hawai'i, served as Volunteer Coordinator for the 2013 Aloha Writers Conference in Kapalua, Maui, and attended best-selling author William Martin's retreat workshop during that conference. Rick participated in best-selling author William Bernhardt's Level 1, Level 2, Level 3, and advanced writers' workshops between 2010 and 2016. Since 2015, Rick has presented seminars as part of the Rose State Writers Workshop (2015), the Red Sneaker Writers Workshop (2018), and the WriterCon Conferences (2020, 2022).

Rick is married with two grown children, Jonathan and Jennifer. He divides his time between Maui, Hawai'i and Southern California with his wife, Christy, with whom he is learning to relax and enjoy the game of golf.

You can follow Rick on his website: rickludwigauthor.com or send him an email at rickludwigwrites@gmail.com.